Also by Dan Malakin and available from Viper

The Box

THE WRECKAGE OF US

DAN MALAKIN

First published in Great Britain in 2024 by
VIPER
an imprint of Profile Books Ltd
29 Cloth Fair
London
EC1A 7JQ

www.profilebooks.com

1 3 5 7 9 10 8 6 4 2

Typeset by Crow Books Ltd

Printed and bound in Great Britain by
Clays Ltd, Elcograf S.p.A.

A CIP catalogue record for this book is available from the British Library.

HB ISBN 978 1 78816 845 8
eISBN 978 1 78283 872 2

FSC
www.fsc.org
MIX
Paper | Supporting
responsible forestry
FSC® C018072

For Regine

PROLOGUE

The Forest of Bowland before dawn is as dark and endless as a nightmare. For two days, a large portion of the Greater Manchester Police force have been reaching deep into its three hundred square miles, hunting with dogs and drones, calling her name.

Astrid Webb. Thirty-two years old, five foot seven, slim build, blonde hair. Missing since Saturday 4 November, at approximately ten forty-five in the morning, when her car was found crashed on the B6243 near Dutton, blood splattered over the steering wheel, the dashboard, across the windscreen.

The search is getting fractious. Yesterday there was a switch to move the teams east towards Bleasdale – greeted on the ground with shakes of the head and mutters that those in charge don't know what they're doing. Most of the orange-waistcoated officers spread between the ghostly trees, their radio static mixing with the squawking birds, already suspect this effort will be for nothing. Mrs Webb won't be the first to vanish into the forest, never to be seen again.

Every hour that passes the pressure continues to grow. Journalists' vans are camped by the striped tape cutting off the country lane where her car was found. Social media ghouls, enticed by conspiracy theories, are lurking in the local area, harassing officers for titbits of information. Top brass want results, and they're getting nothing but bad headlines for these hundreds of hours of effort; a balance must be struck between hunting for one person and helping all those relying on the police service. Some are clamouring for the search to be pared back.

Finally, a call over the radio. They've found a body.

Detective Inspector Ronson and Detective Sergeant Maxwell drive there in grim silence as the charcoal sky grows lighter by degrees. It's so far from the crash site it takes twenty minutes and a further half-hour crossing marshy fields before they locate the dense copse of trees. They find a police dog handler there, gripping the lead of a panting German shepherd, and nearby a young community support officer is covering his face, taking deep quivery breaths, the puddle of vomit beside him misting in the cold air.

Ronson crouches to examine the body. It never gets easier. You'd think it would, but it doesn't. For days he's been parroting the party line – that they might find her, that she could be hurt, disorientated, wandering through the forest tired and scared and still alive, but he knew from the start this was not the case. The truth is clear from the raw pulp of burgundy meat and bone where her head should have been, the clumps of dirty blonde hair still attached to the shards of her skull, shattered like gory pottery. Beneath her pretty dress, her body pulses with maggots and worms.

The person who murdered Astrid Webb didn't just want to kill her.

They wanted to destroy her.

PART I

1

BRYAN

Bryan Webb's swerving his bike round the potholes in the crumbling road leading to their cottage when he sees the police car parked out front. His legs go weak and he stumbles to a stop, twisting his feet to detach the cleats, ending perhaps the most ungainly dismount of all time by leaving the carbon fibre frame to crash horrifically to the ground. He clatters as best he can in his cycling shoes to the young constable about to ring the doorbell. From his forlorn expression Bryan can tell it's bad news.

For twenty-five years he served in the police force, mostly as a station sergeant in Manchester. People think the worst part of the job is dealing with scrotes effing and jeffing, kicking over chairs and acting up, but that was nothing compared to the endless procession of grief: sobbing mums, agonised dads, kids whose lives will never be the same again. Whole families destroyed by an officer waiting at your front door.

Now it's his turn.

'Mr Webb?' the constable asks.

5

Bryan nods breathlessly, wiping his sweat with a Lycra sleeve.

'It's your wife. I'm sorry to say we've found her car. There's been an incident.'

The words arrive at his brain but make no sense. Something about Astrid's car? He glances around to where her black Clio usually sits unused – she doesn't leave the house much – and notices it's not there. She didn't say she was going out when he left.

Bryan realises the constable said *incident*, not accident, and feels a chill deep in his gut. 'Oh my God – is she okay?'

'Her car's been found.'

'Where is she?'

'I'm sorry sir, we don't know yet.' He gestures to the door. 'Should we step inside?'

'Was there a crash?'

'A family liaison officer is on their way. Why don't we put the kettle—'

'I don't want a bloody cup of tea. I want to find out what's happened to my wife!'

The constable isn't sure what to do. He's been given a job and it's not going right, but Bryan doesn't care. He stomps back to get his bike, noting with dismay the scratches along the frame, and shoves it inside.

'Are you going to drive me?' he says. 'Or do I have to find it on my own?'

They head east out of the village. Soon they're flanked by fields. Grazing cattle, drystone walls, Pendle Hill rising in the distance. Why would Astrid even be coming this way? At a pinch she might nip to the shops, though that's unlikely as she would've asked him to pick up what she needed on his ride – even then she'd go to the Spar in Northcote, not deep into farming country . Nothing about this makes sense, no matter which way he slices it.

By the time they arrive at the police cordon he's wrung his hands so hard his fingers feel like claws. He gets out and hurries the rest of the way on foot. Her car's skidded off the side of the road, the front bumper thrust into a hedgerow. A white-suited forensics officer is in the front, leaning over the driver's seat to take a sample. Bryan sees the splatter of red on the windscreen and wails.

Blood. *Astrid's* blood.

The constable tries to lead him back 'This is why we say—'

Bryan pulls away from him. 'Back off, I can handle it. Who's the SIO here?'

There's not much of a set-up yet. No large-scale map of the area propped on a stand, no sergeant beside it, drawing lines and doling out orders. In the distance is the steady throb of an approaching helicopter.

'The senior investigating officer,' Bryan says, giving his best *are you deaf or are you stupid* glare. He may not have been on duty for a few years, but he still knows the right tone to put the fear into even the hardiest plod. 'Hurry up, son. I've got some information about my wife that might help.'

Bryan's first impression of the SIO is that he's scruffy. Detectives don't need to dress in a dinner suit, but tuck your shirt in, comb your hair. Look presentable to the public.

'Detective Inspector Gabriel Ronson, CID,' the man says, steepling his fingers beneath his chin, unshaved for at least three days. 'I'm so sorry this is happening, Mr Webb. It must be terrible for you, just terrible. Please, could you step this way?'

He leads Bryan past the large blue tent they're putting up to the back of a police van. It's reinforced inside, the window to the driver's cabin heavily meshed. Black vinyl benches run down either side. They sit opposite each other.

Ronson has a kind face beneath his ruffled grey hair, and when he smiles it seems genuine. It's enough to make Bryan forgive what he assumes is a thin spill of coffee on his tie.

'My wife isn't well,' he blurts out. While waiting, he'd tried to think of a discreet way to explain about her illness – Astrid hates people knowing what she goes through. That wasn't one of them. 'She gets migraines, nausea, back spasms. She's been depressed. I— I'm worried . . . I . . .'

'Take your time.'

He's worried he missed something is the truth. These last few weeks he's been so caught up with the Foundation, preparing for their government meeting next week. The signs have been there though. Great flashing neon ones. How could he just ignore them?

'She was detained in Manchester,' he says, unable to meet the detective's eye. 'A few weeks ago.'

'What for?'

'Causing a disturbance, apparently – I wasn't there. I had to pick her up from the station.'

'Is she on any medication?'

Bryan nods.

'Would she have taken any medication today?'

8

'This morning, at nine.'

'Painkillers?'

'Others, too – antidepressants, anti-anxiety. Some for the side effects.'

'Does she often drive on her medication?'

'She really doesn't go out very much.'

Ronson nods, makes a thinking noise. Pulls out an A5 notebook held shut with a thick band of elastic and so dog-eared it's twice as thick in the top corner. He licks his finger and flicks through it. 'You said to my colleague before that you weren't sure where your wife was going.'

'That's right.'

'No friends in the direction she was heading?'

Bryan shakes his head.

The detective scribbles something on the pad. 'And you were out when she left?'

'On the bike.'

'Where'd you go?'

The question catches him off guard – this morning feels as far away as nursery school. Ronson tilts his head, hand on his chin, finger crooked below his lips.

'Longridge Fell,' Bryan says.

'You don't seem sure.'

'Sorry, I drew a blank for a second.'

'Were you on your own?'

'I generally go for a ride every Saturday morning.'

'And the officer was already at your home when you got back.'

Bryan nods again, but carefully now. His heart is pounding. His mouth is dry. He knows what's going on here. Ronson is sizing him up, calculating the timings, doing the miles per

9

hour maths. He's thinking, *Could he have done her in and made it back in time?*

Usually if someone's missing you don't have to look much further than the spouse, the boyfriend, the secret lover. As her husband, he's the bullseye in their sights. Especially with no alibi.

Whatever he does next feels charged. If he bursts into tears, if he swears that he would never hurt his wife, anything at all could be seen as a sign of guilt. It seems so cruel that he's got to worry about this while dealing with what surely must be the worst moment of his life.

A clatter outside makes them both turn. Someone has dropped a bundle of rakes by the tent. When Ronson looks back, the suspicion seems gone from his face.

'Let me help you look,' Bryan says. 'I've got experience—'

'Sergeant, right? Denton station.' Ronson lifts an eyebrow. 'Tell me, why'd you leave the job?'

Bryan shrugs helplessly. 'I guess I fell in love.'

'Well, Sarge,' Ronson says, his expression sympathetic enough to fill Bryan with relief, 'I'll tell you what you no doubt would have told a worried husband in my situation – please, leave the search to us. The last thing we need is you getting lost as well.'

'That's my wife out there.'

The detective pushes his palm like it's on a brake. 'Please, Mr Webb. You used to be with the police, but you're not any more.'

Suspicion. Bryan senses it again. Or is he being paranoid? Ronson wouldn't be the first cop to give him grief for handing in his warrant card – some serving officers are like that. Even though he did the full stint, to some of them once you're an ex, you're an ex. You're out of the club. It's not like that with everyone, but more than you'd think.

Either way, he doesn't want to get on Ronson's bad side. He's the one running the case. He says who's a suspect and who's not. A detective takes a dislike to you, they think it's their gut talking, then you're fighting *against* the evidence.

Bryan lifts his hands in surrender. 'There's got to be something I can do to help.'

'Go home, Mr Webb. Try to stay calm. As soon as we find anything, we'll be in touch.'

They get out of the van. It's busier now, a makeshift hub for the search teams. Beside them comes a loud *fzzzz* that makes both of them flinch – a drone lifts off the ground, moves steadily up to head height, then speeds into the distance.

'Still not used to those things,' says the detective wryly.

Bryan's pleased for the opportunity to bond. 'They're alien to me too.'

On the way back to the car, he pauses by the large map of the area now set up at the entrance to the tent. It's been annotated with all the search areas. They're only going on foot a few miles in each direction, focusing especially on the north of the crash site, deeper into the forest. That makes sense if they think Astrid had an accident and stumbled from the car, otherwise they'd be able to pick her up in a field from overhead, but it's clear from the various roadblocks and checkpoints marking the routes in the other directions that the detective suspects something altogether more sinister.

Once Bryan's in the back of the police car, Ronson ducks his head by the door. 'You must be shocked by all of this. It's a horrible situation, awful, but we'll do our best. I can promise you that.'

'Thank you,' Bryan replies, but when he looks out of the rear window as they're driving away, he sees the detective watching the car. Watching him. Wondering if he's the kind of man who'd murder his wife.

2

BRYAN

Where was Astrid going?

Of all the questions clamouring for attention as the constable drives Bryan home, that's the one shouting the loudest. To visit someone? But who? She hasn't made any new friends that he knows of since they moved up here. Because she fancied a drive? Even on a sunny day he struggles to get her out of the house, and this morning was as gloomy as it comes.

Could she have had another funny turn? Like that disturbance in Manchester, or last week when he got home from work – she'd blacked out after having a shower and only come to in the trees behind the house, wearing nothing but her undies. In a proper state. Didn't know what was going on. Most likely it's happened again, except this time instead of going for a wander she got behind the steering wheel.

Back at the cottage, the officer comes inside to get a DNA sample. They go up to the bathroom, and with relief Bryan sees her toothbrush is still there. The tiny white pots of whatever it is she rubs on her face remain clustered in the corner of the windowsill.

On the drive, his mind spinning in all directions, he'd considered the possibility that she'd left him. He's not such a fool as to think she's satisfied with their life in the countryside, at least not yet. *If you can't be happy here,* he'd say to her, *then where can you be?* She'd smirk at that, claiming he'd been brainwashed by the garden centre brigade, but he knew she was disappointed. Like him, she thought moving out here would finally snap her out of her sadness.

Instead Dinckley turned out to simply be the latest place for her to feel that way.

They've only lived here a couple of years, coming in the hope it might help Astrid recover from her worsening illness, away from the noise and pollution of the city, and it's as quaint a place as you can get. Picture-book charming, with the village green, the duck pond, the thatched roof cottages. Yes, it's slow-paced, and the biggest scandal is usually nothing more exciting than the pub running out of dry roasted peanuts, at least until today, but it's calm and peaceful and it honestly puzzles him how she doesn't wake every morning and see the sheep grazing out the front window and feel overcome with contentment.

A terrible thought comes to him as the constable bags her toothbrush and some used cleansing pads from the pedal bin. Perhaps his wife was more unhappy than he realised.

Bryan has never been one to mind being alone but when the constable leaves, the reality of being here, just him and the million unanswered questions in his brain, is enough to send him batty. He tears around the house, looking for clues to where she might have gone. Maybe she left him a note? She has a tendency to overuse Post-its, and those sticky yellow squares containing her small angular writing are always stuck to the fridge, beside the kettle, or in the downstairs computer nook where she works. All are bare.

He sits down in front of the computer and shakes the mouse. The Windows login page appears. They call this Astrid's computer, but that's more because he's got the laptop and prefers to get out of the house to work – he shares an office with a local solicitor on Brownhill high street. He enters the password and the screen unlocks to her Outlook page. The sight of over fifty unread emails, going back to Wednesday, is shocking. No one is more passionate about the work they do at the Foundation than his wife.

Yet another sign he missed.

Keen for the distraction, he scans the emails. He dashes out a reply to the personal safety instructor they have lined up for Monday with the address where she'll be teaching, then a more measured response to Weston Timber, a potential corporate sponsor. As he's typing, he spots the open web browser at the bottom of the screen.

Was she looking at something before she left? Breath catching, he clicks on it, but it's only rainradar.co.uk. Astrid is more British than most when it comes to watching the weather – he swears she spends half her time transfixed by those blue pixels sweeping across the map. He often jokes the Met Office should probably call her for the latest fluctuations in atmospheric pressure.

He checks the address bar to see what else she's been looking at. Nothing there. Strange. He clicks the gear icon in the top corner and squints down the menu to find the History page. Except for the rain-checking website, it comes up blank.

He sits back, neck prickling, goosebumps like scalpels. Why

on earth would Astrid clear her web history? When did she even start doing that? Is there a setting that does it automatically when the page closes? He tries it now, shutting and re-opening the browser, checking the History page. The rain website is still there. She must have done it right before she—

The doorbell goes. He races to open it, praying it's her. Instead, it's Meera and the Carpenters, Lionel and Denise, their closest neighbours.

'Oh, hi,' Bryan says, wishing he'd taken a second to look through the peephole. It's too late now to shut the door in their faces.

'You poor thing,' Meera says, taking his arm and turning him back inside. She's a couple of years older than him, early fifties perhaps, cardamom-scented and ample inside pastel-coloured knitwear.

The Carpenters follow, Lionel sombrely carrying a foil-topped casserole dish which, Bryan knows by the aroma, contains the same Irish stew they bring to all the village pot-lucks. Even though nothing is further from his mind than food, it's a kind thought. He thanks them as he takes the dish, the ceramic still warm, and puts it on the counter.

'Have you heard anything?' Meera asks.

He can't help noticing the dusty blush on her cheeks, the fresh pink gloss on her lips. If his wife were here now her eyes would be rolling so fast she'd have to run to catch them. She thinks Meera has a thing for him, and maybe she's right. They often laugh about it.

'I was at the crash site—'

Meera interrupts: 'You were with her?'

This is probably already prime village gossip, so he wants to pick his words carefully, lest they're twisted in the retelling. No doubt there'll be at least a few people thinking he's done something awful to his wife. Maybe even someone he's shared a pint with at the pub, or played cricket with during the summer.

'The police were here when I got home from my ride,' Bryan says. 'I went with them.'

Meera squeezes his arm. 'I'm sure they'll find her.'

He moves to the kettle, forcing her to let go. 'How did you hear about it?'

'Local radio,' Lionel replies. Then shaking his head, 'Bad news.'

'Terrible,' Denise confirms.

They're harmless, the Carpenters, but quiet. The kind of people that only ever make up the numbers in a conversation. Bryan doesn't mind too much, but Astrid finds them hard work. Nothing has her reaching for a *no* more readily than when he says they're having people over for drinks.

While the kettle boils, Bryan busies himself playing host. Cups, milk, sugar, sweetener for Lionel, and do they have any more of those chocolate chip biscuits? But his hands are jittery, and he fumbles a cup. It falls onto the counter and the handle breaks off.

He sweeps the pieces into his palm. *What if Astrid tried to kill herself?*

Five years ago, when they got together, she was close to her lowest point. All along he thought he could help her – he's certainly tried hard enough. But what if . . . he sees her swerving into the hedgerow, eyes red-rimmed but blank with resignation, her head slamming off the steering wheel.

What if it wasn't enough?

He knows she's thought about it. They've been to joint therapy sessions where she opened up about her suicide ideation. He hoped that with her medication, with the important work they do at the Foundation, with the security and stability of their home – all perhaps a touch dull at times, he's the first to concede that, but maybe not a bad thing considering what she's been through – with all that, he hoped she would find enough in life not just to endure it, but to enjoy it too.

Meera lays a hand on his shoulder. 'It's not even dark yet,' she says. 'There is still so much time.'

Bryan remembers her new doorbell, the kind that takes videos. Wasn't she always complaining about it recording every time a car goes past? Her cottage is at the top of the lane leading to theirs – could she have recorded Astrid's car leaving this morning?

'I'm so sorry,' Meera replies when he asks her about it. 'My son came round only a few days ago to fix it. He changed the settings so now it doesn't work at all!'

He gets back to the drinks, mind firing back through events of the day so far, holding every memory up to the light – what did Astrid say when he took her breakfast? Was there anything he missed? Any clue to where she might have been going? When he turns back with the teas, he sees their furrowed brows and glum mouths and wants to scream. Instead he asks Lionel about his recent success – his landscape shot of the early-morning mist rising from the Ribble to partially obscure the stone bridges in the background came third in a national photography competition. All week it's been the top news story on the village WhatsApp group.

'Pleased with that one,' he says.

'Me too,' Denise chirps in, unhelpfully.

Bryan nods like he's supposed to, his smile rigid. Astrid's missing. *Missing*. What's he doing standing here, making small talk with the neighbours? He saw this kind of thing for years in his old job, people in this situation. It didn't look pleasant then, and it doesn't feel pleasant now. It's like he's frozen. Like he's trapped in headlights. Like he's powerless to stop something dark and vast hurtling towards him.

'Excuse me,' he says, stepping around the Carpenters to get to the utility room. He closes the door and leans against it, the lights off, happy to stay in the dark and shut out the world. Sod politeness. Sod all of them. He pulls out his phone and rings Inspector Ronson. It goes to voicemail. He leaves a message saying to call, please call, let him know what's happening.

The constable gave him a card for the family liaison officer. Maybe they'll have some details. Bryan finds it in his back pocket, flicks on the light. At the same time, he notices it's weirdly chilly – they dry clothes in this room, so it's usually the warmest in the house. Now it's colder than the kitchen.

It looks as though the floor is wet. He realises it's not water, but glass. Jagged chunks of it are spread over the terracotta tiles. The back door has been smashed.

In the frame, caught on the end of a jagged shard, is a scrap of his wife's blue dress.

3

ASTRID

SUNDAY 29 OCTOBER, 10.14 P.M., SIX DAYS BEFORE THE CRASH

Prawn and harissa spaghetti for dinner. Two games of whist and a round of cribbage. *Countryfile*, *Dispatches* ('Undercover Ambulance: NHS in Chaos'), and to round out the torture an old episode of *Midsomer Murders* they'd seen before. Then, finally, thank everything holy, bed.

Astrid shuffles upstairs. Eyes drooping (just in case), she cleans her teeth, scoops and spreads her creams. When Bryan comes up, she makes her voice spacey and mumbles, 'G'night.'

'Night, love,' he replies.

She closes the door to her bedroom and listens while his electric toothbrush hums, while he coughs and hacks and spits into the sink (sounding, as always, like he's swearing in some guttural language), while he takes his final marathon piss of the night, which tails into a Morse code of drips and splashes that seems to go on for ever. One final *hwuf-wuf* clear of the throat and he's off, clicking the bathroom light, plodding down the landing. Quietly closing his door.

Astrid's always been jealous of her husband's ability to sleep.

21

It comes to him as readily as a loyal dog. For her, however, sleep is like a mouse – seemingly innocent, but cunning, annoying, and with the capacity to chew through her internal wires if she doesn't manage to catch it. She gives him another ten minutes, then eases down the handle. Creeps out of the room. Pauses at the top of the stairs.

It's quiet, but that's not unusual. Bryan doesn't snore. The only way you know he's asleep is by being close to him and hearing the texture of his breaths change; go longer, deeper. She's not slept in the main bedroom for months now. Even before the drama of the last couple of weeks she'd resigned herself to the chilly little front room, with its dewy windows, its yellowed wallpaper, the radiator that clunks and clanks sporadically through the night like a lost Aphex Twin track. It meant she could get up and down (and up and down some more) as many times as her insomnia dictated without waking him. Who knew it would have the bonus of allowing her to sneak around unseen?

Astrid drifts downstairs. She knows every creak of the staircase, and reaches the bottom without making a sound. The door to the storeroom, or the Palace of Failure as she calls it (to herself, of course; Bryan would not approve of the negativity), is already ajar. She slips inside.

She pauses to inhale the soothing aromas. Floral chamomile and fruity citrus and at the pungent end a top note of liquorice. Mixing herbal teas started as a hobby, something to both pass the time and indulge her love of them. And perhaps it could have worked as a business, if she were different, and her husband were different, and the entire world were different. Now the boxes of loose teas are stacked beside the boxes of cotton rope for her (failed) macramé therapy business, the crates of multicoloured gemstone nuggets for her (failed) bracelet business, and the rest of her Bryan-inspired attempts to bring money into the house.

Money.

She tries not to think about it.

Bryan never comes into this room, which makes it perfect for hiding things. She glides in the dark to the right stack, eases the top box to the floor, then opens the flap of the one below. A waft of star anise hits her nose. She slides her hand down the side of the bags, alert to any crinkle of plastic, until her fingertips touch the phone hidden in the bottom corner.

Back into the hallway. Through the kitchen, the utility room, to the back door. She turns the key in increments, the pressure of the lock building, until the faint click as it falls away. Pulling up to avoid the wood sticking at the bottom, she tugs the door open. Then she's outside, embraced by the night, the chilly air, the darkness. A week ago if someone had shown her a snapshot of this moment she would have declared them certifiable – standing in the back garden with just a cardigan over her pyjamas, the temperature no more than ten degrees. As a child, proud of her Nordic roots (despite her mother) she'd never minded the cold, but as her health plummeted she'd grown to loathe it. These last few years, she tramped around the house in a hat and scarf unless the thermometer topped twenty. Now look at her.

The garden is open to the trees beyond. She creeps between them, stepping over roots and fallen branches, the moonlight enough to guide her. Bryan doesn't know about the air-raid shelter. Rather than exploring his own back yard, he prefers grand hikes, expeditions to new places. She only discovered it by accident last year, tiredly tripping over what she later realised was a periscope, finding the entrance hatch submerged in shrubbery. Inside is a domed corridor, stretching about six metres, the floor messy with twigs and rusted beer cans. Graffiti tags cover the walls, and while not pervasive, there's a definite tang to the musty air from years of accumulated piss.

Sitting on the concrete lip, fingers stiff from the cold, Astrid turns on the phone. All the messages are there. She flicks through them, suddenly nervous, unsure. What if it's all a lie? Or a trap? And here she is stepping straight into it. They've had threats to the Foundation before this – abusive men have gone to prison because of their work.

Is it too late to call? She takes a chance, and once they're talking her anxiety melts away.

'I thought you might be asleep,' Astrid says. 'You're an early riser, right?'

'I'm very much a creature of the night,' he replies. 'Usually, I'm waking up about now.'

'You hide your fangs well for a vampire.'

'I'm only an emotional vampire. Here to suck your remorse away.'

Astrid laughs. 'You're weird.'

'Takes weird to know weird.'

So much has changed in the last week. Not least the rediscovery of herself as a sexual creature. Even now, uncomfortable on the rigid concrete lip, her bum rapidly becoming ice, itchy tingles are springing to life in places she'd long given up as being for functional use.

They chat some more, but there's a disturbance at the other

end of the line. He says he'll see her soon then hangs up. It's enough to quieten her fears, to remind her that she's doing the right thing.

All she can do now is wait.

At eight forty-five the next morning, so accurate to the second you could plan a prison breakout by it, Bryan edges backwards into her bedroom with the tray. On it is her usual breakfast of tasteless oat things (no butter, can't be too careful with lactose!), apple slices, a cluster of grapes still on the stem, two mugs of tea, a glass of water, and of course the Lilac Monster: a pill box the size of an iPad. Four times a day, seven days a week, she raids those tiny compartments for relief.

'Morning, love,' he says, placing the tray on her lap. He retrieves one of the mugs and falls back into the chair next to the bed, all in one smooth machine movement. 'Status report?'

She forces a wan smile. 'Sporadic showers. A cold front came in from the east.'

'The Beast from the East,' he says, but he's distracted. He's barely looking at her as he puts his mug on the floor and fishes his phone from the pocket of his grey moleskin trousers. 'That stupid woman better confirm today.'

'It's never easy,' she replies, squeezing her forehead, jaw crunched in supposed pain, hoping to pass their fifteen minutes together without giving anything away before he sallies off to save the world. Thankfully he's so wrapped up with the upcoming government meeting that his police radar might not be pipping so loud.

He stops scrolling. 'Listen to this. *So lovely to talk yesterday, will get straight on to E.B. to organise the meeting.* Guess when that was sent? Last Tuesday! Six days ago.'

'Sounds stressful.' She sways her head, eyes slipping shut, as though she may faint.

'Kept me on that bloody video call for nearly an hour. An hour! Looking at her stupid old face and listening to her prattle on about her church social club. Like I give two hoots about their themed curry evenings, or their *fascinating* talks from the Wildlife Conservation Society . . . Am I boring you?'

She thought she was getting away with it. Cracking an eyelid, she sees his upright posture, his alert gaze.

'Sorry,' she says. 'I'm still not feeling too good.'

'You're looking better. Got some colour in your cheeks.' She's been struck down with flu all week (so he thinks). When he leans forward to rest the back of his fingers on her forehead, she clenches to stop herself jerking away. 'A bit hot, but I think the fever's gone.'

'I'm definitely on the mend.'

'You haven't touched your breakfast.'

Despite her churning stomach, she takes a bite of apple. 'You were saying about the meeting . . .'

'What's going on, Astrid?'

Her mouth freezes mid-chew. Does he know? Or can he simply sense something is wrong from the vein throbbing in her forehead? *Act normal!* But how can she, after what she's found out? How can anything be normal again?

She finishes her mouthful, sips her water. Manages to say, 'I don't know what you mean.'

'Has something happened?'

'Like what?'

'You seem . . . off.'

'I'm just tired.'

'You're always tired.'

'Sorry, I'm listening now. I promise.'

'Why aren't you interested in this?'

'I didn't sleep well.'

'You never sleep well.'

She makes a show of sitting forward, blinking herself awake. 'Call her back today. I'm sure it's just slipped her mind.'

A long pause. Bryan holding her under his microscope stare. When they first got together, she marvelled at how all he had to do was turn his lean face towards an underling at the station and they'd spring to attention. His ability to get things done (well, one Niall-shaped thing in particular) was what made him so attractive. That and his thighs.

'I thought you were passionate about this,' he says, sighing, shaking his head as he looks away. 'I thought you cared about women who've been through the same thing as you.'

Could she be wrong? Is she being duped into destroying her own marriage by someone she barely knows? These last few days, as she's come out the other side, her head has been clearer than she can remember. It all seems to make so much sense.

But doesn't everyone feel that way when they're being scammed?

'I'm sorry,' she says. 'I promise I'll—'

'All right, forget it. If you *are* feeling better, maybe you can get on top of the house.'

'You might have to hold the ladder.'

He snorts a single, seemingly unwilling laugh. 'The towels need doing. And let's get the windows open in here.'

'Yes, Sarge,' she says, throwing up a salute.

This time his chuckle sounds genuine. 'At ease, officer.'

Soon it's nine o'clock, time to cycle to the office, but she can tell he's still unsure. To hurry him along she takes her pills, hands him the tray, and swings her legs off the bed like she's ready to take on anything. It takes all she can muster to keep her smile relaxed as he kisses her goodbye.

After he slams the front door, she looks out the window and watches as he swerves around the potholes, racing up to the main road. She looks over the green fields, the higgledy-piggledy stone walls, that famous hill in the distance the name of which she can never remember, the top already white with snow.

God, I hate it here.

She spits her pills into a tissue. Not long now.

4

CELINE

She needs to relax. Seth will hate it if he gets here and she's all manic. Instead Celine's up again to check her face and tease her hair and straighten her dress and sip her vodka Coke and light up the rollie gone cold in the ashtray, wishing for probably the billionth time in the last hour that she hadn't been such a gannet and saved a bit of 'the good stuff', as he called it, so she could've sprinkled some into her ciggie and been much calmer than she's feeling now, which is not calm at all, thanks for asking.

Smoking gives her something to do for oh about twenty seconds then she's off again. Stirring the saucepan on the hot plate, adjusting the cutlery on the table, straightening the photo album they're going to look through after dinner, arranging the wildflowers in the tall glass in the centre. Does everything look okay? Classy? Literally, that was what she searched for online. *How to plan a classy date.* Not that Seth asked her to do this, but she's scared he's losing interest in her, that he thinks she's a silly little girl, that he's going to go back to the cottage, back to that woman, because what other explanation can there be? At the start of summer, when they first got together, he called her all the time. They'd sit up half the night, just by candlelight, staring into each other's eyes. *I'm yours and you're mine,* he'd say to her. *I'm totally addicted to you.*

Roll forward to late autumn and it feels like she barely sees him; when she rings, he's always 'up to his neck' in work. After the disaster last weekend – the screaming bust up when they got back from the party – she needs to do something to put things right. To show him she's not just a silly little teenager.

To prove she's mature enough to be with him, so he chooses her instead.

Celine glances at the travel clock on the nightstand. 8.47 p.m. *Ugh.* He said he'd be here at half seven. She wrings her hands, rolls another ciggie, forces herself to take a small sip of her vodka Coke, not the big glug she wants.

What if he's been in an accident? She imagines Seth checking his watch, realising he's late and rushing across a busy road, a car skidding to avoid him, but it's too late; she can almost hear the screaming ambulance, the clattering stretcher, the paramedics arguing whether it's safe to move him.

At the table, desperate to see his face, she flips open the photo album. She thought it was a bit cheesy when he first gave it her, like, isn't that what your grandparents do? But he's older than her – he's just turned thirty – so she assumed it was something you do at that age. Now it's her favourite thing ever. Sometimes she'll happily flip through it for the whole night.

Celine starts at the beginning, forcing herself to pause and take in their journey together. It's amazing how she always looks better in the pictures when she's with him. On her own she just sees her bit of a belly, which she hates no matter how often he calls it cute, or that her hair's dull; its better now she's lightened it. He prefers it that way.

She turns to her favourite picture of him. He's leaning towards the camera in some swish bar, glass of fizz in his hand, his curly black hair falling cutely over his forehead, with that look, the one that makes her calves stiffen just thinking about it. She could die he's so fucking fit. *Please don't let him be hurt. Please don't—*

A scrape of metal by the door. His key! She jumps up from the mattress, smoothing her dress, her hair, furious with herself for being so dishevelled. So much for looking classy.

Seth doesn't even manage to say hello before she launches herself at him. He grabs her smoothly round the waist, kissing her in mid-air. She wraps her arms and legs around him; he pushes her against the wall, grappling one-handed with his belt, kicking off his work trousers.

'No knickers,' he says, pushing into her. 'Dirty girl.'

Afterwards Celine asks if he wants to sit at the table to have dinner, but he says he's too tired. Can they chill in bed? He's got a new film for them to watch. *Your Final End.* Korean, super bloody. She tries to hide her disappointment, which only makes him laugh.

'Come here, sourpuss,' he says, crouching by his bag. He digs around inside, brings out a battered tobacco tin, and takes out a plastic baggie half full of a cream-coloured powder. 'Got you some of the good stuff. There's quite a bit there, so don't go nuts on it, okay?'

She holds up three fingers, Girl Guide style. 'I promise that I will do my best.'

They settle on the bed and he puts on the film. He's shown her how to do bumps, but even though it hits her stronger she doesn't like how it burns her nose. Instead, she rolls a new cig, fingers quivering so much she can barely get the miniature spoon he gave her into the baggie, let alone sprinkle the powder over the tobacco without dumping it onto her lap. The first drag feels like a long, glorious sigh of relief.

Soon she's drifting. On the screen someone's getting taken out. A shot to the back of the head, his body slumping to the ground. *Gangland style*, Seth said, or maybe she imagined it; maybe he said it when they were watching a similar film, a similar killing.

It's a bit weird, she can see that, having a shag then watching people being murdered, but she supposes that's what binds them together. That's what makes them dark stars. Twin souls drawn to each other in this horribly cruel world. Like that poem he wrote for her; she'd memorised every word.

> *Two dark stars dance and spin,*
> *Together they burn bright, defying time,*
> *For ever they swirl and twirl,*
> *Lovers enfolded in an eternal sky.*

What would she do if she lost Seth? If he chose that blonde woman in the cottage instead of her? All told, things were pretty grim when she ran away from home. She got the job at the pub and met a few people, but it didn't really start turning around until she met him. He helped her find this flat, which while *petite*, okay, one room, is enough for them; he borrowed his mate's van and drove her to a dead cheap charity shop that sold furniture so she could get a nightstand and a clothes rail. Add to that the stuff she's found in the market – the vintage gilt-edged mirror, the amazing mannequin jewellery stand –

string the lot in fairy lights and yes, it's still in a dingy block in Ardwick, but once you're inside its proper nice.

He's nudging her. 'Hey? Earth to Celine. What's that smell?'

She shakes her head to clear the fog. Something's burning – dinner! She staggers from her bed to the kitchenette; her eyes aren't working right and ghost auras surround everything. *Oh no!* The pan is still on the hotplate. She'd left it on low to keep it warm.

Thankfully it's only the bottom that's burned. She spoons it into two bowls and brings it over to the bed. Seth pauses the film to light a Silk Cut; he leans forward to look at the food.

'What's that?'

'It's fancy,' she says, offering one of the bowls. 'M&S.'

He takes a drag and grimaces. 'Looks like you dug it up from outside.'

'It's that beef thing you got in the French restaurant, remember? Beef bunions, or something.' When she said that over dinner he laughed. This time he frowns, not mean, mostly disappointed and only a little amused, like he's wondering why he's with someone not even grown up enough to make him a nice meal after he's been working all day.

'Put them down,' he says, 'and look at me.'

Celine places the bowls on the table and turns back to him, but it's hard to meet his eye without crying. *Bet* she *knows how to cook.*

He slides to the edge of the bed, and lifts a hand to her. 'I don't come here for the food.'

She steps towards him, takes his hand. 'What do you come here for?'

'You,' he says, pulling her onto him.

They start kissing, slow, gentle, his hand cupping her cheek. She feels dreamy as he lowers her down.

'You are the most beautiful creature I have ever seen,' he whispers close to her ear. 'I don't think there's another girl in the world as beautiful as you.'

All doubts are gone. It's just the two of them, how it's meant to be. As he kisses down her belly, she recites the poem to herself. *Two dark stars dance and spin*— His head settles between her legs and she gasps, the first waves of pleasure quick to crest.

A ringing phone snaps her out of it. Seth looks around, finds it on the floor, stares hazily at the screen.

'Sorry,' he says, getting up. 'Bloody work. Won't be a minute.'

Celine goes cold. Her head is instantly clear. Seth grabs the lilac throw he bought for her at House of Fraser and excuses himself to the bathroom.

Don't move, she tells herself. *Stay where you are.* But her bad self is twitching, electrifying her limbs to life, like Frankenstein's monster. *I will never forgive you if you ruin this for me!*

Too late.

She creeps to the bathroom door, presses her ear to the wood. His voice is muffled, she can't make out the words, but his tone is too honeyed; it's the same voice he uses when he wants her to try something new in bed. She strains to hear. Surely he wouldn't take a call from her while he's here?

His voice is suddenly closer. 'Won't be long. I promise.'

Celine pivots on her heel, but she's half-cut and stumbles, banging her shin on the nightstand and landing on her knees.

'Useless bunch,' he says, coming out. 'Don't know what they'd do without me.' He sees her on the floor. 'What's going on here?'

Won't be long. I promise.

It must be her.

He's not smiling now. 'What were you doing, Celine?'

'I— I remembered I didn't have a shower after work, and—'

'You were listening?'

Her heart's pounding high in her throat; she's imploring herself to keep her mouth shut. 'Who were you talking to?'

The muscles around his eyes tighten. She may be young, but she knows a lie when one's coming. She's seen enough of them in her time.

'One of the lads needed to check something,' he says.

'You said you won't be long.'

'I was talking about his shift. I told him it won't be long until he's finished.'

She nods, but she's trying to remember the tone of his voice when he said it, to see if what he's saying now makes sense.

'That's how it is, eh?' Seth stabs at his phone. 'Got to prove to you I'm not a liar.'

Celine scrambles to her feet, feeling ridiculous in her dress, a child playing adult. Has she learned nothing since the party?

'Don't,' she moans, trying to drag his hand from the keypad, desperate to wind time back so she won't be able to ruin yet another night. 'I believe you.'

The call goes through. Seth puts the phone on speaker. 'Phil? It's me.'

'Evening.' Phil's voice is so rough it's more of a growl.

She grabs again for his phone, to end the call, the horror, and get him back to the safe ground of the bed. He shoves her away and jabs a finger. Stay.

'Sorry to do this,' Seth says, eyes coldly locked on hers. 'Got someone here who thinks you might be my piece on the side.'

Phil laughs. 'You're a bit flat-chested for me, mate.'

35

'Did you just call me about work?'

'All fixed, thanks to your help.'

Seth lifts his eyebrows to ask if she's satisfied.

'Yes – yes,' Celine says, reaching for him. 'I'm sorry. I'm so sorry.'

Seth finishes the call, but when they kiss she can tell things aren't right. She pushes him back on the pillow, straddles his waist, licks her lips like they do in the pornos they watch.

'You know what,' he says, sliding her off. 'I'm knackered. Think I'm going to head home, get some kip.'

'But I've not seen you all week.'

'I'm tired, Celine. I've had a killer day and I don't have the energy for your paranoia right now.'

He's going to *her*. She knows he is. He said that once men get horny there's no stopping them, they've got to have it; if he's not going to have it here, he's going to get it there.

'Please,' she says, scrambling to her feet. 'Don't leave me.'

'Look at yourself. Look how you're acting.'

He grabs his trousers from the floor, but she gets there at the same time, holding onto one of the legs.

'Don't go,' she says. 'I won't do it again.'

'Come on, that's enough.'

'I love you so much.'

Seth crouches to her. He takes her hands in his and says, 'All I want is to love you, Celine. But you make it so hard for me.' He leans forward, lays a tender kiss on her lips. 'Don't stay up too late.'

She's able to hold back the tears until he's gone, promising to call tomorrow, although he's on shift again next week so he might not be able to see her until Thursday at the earliest. As soon as the door shuts, she allows the first sob to escape. The tears come so hard the world looks fractured. She lurches to the bathroom, holds onto the sink, sees her streaked, blotchy face.

Look at you. No wonder he left.

She shouldn't have said anything about the call. She should have kept her head together, played along, made it so good for him here that he didn't *want* to leave. Instead, she's driving him away.

If he dumps her, it'll be no one's fault but her own.

She's not supposed to have any knives. Seth said he'd kill her if he found her with any, but these last few weeks her head's been so in the bin that she found herself in the army surplus shop. She found herself checking out the blades, buying one. Stashing it in a secret place here at the flat.

To win Seth for herself, she needs to be decisive. She needs to be like he was with that young bloke who tried to chat her up in the bar. Show no mercy.

Anyone wants him, they've got to come through me first.

5

BRYAN

Who would want to hurt Astrid?

Bryan stares at the smashed back door, the shattered glass on the tiles, the fragment of his wife's dress caught on the frame. She's not been in an accident. She's not banged her head on the steering wheel and stumbled concussed into the trees. She was kidnapped in their own home.

How's this possible? It doesn't make any sense. That feeling again, dislocation, his life coming apart – he's snatching for the pieces as they fly away, but they're going too fast, or he's too clumsy, too out of practice, gone soft. This wouldn't have happened if he was still on the force. No one would've dared mess with him like this back then.

This can't be a coincidence. Something's going on behind his back, and he doesn't like it. Not one fucking bit.

Detective Sergeant Maxwell is the first to arrive. She's tall, strong-featured, her hair pulled back and hands expressive as she goes over the next step – they'll be conducting a full search of the property, with his consent. She slices the air to emphasise

39

that he can request it to stop at any time, although this will require them to return with a warrant, the sequence of which she explains by jumping her finger and thumb along an imaginary line. Her presence is immediately reassuring, much more so than that of Inspector Ronson. Although Bryan's head is so filled with frenzied conjecture about what's really going on that barely hears a word of what she's saying.

'Scenes-of-crime officers will be here soon to get to the bottom of it,' she says, underscoring her certainty with a swift chop.

As the police numbers swell, Bryan follows them upstairs, waiting on the landing as they carry out the search. He knows all too well how some officers get a voyeuristic thrill going through people's private things, hunting fodder for a 'guess what we found' canteen story, and he's in no mood to have his dignity ransacked along with his drawers. There'll be no holding up of his wife's lingerie and making saucy comments, not that Astrid wears much of that stuff. Like any good marriage – like his parent's marriage, and they were together for over forty years – their relationship has always been more about support than sex. That's what keeps people together through the bad times.

The front doorbell. Inspector Ronson's voice in the hallway. Bryan goes downstairs, holding tight to the banister, as though some of the steps may have vanished. The way this day is going, it wouldn't surprise him.

In the kitchen, Meera is manning the kettle, a row of mugs lined up and waiting for the hot water. Lights have been set up in the utility room – flashes come from the open door when photos are taken. There's talking inside. Bryan strains to hear what's being said above the clumping of boots in their bedroom, the water bubbling in the boiling kettle, Meera's inane prattling about how everyone likes their tea, and isn't it interesting how older people prefer it darker?

'The tea, I mean,' Meera says, her tinkling laugh so annoying he wants to scream at her to get out, get out *right now!*

Ronson shambles out of the utility room, blinking like he's just been for a kip in there. If he looked the wrong side of bedraggled before, at least by Bryan's standards, then he's positively dishevelled now. Shirt untucked, eyes bloodshot, rucksack hanging limp from one shoulder. The difference between him and that Sergeant Maxwell could not be more pronounced than in this moment.

'I'm so sorry to be a bother,' he says, massaging his temple with his thumb. 'Can I trouble you for some aspirin, or paracetamol? Anything, really.' He offers a strained smile. 'Sometimes cases stay with me, and I don't sleep so well. Did you ever get that? When you were in the job?'

Bryan gets some painkillers from the cupboard. That's one thing they're not short of in this house. 'I wasn't a detective. I rarely got that close.'

'Lot of officers in the area remember you. Quite a few volunteered to come in on their day off to help when they heard it was your wife.'

'How's the search going? Where are you focusing?'

'We'll probably move deeper into the forest.'

Bryan hand him two pills and a glass of water. 'Towards the north and west?'

'It makes sense to focus on that part – especially if she, or they, are on foot.'

That's true – in the other directions are mostly fields, leading to villages and towns. Hard to stay out of sight if you're with someone dripping blood. 'What about the roads?'

'We have patrols and checkpoints stationed on all the routes into and out of the area.'

Ronson finishes his water and washes the glass. There's no drying rack – Meera must have moved it when she was tidying – so he looks from the sink to Bryan and back again, as though unsure what to do next. Bryan takes it from him and places it on the counter. Is this really the person who's going to find his wife?

They move to the front room, Bryan taking an armchair. Ronson staying by the mantelpiece, ruffling his greying hair, taking in everything with appreciative lips, as though considering putting in an offer on the place.

'Beautiful home you have here,' he says, 'just lovely. These old beams, are they original?'

'They were certainly here when we moved in.'

Seemingly oblivious to the sarcasm, Ronson laughs. 'I like that one. Oh, and thanks again for not going out on your own today. We had one man looking in the same part of the forest for a missing dog once, and he never came out. Dog returned home that night.'

'My wife is not a dog.' This was why he'd taken such a dislike to the detective in the first place.

'Some people prefer their dog to their wife,' Ronson quips, which doesn't help.

He settles on the sofa and fishes around in his rucksack, pulling out the same worn notebook as earlier in the day. 'I'm sorry about this, but the superintendent is very keen on details.' He licks his finger and flicks through the pages. 'What time did you say you left the house this morning?'

'About nine, I think.'

'Can you be more exact?'

'I think it was a few minutes after.'

'You went up and down to Longridge Fell, back at eleven forty-five?'

'More or less.'

'Did you come in the house?'

'Just to put the bike away.'

'You didn't see any sign of disturbance?'

'Nothing.'

'How about when you got back this afternoon?'

'Not until I found the broken door.'

'Strange there's not more sign of a struggle.' Ronson taps the tip of his pencil to the notepad, then closes it, wraps the elastic round to keep it shut. 'Could I take a look at your bike?'

Everything moves into such sharp focus that Bryan is momentarily giddy. He thought he was perhaps overthinking it at the crash site, when he wondered if he was in the detective's sights, but now he's certain. Ronson is wondering whether he staged the break-in at the back door. Whether he could have crashed Astrid's car as part of a cover-up and cycled back in time.

They go through to the hallway. Bryan winces at the scratches on the side of the bike from when he dumped it before. When they moved to the countryside and decided to 'go green' he invested in a Montague M-E1, a full-sized carbon fibre foldable e-bike that competes for his attention with Astrid as the greatest love of his life. With shipping from America, it cost over four thousand pounds – but since getting it he's barely used his fifteen-year-old Fiesta, so much so that he's been thinking recently of getting rid of it while someone will still pay him to take it away.

'Wow,' Ronson says, passing a hand along the frame. 'I'm no expert, but this looks nice. What speed does it go?'

'Electric assistance? About twenty-five I think.'

'Any faster and you've got to pedal, right?'

'My legs are not going faster than twenty-five miles an hour.'

'Folds as well,' Ronson says, examining the mechanism. 'Probably easy to pop in the car.'

'I wasn't with her, if that's what you're asking.'

'I tried to get into cycling,' Ronson goes on, 'but I ended up just riding to the pub.' He turns his head and jogs his bushy eyebrows. When he sees Bryan's expression, his smile wilts, and he goes back to the bike, opening the built-in toolbox below the seat. 'This is great. You've got everything. If I ever break down, I'd like it to be with you.'

Bryan wants to drag him up, push him against the wall and scream in his face that he's wasting precious time. He's not done anything to his wife. 'Could we please focus on Astrid?'

Ronson closes the toolbox and straightens up. When he regards Bryan there's a new bite to his eye. 'Not to be rude, but she's quite a bit younger than you, isn't she?'

'That's hardly relevant.'

'I'm just trying to get a picture of the two of you.'

'She's thirty-two, I'm forty-seven. Not what you'd call a cradle snatcher.'

'Fifteen years is a big gap.'

'We don't talk about it on a daily basis.'

'Would you say your marriage is a happy one?'

What a question. On his part, yes. Being with Astrid has changed everything – he's moved out of the city he believed he'd never leave, he's given up the job he was even more certain he'd never leave, he's with a woman more beautiful than he thought possible. But he knows it's hard for her. He knows what she struggles through, every day. Is she happy with her life? Probably not. Their marriage? The detective would have to ask her that, but the hope is she'd say yes.

That's hardly the point though. Bryan knows a detective's line when he hears it. Ronson's wondering if perhaps Astrid was going to leave him for a younger man. If Bryan uncovered an affair and fixed it himself.

'It's not always easy,' he says. 'But show me a marriage that is.'

It's chilly in the hallway. What if there was no break-in? What if she was out the back and forgot the door was closed? Some of the pills she's on makes her a bit loopy at the best of times. It's possible she stumbled into it, shattered the glass, spaced out on the drive to hospital and skidded into the hedge. He pictures her lost in the forest, shivering in the dark, desperate to come home. Usually at this time of the evening she's bundled on the couch in a carefully constructed pile of blankets and hot-water bottles. He covers his face and makes a noise somewhere between a growl and a whimper.

Ronson touches him warmly on the shoulder. 'It's okay, Mr Webb. There are people looking for her right now. Every single one of them is desperate to find your wife.'

'Thank you,' Bryan says, wiping his arm across his eyes. 'Sorry.'

'Nothing to be sorry about.'

Ronson shakes his head, takes a deep breath. There's a debate going on in there. Bryan wishes he knew which side was winning.

'I'm just thinking,' the detective says. 'Is there a past relationship? An old boyfriend? Anyone who might want to hurt your wife?'

Bryan's face goes slack. It's been a long time, years, but how could he not have realised before? It's like when you're looking for your keys. You run around the house, you root through your jacket pockets, you check the front door, the driveway, the car, then finally, exasperated, in defeat, you go back to where you started and find the damn things hanging where they always are.

It *can't* be him – but it must be.

Who else has ever wanted to hurt his wife?

6

BRYAN

He always wanted to get married, to have a relationship like that of his parents. One able to last past the initial passion, past the rocky times, the uncertain times, one that provided a safe and stable haven in which to grow old. His mum held his dad as he passed away, and within a week was gone herself of a broken heart. That's the kind of love Bryan wanted.

For forty-plus years, it eluded him. He had flings, of course. A few even became girlfriends, but something always went wrong – feelings faded, or they got funny about the job, asking him to choose. Then he met Astrid. From the moment he saw her, he was transfixed. The same, however, probably couldn't be said of her.

To her, he was the plod behind the desk dealing with her enquiry.

'Don't get me wrong,' Bryan says to Ronson, 'I didn't make any moves on her.' They're back in the front room, facing each other on armchairs. 'Quite the opposite. I was probably more clipped than I should've been. She was very upset. Someone was stalking her.'

Niall Turton, that was his name. Medium height, medium

build, cropped brown hair. Nothing looking. At the time Bryan was shocked she'd even given him a second glance, a looker like her. Niall had been a supply teacher at the primary school where she worked – but they ended up in bed after some leaving-party drinks. Next day, she tried to laugh it off, but he was smitten, unsurprisingly, and didn't understand the word no. Then he took to following her around.

It had been late, that night at the station, past eleven. The creep had showed up at the restaurant where Astrid had been with her mates, then got on the same bus as her, even though he lived in the opposite direction. She'd hopped off when they went past the police station and run there.

This Niall wasn't outside when Bryan poked his head out, so he logged the incident and went through the next steps – how to record evidence, how to increase personal protection. When they finished, she looked at him with those scared blue eyes, and asked, 'Is that it?'

What else could he do? Send some officers to speak to Niall? Perhaps. She knew where he lived. But Bryan had very little grounds, and he was still a bit wary about giving her preferential treatment because he was attracted to her. For all he knew, she could be lying to get him in trouble. It happens.

'Can I at least stay here for bit?' she asked, settling on one of the grey plastic chairs.

'Let me get you a drink.'

Bryan made a round of tea and they started chatting. Not about much, small talk. The weather, work – she was interested in the station, and he did his best to dredge up exciting stories. Before they realised, it was two in the morning. He had a car drop her back home.

Ronson glances up from his notepad, pencil poised. 'What happened next?'

'I forgot about her,' Bryan says. 'Or perhaps more accurately, I stopped myself thinking about her. That lasted less than a week – right until the moment Astrid came back to the station in tears. The situation had escalated. As well as following her, Niall was now calling and texting incessantly, trolling her on social media, banging on her windows during the night. She'd not slept for days.

'I escalated it from our end. We sent some officers to speak to Niall, and I gave her a direct number so they could get a car to her as soon as she felt in any danger. None of it did any good. The harassment escalated.'

'Why didn't you bring him in?' Ronson asks.

'Niall went to ground after that first visit from the police. Couldn't track him anywhere. Eventually we found he'd bought a one-way ferry ticket to Ireland, but no matter how long we scoured CCTV we found no evidence of him ever boarding.'

'And that was it?'

'He was just getting started. He created fake email accounts for Astrid's friends, then used them to spread lies about her – daft stuff, like she'd been arrested for shoplifting, or she was sleeping with such and such's husband. A picture of her undressing was emailed to all the teachers at her school, and it turned out he'd hidden a webcam outside her bedroom window. Can you believe that?'

'Sounds like a horrible thing to go through.'

'She's never really recovered, if I'm honest.'

'Tell me about it.'

Bryan squeezes his fingers, looking down. 'She's had it tough, my wife. It's not my place to go into it, but she didn't have a happy upbringing, not like I did. Her parents weren't bothered – it was her grandad mostly who raised her. I don't think her mum was even in the country.' He waves his hands. 'It doesn't matter. What's important is the thing with Niall must have triggered something in her body. Once the floodgates opened, well, let's say we've struggled to shut them.'

'This is the medication she's on?' Ronson asks. He's got a soft tone, a therapist's air. It's not hard to see how he'd be able to get many a criminal to spill the truth.

'It started with antidepressants, then she got migraines. The worst is these muscle spasms in her spine – they got so bad that before the wedding we were worried she'd have to go down the aisle in a wheelchair.'

'And how is that now?'

'It flares up sometimes when she's stressed, but we keep it under control with her medication, and she does yoga, and we eat so healthy these days. No more bacon baps for breakfast.'

Ronson makes an amused sound. 'That's dedication.'

'I'd do anything for my wife.'

The same chilling thought comes back to Bryan. *What if she killed herself?*

What if she was too ashamed to admit she'd had enough? What if she thought he would somehow get over it easier – maybe blame himself less – if he thought she had been murdered? Could she have staged the whole thing herself?

He should have been more on it when he got that call from Manchester police. *Come get your wife, she's caused a disturbance.* That should have been a sign something serious was wrong – same with last Wednesday when he found her wandering confused behind the house. He thought he was on top of it, that he knew what was going on. He thought he could focus on this meeting with the Department of Crime and Policing next week and not have to worry about his wife. Turns out he was wrong.

'What happened with Niall?' Ronson asks. 'He doesn't sound like one to give up easily.'

Bryan sighs. 'He kept it up for six months or more. We collected evidence, but it was hard to do anything. We didn't even manage to get a restraining order – couldn't find him to serve notice.'

'That doesn't explain why he'd stop.'

'That might have been because of me,' Bryan says. He knows some officers don't like this kind of thing – dating the public, especially if the case is active. When asked, he's always just told the truth: she kissed him first. 'You see, I don't think Niall ever went to Ireland. In my mind he bought that ticket to throw us off the scent. He was still around, that's what I reckon, and once he saw us together he backed off.'

'Niall Turton, eh?' Ronson ruffles his hair and blows out his cheeks. 'You don't happen to have any of that old evidence you collected?'

'Sorry, we binned it in the move.' They actually burned it in the back garden as part of a cleansing ceremony, but Ronson doesn't need to know that. He's probably already got them marked down as a couple of kooks.

'You've been of great help, Mr Webb,' Ronson says. 'Let me check how the rest of them are doing, then we'll be out of your—'

He's interrupted by a young constable hurrying down the

stairs. He's holding a pale green notebook that it takes Bryan a moment to realise is Astrid's journal. 'Boss. Look at this.'

'Excuse me a moment,' Ronson says, then goes into the kitchen with the constable.

Bryan paces the hallway – that should have been the first thing he looked for when he got home. When's he going to start getting his head in the game?

A few minutes later Ronson comes back out, holding the journal aloft like it's a winning lottery ticket. 'I think we may have found our Mr Niall Turton.'

7

ASTRID

SATURDAY 21 OCTOBER, 5.57 P.M., FOURTEEN DAYS BEFORE THE CRASH

Astrid knows she should be ashamed. It should, she knows, be a humiliating experience to sit in this police cell, with its inch-thin blue mattress, the metal toilet sticking out of the wall, the bars across the frosted window. She even *wants* to feel that way. To feel that way would be normal, predictable (even for her), and wholly preferable to how she actually feels, which is as though she's in a car poised on the edge of a cliff, the front bonnet teetering up and down, so unsteady that even pulling the door handle could be enough to make her plummet.

A rattle of the key in the lock. The door opens and an officer, dark hair, cautious smile, asks her to follow him. Was he there when they checked her in? If so, she should apologise – the last few hours are coming back to her in a series of increasingly awful montages – but she's not sure, and she doesn't want to focus her mind on it in case more horrors are unearthed, and she doesn't trust her mouth to work anyway. So instead of apologising as she no doubt should, she drags herself up like a woman twice her age, wincing against the

53

pain spreading down her spine, the migraine gathering force to compete against her (ridiculous) hangover. Even a decade ago in her drinking heyday she never knocked back doubles at lunchtime. How did she *expect* today to turn out?

She follows him along the long cream corridors back to the booking desk, heart yammering high in her throat. There he is, her husband, in his muddy jeans and wax jacket, as though he's been called away from the farm to collect his errant wife. He's chatting to the woman behind the desk, and has to do a double-take.

'My good Lord,' he says, rushing over. 'What happened to you?'

Astrid can't look him in the eye. 'I— I don't remember.'

'It's okay. You're okay now. Let's talk about it in the car.'

She sits while Bryan organises her release. An older officer comes out from a back room and takes him to one side. There's a hushed discussion, a mutual laugh, then Bryan comes back and helps her up from the chair. Says a hurried, 'Let's go.'

On the way to the car, he explains that due to the severity of her actions, including scratches so deep they broke skin, the police were strongly considering pressing charges. 'I had to call in an old favour,' he says. 'You're lucky he was working today.'

She should ask for the story. That's what he wants. He can't wait to tell her how he and the officer who got her off bunked together in their training days or worked on some sting, but honestly she thinks it might have been better if he'd left her in the cell.

Almost anything would be preferable to returning to Dinckley.

'Thank God it's Manchester,' Bryan says, driving back. 'They know how to deal with people on medication.'

Again, he waits for her to respond. Again, she keeps her head turned to the window, her gaze glued to the passing green blur. Tiny spasms like electric shocks fizz down her spine. She's fighting a battle between the panic rising in her chest and the dread of her desperation for the relief of her (now very late) five o'clock meeting with the Lilac Monster.

He switches his voice to the *don't worry I'll clear up your latest mess* tone, mollycoddling with a touch of despair. 'At least tell me why you were drinking. You know you shouldn't, especially on your own – especially after you've been so sick all week. Please, help me understand.'

This time all her silence elicits is a growling sigh of exasperation. She knows this is unfair on Bryan, but she's so confused, and the further she goes from the excitement of this afternoon, the more ridiculous it seems. How does she know any of what she's been told is true? It all sounded so plausible earlier, exciting even. An explanation for everything, a path to a happier life, all within her grasp, as long as she trusted the person offering their hand.

What if she's so keen for it to be true that she's stumbled into a trap?

'For God's sake, Astrid. I know you're embarrassed, but the least you can do is say something. It's like you're annoyed with *me*.'

It's easy to give in to the tears. They've been beating on the back of her eyes for hours. The ferocity of the first sob sets off stabbing pains in her skull. She digs her thumbs into her temples, letting out a wail.

'Let's get you home,' he says, switching to the fast lane.

What was she thinking? This is the truth of her life. She couldn't leave it any more than she could rip out her heart and grow another. The physical pain may have started only five years ago, when Niall dug his tentacles into her world, but the mental torment was there from day one.

Her parents never wanted her, it's as stark as that. Her father was a university lecturer in Law at Durham University (and already married); her Norwegian mother had been studying there for her MSc in International Human Rights. When they found out she was pregnant, he left his wife and teenage children to start a new family. Her mother, however, had long-standing and previously undisclosed mental-health issues (big surprise, genes have been mentioned many times), and absconded back to Bergen the day before Astrid's first birthday. Her father had no interest in playing a single dad. One of the luckiest breaks she's had in this overall disappointing life is that she had a lovely grandpa willing to step in and raise her. He passed away when she was seventeen, leaving her enough of an inheritance to go to teaching college.

'You carry a lifetime of trauma,' intoned Shri Vashangha, the spiritual healer Astrid visited for a while, a wizened old man with finger lines of white paint on his cheeks and forehead. 'You are learning to free it, but sometimes trauma has nowhere to go. So, it sits in your body. This is the cause of your pain.'

And yet, her twenties. Living in the Whalley Range apartment with Vivien. Working in the cafe and studying for her PGCE. Going out on Friday (and sometimes Saturday!) night, and spending lazy Sunday afternoons flouncing round flea markets in chiffon tops and ballet flats. She would wake up in the morning anxiety free, agony free, able to pass through the hours like a normal person. Why wasn't trauma beating down her door back then?

Until this last week, she'd assumed it was because she hadn't yet met Niall. That he was the catalyst.

Now she's not sure what to believe.

The first time she saw Niall, she thought he was cute. Not tongue-lolling, but with his neat features and preppy black V-neck, he caught everyone's attention when he leaned confidently into the staff room on his first day. It helped that aside from Thabo, who taught music three mornings a week, there were no other male teachers at the school.

He joined for six months to cover a maternity leave. Astrid didn't speak to him much besides to say good morning, although she did notice his eyes linger on her. By then, Vivien had nearly saved enough for a deposit on her own place, so it was fresh in Astrid's mind that she had to do something to progress her life. That she was being left behind, once again. This time by her best friend instead of her parents.

She'd never been keen on one-night stands. She found sex intense and stressful and she preferred the intimacy of the bedroom more than the act itself, a point of view that wasn't conducive to taking strangers home. She'd tried it once on New Year's Eve, taking the bloke she'd snogged outside Manchester Town Hall at midnight back to hers, but the act may as well have not happened for all she remembered of it in the morning. She'd scrubbed her mouth to get the taste of his morning-breath kiss off her lips. So no one was more surprised than Astrid when she found herself and Niall tipsily staggering to the taxi rank at 2 a.m. after a work night out. They got in a black cab to his place in Bury.

They'd already been kissing, that was her reasoning. And he was hardly a stranger (oh, the innocence! She wishes she could go back and slap her younger self). The event itself, of course, was a flop. Not literally. He paraded round the room adjusting the lights and the music with it waving away. Once it was done she lay awake, feeling increasingly sick as the alcohol wore off and wondering if it was acceptable behaviour in a one-night stand to stuff your lover's mouth with a sock to stop his snoring. At dawn she crept out to get the first tram home.

That, in her mind, was that. The same was not true for Niall, who seemed to think they were now in a relationship. It didn't help that they'd (rather humiliatingly) 'gone at it in front of everyone' as the deputy head put it. The whole school assumed they were an item.

'I can't date another teacher here,' she'd said.

'I'm finished next month anyway,' he replied.

'I recently got out of a long-term relationship.' That was true, if you classed two years ago as 'recent'. 'I'm not ready to see someone else.'

'We'll take it slow. Get to know each other.'

She had to be straight with him. 'Niall. I don't see any future for *us*. Is that okay?'

He assured her he understood. That night she looked out of the bedroom window and saw his car parked up the street. He left her long voice notes on WhatsApp that vacillated from maudlin to vicious. On two occasions he (unconvincingly) just happened to stroll into the same pub where she was drinking; the third time at El Capo for Zack's birthday, a local Italian restaurant on the other side of town for Niall, she told him enough was enough. Next time she saw him she'd be calling the police.

She hoped that would be the end of it, but it was only the beginning.

Back home, Bryan tells her to run a bath. 'I'll bring you some tea. Chamomile and passionflower?'

It's all she can do to moan her agreement as she limps up the stairs. If anything, her hangover is intensifying, and she has to turn the lights down to the dimmest setting to bear them. Forget the wishful thinking of this afternoon, this is her reality. Hauling herself around like an eighty-year-old.

Who else would care for her? Who else would put up with her? Who's to say what life would be waiting if she leaves this one?

She turns on the hot water, warms her hands under it. And then, of course, there's the chance this might all have started from some scam. Not today (well, hopefully), but those first messages. Putting evil seeds in her mind. To be safe, to be looked after, these are not things to simply be tossed aside, not for someone with her condition.

Bryan comes in with a steaming mug and the Lilac Monster. Seeing as it's already eight he suggests doubling up the five and nine. She's not complaining. He tips the mix of pills and capsules into her waiting hand.

'Hot bath,' he says, lingering in the doorway, 'you'll be your old self. I'll put dinner on.'

It's meant to be comforting, but all she can feel is horror. That she's back here, that she'll always be here, that for the next twenty, thirty, maybe even forty years (God help her) she'll be stuck in Dinckley, stuck in this cottage, stuck with this man, doing the same chores, taking the same pills. Her *old self* always and for ever. Stuck, STUCK, *STUCK!*

His footsteps clomp down the stairs. Why is she even considering any of this? Ruining a marriage to someone who's always been there for her, who's loved her like no one has before, who's essentially uprooted his whole life for her. This isn't a prison. She can leave through the front door any time. Will she really be the one to ruin it all?

What do you call a decision that's one step up from reckless?

The bathroom mirror has steamed around the edges. Astrid takes in her drained eyes, her sunken cheeks, a mouth so used to being turned down that when she smiles her lips don't quite seem to know what to do, so the end product looks unnatural, fake. It's the kind of smile people back away from, slowly. The kind of smile that makes someone asking for directions say, *Don't worry about it*, and ask someone else. She's had enough of that smile. She's sick of it.

She closes her fingers into a fist. She doesn't know if everything she's found out in the last week is true – if they have her best interests at heart. Even today, it could all have been a lie.

It's like scratching an itch, he'd told her. *You stop scratching, you stop itching.*

She opens her hand and stares at the medication nestled in her palm.

If not now, then when?

It won't be easy. Like jumping off a moving treadmill.

If not now, then probably never.

8

BRYAN

For probably the first time in his life, Bryan feels utterly powerless.

Once the police are gone and Meera has been forced out of the door, telling him to *call, any time, day or night*, he paces the front room, trying to fit together the events of the day into a single theory. Does it make any more sense if Niall is involved?

How about if Niall's motivation isn't so much desire for Astrid as revenge against Bryan?

The story Bryan told Ronson about how he met his wife was accurate, but only to a point. It missed out the last words Bryan said to Niall after he tracked him down. The real reason that scrote left her alone.

If I ever see you again, it'll be worse. Much worse.

Back when Bryan was a sergeant, they used to call him Clipboard at the station. He knew all the rules and came down hard on rogue bobbies under his watch, the ones that liked to intimidate ordinary citizens, dishing out public order offences because they didn't like the look of someone. That didn't mean

61

he wasn't aware of more old-fashioned police methods. Or above using them.

He'd never worried about Niall coming back at him – the creep had disappeared fast once he knew what was on the table. Could it really be him? Astrid didn't mention him by name in her journal.

Wouldn't Niall be the first person she suspected?

Someone had been stalking his wife, Ronson had explained. She'd recorded all the incidents in her journal, remembering how they did it for their investigation last time, formatting the page into columns: date, time, description, location, notes. The first occasion was in Manchester, the day Bryan had to pick her up from the police station. Some dodgy-looking bloke with his hood up and face covered, following her round the shops – is that why she had a few drinks that day? To calm her nerves?

The same question, persistent as a rotting tooth, since Ronson came out of the kitchen holding the journal aloft: *Why didn't Astrid say something?*

She'd seen the stalker twice more, outside the cottage. A shadowy figure in the trees past the back garden.

Bryan drops into the armchair. He grabs his head and squeezes it between his fingers. Maybe she didn't want to worry him. Maybe she thought he was too busy. It's true the Foundation has been mad of late, with the run up to the government meeting – on Monday! They're in the late stages of negotiation to head up a new taskforce to raise awareness on stalking and harassment in the North. What if someone wanted to sabotage that? They've hardly kept it a secret. He told their PR company to make a big deal about it on social media, keep the attention up.

They started the Victim Relief Foundation when they moved to Dinckley. Bryan thought it would be a way for Astrid to get involved in something, give her a focus, and it's not like they needed to get jobs – with his police pension and the profit from selling his house in Hale, they had a comfortable life, as long as they lived within their means. For two years now they've worked hard to build something that is finally getting the recognition it deserves. Their website is packed with easily digestible information about all the stages of getting help, from first logging a complaint, to taking the perpetrator to court and preparing for a trial. They're involved in fundraising all over the North West, and offer financial relief for those people who are going through the very worst time of it. Who often have to start again with nothing.

More than a few domestic abusers have ended up behind bars thanks to the advice and support the Foundation has given to victims. Could one of those stalkers be out? You ruin my life, I'll ruin yours, that kind of thing? And the timing of it, this happening two days before the meeting with the Department of Crime and Policing – another coincidence?

By midnight, it's enough. Any more thinking and his head might pop. He races upstairs, rams a rucksack full of warm jumpers, and dumps it by the front door with the other stuff. Into the kitchen, grabbing protein bars from the shelf, dithering over the tea and stuffing a handful of her favourite camomile into his jacket pocket. An enraging hunt for the car key, and out the door.

Say it is Niall, what could have happened? He breaks in through the back, probably with a knife, forces Astrid into the car. She's driving, still a bit out of it from her morning

63

meds – does she crash on purpose? To get away from him? Or do they have a scuffle at the wheel? The police should get the forensics back from the car by morning, so that'll give a better idea of who was with her.

Bryan pulls up by the cordon at the top of the country road. There's no one standing point, but further on he hears voices, sees the glow from the light stands. He gets out with the rucksack and lingers by the tape, trying to picture what the reaction will be to him showing up. Is it even worth approaching them? It's a fine line between natural concern and being a nuisance, and the last thing he wants to do is step over it.

He climbs back in and drives. By the time he gets home it's gone four – he's so tired that he takes the turn onto their lane a fraction late and almost slams into a tree. Wouldn't that be an ironic end to the worst fucking day in his forty-seven years?

Usually, he has brandy before going to bed. Just the one, a glass of St-Rémy XO – it's the only time he drinks these days – but tonight he's too knackered even for that. Heading upstairs, he's sure he's going to pass straight out. Every night in his life so far has ended with him closing his eyes one second and opening them the next to see the new morning. Tonight, he can't find the off switch. His body's aching, he's desperate for rest, but instead he tosses and turns and tosses some more, twisting himself in the duvet, locked in a mental argument of such intensity it leaves him dizzy. Around six he falls asleep, he must do, because he's jerked from somewhere vague and unpleasant by the sound of someone hammering on the front door – *bang, bang, bang!* Like they're freezing. Desperate to be let in. He races downstairs, tripping over his feet, stumbling to his knees on the hallway flagstones and scrambling forwards to fling

64

open the door – to no one. Just the smell of the countryside in the dark grey morning.

He gives up on bed and makes a cuppa. How does Astrid do this? One night of insomnia and he's not sure he's ever felt worse. Eyes heavy, head spinning, barely enough energy to raise his face out of his hands, let alone the orange and fennel tea he's so desperate to lift to his mouth.

He prods his phone on the counter, bringing the screen to life. Not even seven o'clock. This is hellish. This can't be his life now – insomnia and anxiety, his insides fizzing as though they'd been removed, marinated in acid, then shoved back inside.

Outside the blackcaps are starting to sing. It's strange being here alone. The place feels empty without Astrid, even though she's never up at this time. He calls Inspector Ronson – maybe they got a lead on Niall? Or results back for the car from forensics? It goes to voicemail. He doesn't leave a message.

That powerless feeling again. The authority he used to have, the ability to dictate a situation, all of that's gone. He's just another civvy, another victim. Same as the rest.

Or is he?

Bryan sits up straight, rubbing his face as the idea takes hold. He's surprised he's not considered it before – although it would definitely cause a ruck if it got out.

For the first time since last night, the haze clears. He can see a path ahead. It's not the done thing, but desperate times and all that.

Let's see what's really going on with this case.

9

BRYAN

He's got to be careful. If it gets back to the detectives running the case, he'll be in serious trouble. Criminal trouble. But what choice has he got? He can't sit here doing nothing.

Bryan races upstairs to his office. Using his own phone is out of the question. It's not a given that his records have been requested – although if they do consider him a suspect then that warrant won't be far away – and there's always the option of driving into Blackburn and using a phone box or internet cafe, but all it'll take is for CCTV to catch him shiftily entering some backstreet phone shop and that'll be him in the spotlight. Fortunately, he's had an idea that just might work.

At his desk he drags out the drawers and claws through coins and keys and stamps. Why does he keep all these bloody receipts? What's the point in having one from the petrol station last year? He finds the clear plastic case right at the back and carefully opens it. Inside is a USB flash drive, an adaptor to split headphones, and the pay-as-you-go SIM card he bought for their anniversary trip to Paris last year.

67

He fits it into his phone, and makes the call.

Bryan and Douglas Hooper – or Dangerous Doug as they used to call him – started as cadets together at Warrington, and worked at the same station afterwards, although their trajectories ended up being very different. Bryan was happy at the station, staying until he left the force a month shy of his forty-fifth birthday, but Hoop had loftier ambitions.

Or Chief Constable Hoop, as his underlings call him now.

'Who's this?' he answers, understandably cautious. It's his personal mobile number.

'Hoop, it's Webb.'

There's a pause. Has he heard about the case? He must have done, especially if they're pulling in off-duty officers to help with the search.

'Hello Bryan,' he says, his voice grave. He's heard then. 'How you holding up?'

'You can't begin to imagine.'

'It's a horrible thing to happen, awful.'

'I'm just hoping – praying even. If you can believe that.'

'I'm sure everyone does the same in your position.'

Another pause. Hoop's not giving him much. He must have an inkling why he's getting called, though, which makes the fact he's not immediately offering help more concerning.

'Listen, Hoop . . . I'm not sure about the SIO running the case. Ronson. You heard of him?'

'Been told he's decent. Gets good returns.'

'You should see this bloke. Coffee stains down his bloody shirt.'

'Everyone spills coffee.'

'These were old stains.'

Hoop sighs, giving in. 'What do you want me to do? Try to get a different detective assigned?'

'I just want to see the case file.'

'Fucking hell, Webb. Not asking for much, are you?'

'My wife has been missing for nearly *twenty-four hours*.'

'I know, I know, but—'

'I wouldn't ask you for help unless I was desperate.'

'How do I know you're not going to take the information and—' Hooper's voice cuts away from the phone as he wishes someone a breezy good morning. When he comes back it's muffled and he's walking fast. 'How do I know you're not going to interfere with the case?'

'I just want to find my wife.'

Hoop's stopped and breathing hard. He'd always been keen on a pub lunch or two, but the last time they met up he was probably edging eighteen stone. 'I want to help you, Bryan, you know I do . . . But my name's on the shortlist to be the next chief super—'

'Imagine if it was Sophie, or one of the girls. You'd expect your oldest friends—'

'If I get caught, I'll lose—'

'*Please*, Doug. I'm desperate here.'

Bryan listens, tense, to the laboured breath on the other end of the phone. Finally, Hoop says, 'All right. Let me see what I can do. But it's not easy these days. We use digital case files now, and everything's audited. They'll be able to see who accessed it.'

'Thank you, thank you. You're a good man. A good—'

'I've not sorted anything yet,' he says, but Bryan can hear he's smiling.

They hang up and Bryan goes to make another brew. He's

energised knowing Hoop's going to help, and heads back to the nook to do some digging. Start simple. A Google search for Niall Turton. He gets back some Neil Turtons and a Niall Tatton. No direct hits. Bryan freezes, fingers over the keyboard. What next? He searches for *How to find people online*, clicks onto a website called peoplefinder.com, and puts in Niall's name. This time he gets back twenty hits, but first he has to sign up for a newsletter, which he does. He's supposed to get an activation email. For the next five minutes he refreshes his inbox. Finally, he finds it in the spam folder, which seems dubious, but sometimes perfectly normal messages end up there, so he clicks on the link. The page that opens says congratulations, he's now registered. To access the results, he needs to pay either a one-off fifteen-pound fee, or a recurring monthly charge of five ninety-nine. That option is starred and underlined.

Bryan shoves the keyboard away. The hopelessness from this morning is suddenly back and spreading through his body along with a bone-deep lethargy that makes him want to sink to the floor. Sometimes when you see the family of the missing, you know they're going to be okay no matter what happens, because there's plenty of them around and they're all in it together. Then you get the ones who don't have many people in their lives. The ones who must live with the not knowing all on their own. His mind winds forwards, and he sees himself growing old here, still looking for his wife, still probably in this same computer nook paying scammers for a peek at information on Niall Turton they don't really have.

The computer pings. Bryan lifts his head and takes in the screen. That's probably the scammers now, reminding him to finish his payment.

His email tab is flashing. He clicks into it and finds a message from Meera.

Hello Bryan, how are you? Did you see it's in the *Manchester Gazette*?

He clicks on the link. Maybe the police gave the papers something? It's mostly boilerplate reporting, the only quote from Ronson being that they are investigating several leads. The picture of Astrid is nice, though, from the barbecue they threw their first summer in Dinckley.

The picture's credited to Meera's Facebook account. No wonder she was so keen to send him that link – she's probably forwarded it to everyone in her address book. Without doubt she's been bending the ear of any journo who makes the mistake of knocking at her door.

On a whim, he opens Facebook in a new tab and goes to Meera's page, where she has posted the same link. Bryan hovers the cursor over the reactions, looking for – what? A strange name among the likes? A clue in the comments section? He notices the small circle in the top right-corner showing a wall hanging made from rope. When he clicks that it takes him to Astrid's profile. He's logged into her account!

He didn't know she even used social media, so hadn't thought to check. Scrolling down her profile, sure enough she hasn't posted for well over a year, and even that was only about the macramé business she was trying to get off the ground. He checks her messages and pushes away from the desk in shock.

How can she not have told him about this? Same as being stalked. It seems impossible that this was happening to his wife and she chose to say not a single word about it. He reads the messages again, all received in the last couple of weeks:

I'm watching you

Don't think you can escape me

I won't stop until you're dead

And the last one, sent late on Friday night:

Time's up bitch

10

ASTRID

Finally, time is fluid. Its ice grip has melted.

Astrid stares at the women on the screen, the sparkly marble-toothed housewives of Milton Keynes, or some such nonsense. *Brain mush*, as Bryan would say. Far from the oh-so-serious Second World War documentaries he's prone to frown at for hours on end.

He's at the office so she can fly free, watching without guilt as these sunbed-scorched women prattle away about their meaningless grievances. She can skirt somewhere around the left side of her conscious mind, astrally bound, wondering if she has a soul, and if so what the nature of it might be. Is it something that has evolved over time, like the eyeball, going from a lucky collection of cells reflecting light (or in this case generating thoughts) to something complex and immutable and unique to each person? Or is she making a mistake equating the soul to consciousness, which may well simply be noise generated from the mechanics of the mind?

One of the women (Rayleigh or Kayleigh or Jemima, their

73

faces are all melding into each other anyway) is hooting over some perceived slight that has zero importance. Astrid floats in that moment, pondering the implications of their anger. It brings her back to the same question as always: is the conscious mind choosing our actions, or reporting on them? Does Ray/Kay/Jem (as they call each other) have a choice to be in the life she has found herself living, or could it not have been any other way?

What about Astrid herself? Did *she* choose this life? Trapped in the bum end of nowhere. Trapped in this bum end of a body. It's easier (better?) to imagine that every moment from her birth (and perhaps even before then) has been leading to this, that she (an immutable core-Astrid that never changes) is a passenger, and this is simply a troublesome leg of her journey, like a long bus ride on uncomfortable seats or an overnight layover in a provincial airport, and not because she in some way deserves this. That she has done something terrible for which this is her penance. That . . .

That . . .

That . . .

Her thoughts vaporise. Next time she comes around she's disorientated, dry-mouthed.

Crash-landed.

Astrid blinks the sleep crusted in her eyes. She drags her head from the sofa cushion and stares at the screen, where a lively chef is flipping a pancake to a great hurrah from the other people in the studio. Her head feels as though someone has been cracking it like a soft-boiled egg. She squints to see the time – nearly midday. Not too bad. Only an hour to go.

Occasionally when her back isn't playing up, and she's able

74

to function through the constant throb of a migraine, either impending or descended, she puts aside a quarter or a half of an OxyContin. A stash to have for when the gloom is too much to bear – a little secret that's hers and hers alone. It's not good, she aware of that. She knows she has a problem. But then she thinks, *Oh well, one more to add to the pile!*

This morning has been particularly bad. She has so much to do today, so much she (should not have) promised she would try her best to get done. What was she thinking? Stupid question. She knows what she was thinking: *I can't take any more!* And, *Get me out of here!* And, *If I don't get a break from my life then I swear I don't know how I will make it through the day alive.* Commuter time is always the worst, when she thinks of everyone out there, busy people rushing around their busy lives, doing not thinking. Not wondering what could have been.

Hauling herself from the sofa, she scans her mental to-do list. Even the basics such as brushing her teeth or taking a shower seem like distant aims requiring months of rigorous planning. As for the rest of it, the boredom of laundry and tidying and preparing dinner, the soul-crunching dismay of having to deal with the overdue emails from Zulma, the Kashmiri web developer tasked with building the tea business website – Bryan found her on one of those ethical freelancer platforms, which is wonderful in principle, but he isn't the one who has to decipher her Google-mangled and overly technical messages. Just reading them is enough to bring on the thunderclouds. So she doesn't.

She lumbers out of the living room like a rusted machine. Into the kitchen to start cleaning. To make the hour pass quicker she tries to jolly her mind back towards her thoughts before, about

75

the soul, but they've lost their vitality, and sound more like the stoned 2 a.m. chats she used to have with Vivien.

A glance at the wall clock: 12.19. She considers hitting the stash again, but it's already dwindled down to the crumbs. Besides, if she can't make it through forty minutes then there really is no hope for her.

If you've got the mental space to think about the nature of your being, she hears Bryan say, *then why do you find it so hard to get organised?*

Leave me alone, she replies.

That's not very nice.

I don't want to be nice.

I've cared for you, supported you. I pay all the bills. And what do you do? Moan, moan, moan—

It's not my fault.

When are you going to take control of your life and stop being such a burden? You're pathetic. A waste of space. Just think how much more we'd get done at the Foundation if I had an even semi-competent wife instead of this shrivelled—

Astrid leans over the kitchen counter and groans. Bryan has never said those things to her, but she knows he thinks them. How can he not? It's so unfair on him. He does so much, not only for her. She reads the emails of gratitude they get from the women the Foundation helps with tears in her eyes. She just doesn't love him. That's all it is.

She covers her mouth with both hands, as though she's said it aloud. That's the root of it: her biggest fear. That she made a mistake marrying him. That she settled for someone she loved the idea of, instead of the person himself. Is her illness a reaction to that? Her back spasms especially are always the worst after they've been arguing. Could they be coming from her subconscious mind insisting that she'll never be comfortable until she sees the truth?

But if that is the truth, then what's the answer? Pack up a knapsack, slap on some boots, and hobble off to a better life? She knows only too well from the Foundation that there are worse places to be than here: damp halfway houses, homeless shelters more dangerous than being on the streets. And how would she explain herself to the desperate people there, the battered spouses with no other place to go? *I left my caring husband and lovely cottage because I didn't like doing the dishes.*

Is it Bryan's fault she took up with Niall? Is it Bryan's fault that Niall ruined her job, her friendships, and left her so mentally scarred that she can't even get going with her day without a three-hour detour to oblivion?

She checks the clock: 12.28.

Thirty-two minutes to go.

How is it possible for time to pass so slowly?

She slopes to the computer nook. On a Post-it beside the keyboard, Bryan has left her a note in his spacious, slanted writing: *You've got this!*

Perhaps the pain is something she deserves? Look at how he is, even in the face of her utter inadequacy. When they first got together, he called her beautiful at every opportunity, while she had to sift through his individual details to find the bits she found attractive (his hands, his voice, his particularly well-toned calves). Really, she used his presence to protect herself from Niall.

Is it a crime to mistake extreme gratitude for love?

Twenty-seven minutes to go.

She opens the Foundation admin folder. So much to do, and she can't be bothered to do any of it. Instead, she checks some celebrity gossip websites and wants to weep. A tired voice is getting louder by the second in her mind, saying, *I can't do this any more, I can't do this any more. When is this going to stop?*

Twenty-one minutes.

Surely this can't be her life? These endless four-hour countdowns to relief, and the nullity in between. How long can someone live this way?

Something needs to change. She covers her eyes, wanting to cry, but she's too tired to even push the tears between her eyelids. *Please, if there's anything out there, anything at all, help me, because I can't go on like this. It's too much. Please, help—*

There's a ping from the computer. She jerks the mouse, hunting for the source of the sound. It's nothing, it's probably nothing, but you never know. It could be something.

Her soul deflates when she sees it's just an email from the tea wholesaler, an issue with the last order they delivered. It's only the faintest spark of curiosity that causes her to open it.

When she does, her life changes for ever.

11

CELINE

The Three Bells is an old-fashioned boozer with old-fashioned regulars, wrinkly soaks that come in at eleven in the morning and sit there for most of the day nursing pints of bitter over the *Racing Post*. It's not cool and trendy, like the bars she goes to with Seth, but it's friendly, it's easy, and no one cares if you've had a late one and pop upstairs for a disco nap.

As soon as her shift finishes, she races up there for a shower. Big night tonight. Renata's birthday. Celine's always on at Seth to come out with her friends; this time he promised he'll be here. He said nothing will keep him away.

Ren's already by the sink, wielding her mascara close to the mirror. She's the queen bee of the Salford crew, bubbly and busty, her face a perfect heart beneath those big brown curls, her left ear lined with small gold hoops. The night doesn't start until you hear her smoker's cackle and the clatter of her bracelets. When Celine arrived in the city – from Chester, but she told people *near Liverpool* – barely sixteen and without a clue, Ren took her under her sizable wing. She'd been like a big sister ever since, even getting her the job at the pub.

Celine goes into the shower stall, drags off her clothes. Ren's only just got out so the spray's warm straight away.

'We finally going to meet this stud?' Ren asks.

Celine rasps the luminous pink dregs of the shared bottle of Superdrug Cherry and Almond Body Wash into her palm and scrubs her face.

Ren laughs. 'I know you can hear me.'

'Sorry, what was that?'

'Give over.'

Celine's throat clenches as she remembers Seth strolling up to the door of that cottage, bottle of wine dangling from his fingers. 'Stop mithering me, will you?'

She stays under the water, letting it hit her forehead, hoping the beat of it is enough to drive away the pointless paranoid thoughts infesting her brain. Who's to say he wasn't visiting an old friend? Except the look on his face as he approached the door—

Enough.

Seth loves her and she loves him. End of.

Out of the shower she dresses in party gear. Glittery top, bum-hugging black miniskirt, white trainers in case they make it to a club.

Ren glances at her sideways. 'I'm only joshing.'

'He'll be here.'

'You said that last time, and the time before that.'

Celine bumps her with her arse. 'You're being mean.'

'I'm playing.'

'Not everyone has to spend twenty-four hours a day with their fella.'

'I'll stop teasing you,' Renata says, capping the mascara. She blows herself a kiss in the mirror then turns for the door. 'Once his lordship has decided to show his face to the commoners.'

'Bugger off!' Celine calls after her.

He said he'll be here for seven. She'd better rush to get down in time.

Downstairs, into the snug. Celine squeezes round a table next to Flynn while Ren heads to the bar. Flynn's a good laugh, and he and Ren make a sweet couple, but looks-wise he's the opposite of what Celine finds attractive. Even though he's about the same age as Seth, that's about all they've got in common. Flynn with his cheap gold chains and Adidas gear; her man wears no jewellery and buys his clothes from boutiques in Barton Arcade.

'Ah fucking love you,' Flynn goes, grinning sloppily, his pupils already massive. He throws an arm around her shoulder and squeezes her close, smelling of talc and tequila fumes. 'You're my fucking favourite, Celly.'

'You're not so bad yourself.'

'I hear your man is making a guest appearance. One night only. Top billing.'

She's been avoiding the clock beside the dartboard until now, but finds her eyes gliding there. Ten past seven. She feels herself deflate.

Flynn pushes her back and looks at her as though she's approaching at great speed. 'You all right? What'd I say?' He blinks one eye, then the other, then both. 'You don't look right, but I could be wrong.'

'It's fine, it's nothing.'

'Man trouble?'

She feels the pressure building in her sinuses and flaps her hands, focusing on a spot high up the wall. No way she's going to ruin her face before the night gets going.

81

Flynn gives her another squeeze. 'Ahh . . . You're a great kid, and I hate to see you getting upset.' He lifts his hip and digs around the back pocket of his joggers. 'Here, let me get you . . .'

He dumps a tram ticket, a ratty tissue, some coins and a wad of cling film on the table. 'Here we go,' he says, rooting inside the cling film. Inside are a bunch of blue pills stamped with a cloud. 'Blue Skys. These are primo.'

Before running away she'd only really smoked weed regularly. There'd been other stuff around, mushrooms, some capsules called Yellow Submarines one of the boys in school was selling that at the time she thought were caffeine; now she's more experienced she reckons they were speed. Pills are fun, if a bit full on; she's had quite a few since getting to Manchester. Great for sex so she'll definitely have one later.

'I'm going to hang on for a bit,' she says.

Flynn picks out two and swills them down with his bottle of Becks. He shakes his head, making a *whubba-whub-whub* sound with his lips that has her laughing, and leans in to leave a wet kiss on her forehead. 'You know where to find me.'

Ren comes back with their pints of cider on a tray, and even though Celine had said not for her, a round of tequilas. There's one for Flynn too, which he flings down before they've even done the salt.

'This'll stop you stressing,' Ren says, toasting her shot glass.

Soon enough the Salford crew arrive in a cloud of Lynx and hash. Celine lived at the squat for nearly a year; that's where she met Ren, Flynn, and pretty much everyone else she knows in Manchester.

More pints, more tequila. *Cream Anthems* blasting over the speakers in the snug. The Three Bells isn't a Saturday night place, but none of the regulars mind; a couple of old lags come to hang around the door, laughing at the messiness inside. Everyone's getting stuck into the Blue Skys.

When they come Celine's way she smiles and shakes her hand. Mouths, *soon*. Keeps moving her body to the beat and tries to stop wanting to check her phone. The last time was outside smoking a rollie; it was gone nine then and that was at least three tracks ago. Seth hasn't rung or messaged. It went to voicemail when she called.

That's it, he's dead. Or he's dumped her. She turns away from the music, a finger up to her eye to catch the tear before it can fall.

'Oh no! No way.' Ren wraps Celine in her arms. 'I'm not letting him do this to you again.'

'It's okay.'

'It's not okay.'

'I'm being silly.'

Ren presses a Blue Sky into her palm. 'Fuck him.'

'I'll give it a bit longer.'

'They're all fucking losers,' Ren says, taking Celine by the shoulders. She glances at Flynn, chatting in the corner with the scrawny goth girl Holly. 'Even the good ones.'

It's too heart-breaking. Ever since Celine saw Seth at that cottage, she's been telling herself that she was wrong, that it was all in her head, that the reason she wasn't seeing as much of him as over the summer was because his work was crazy, but tonight is finally the proof she needs. He's just not into her any more.

She pushes her palm to her mouth and swallows the pill with a swig of cider, but starts to cry as it's going down. Cue a drooly and decidedly unsexy coughing fit. When she's able to catch her breath, she sees someone standing there, arms folded, head cocked, taking in her performance with an amused smile.

'Sorry I'm late,' Seth says, 'I—'

But he's cut off by Celine shrieking and flinging herself into his arms.

She'd been worried about whether he'd get on with her mates, being a bit older and with a real job, but she needn't have. He tosses a bag of weed on the table, says, 'Anyone fancy rolling?' After that everyone loves him.

It was work, of course. A long day because of the new trainees he has to supervise. His phone died at lunchtime and he didn't realise until he was on the train. She watches him chatting with some of the lads as her pill kicks in and her head goes *wooah* and she realises she's grinning so frigging hard she's slightly worried her teeth might shatter.

'You coming up, love?' Flynn asks, appearing beside her. He massages the back of her neck.

Celine nods, her legs quivering. She lets go a fluttery breath. 'Think . . . I might be . . .'

'After-party back at ours.'

It's impossible to speak now. She's rushing like a rocket, trying to ride it, her heart going hard and chest sweaty. She's not really sure what's happening when Flynn moves his hand towards her face until she sees the flash of blue but it's too late to stop it going between her lips, and she can hardly spit it out.

'Here you go,' he says, lifting his Becks to her mouth.

The last thing she thinks as the pill goes down her throat is: *Big mistake.*

12

CELINE

Spangled o'clock in the morning. Back at Flynn and Ren's in Levenshulme, the usual party place. It's mostly furnished with stuff found on the side of the road, a long velvet sofa that has burst bits of stuffing coming out, a coffee table rained on so many times the top is water-stained. In the corner a stereo's blasting tunes from a surprisingly nice garden set. UV lights, bedsheets painted with star signs covering the windows. Rave on.

Time goes into the tunnel. Celine is dancing to a trance version of New Order's 'True Faith'; she's crowded in the loo, taking a rolled tenner and ducking her head to the scruffy lines on the toilet lid; she's breathless with Ren in the kitchen over their inability to either work the Venetian blinds or say the word Venetian; she's kissing Seth in the hallway, mashed into the hanging coats, her skin tingling beneath the soft touch of his fingers, and saying to herself that right now, this exact moment, is the best moment of her entire life.

How stupid she's been acting. How *childish*. She put two and two together and came up with bollocks. How long has she known Seth? Not even six months? There are so many reasons for him going to that cottage; there are so many people that woman could be. A friend, a cousin, someone from work. And it's not like he *actually* lied to her that afternoon; he just said he was busy. If she's not careful her paranoia will ruin everything.

He tips her head to the side and runs his tongue thrillingly up her neck. Close to her ear he whispers, 'You're so fucking hot. None of the girls here compare to you.'

She wants to say something similar to him, that he's a super-fit bloke among these pasty lads, but when she tries to speak she realises her sight has gone very strange. In the dim hallway Seth's face is a tanned pixilated blur. Too wasted. Or maybe just wasted enough.

There's a rattle of bangles, a laugh that could sand walls. 'There you are!'

Celine flops into Ren's open arms. 'Here I am!'

'I'm stealing this one away,' Ren says to Seth.

Darude's 'Sandstorm' is on and everyone's going for it. All the staff from the wine bar round the corner have turned up; the living room is rocking. Dancing on the sofa, on the coffee table. Laz, one of the chefs, is up beside the speakers, sunglasses on, cheeks hollow, throwing shapes.

Eyes closed, Celine shimmies to the beats. Too boxed to dance proper. She feels an arm around her waist and pushes into Seth. They groove for a while until she senses something's not right about the feel of his body. She staggers around and sees Flynn behind her; he's flinging his fingers and thrusting his neck, his mouth going *whoop whoop*. She leans forward to ask him what just happened, but he thinks she's doing a dance move, leaning in and pulling back again. Way too weird for her. She pushes through the bodies.

She needs water. In the kitchen the sweat cools on her skin. She blinks to adjust to the light; it feels like someone has shaken her head, and her eyes have yet to come to a stop. It's quieter in here, some people chatting, their voices echoing as though they're all in the bath. She spots Seth's black polo shirt by the sink and picks her way towards him, not wanting to stumble and embarrass herself.

'Hello, lover,' she says, sounding in her head demure, sophisticated.

Seth does a double-take over his shoulder; he was on his phone, and slips it into his pocket. She still can't quite see his face, but senses something is wrong.

'Having fun in there?' he asks. She leans on him and tries to dance, but he stays stiff. 'I think we need another drink.'

She trails him to the counter. So much booze has been spilled you'd probably be pissed for a week if you licked it up. Seth finds some vodka among the few remaining upright bottles, and a couple of plastic cups that he rinses under the tap.

'No mixers,' he says, looking around. 'But I know a way to spice it up.' He takes a baggie from the back pockets of his jeans, crumbles something between the two cups. He holds his finger out to her when he's finished; she can see the pale dusting around the rim of his nail; she sucks it off, wanting to look sexy, but the chemical taste makes her heave. She pulls away, hand over her mouth to stifle the retch.

Seth laughs and holds out one of the cups. The other is gone.

'I don't know,' she says, her voice coming from far away, her stomach twisting at the thought of the neat vodka.

'I've had mine.'

'I just feel . . . I just . . .'

'Come on, Celine. Don't disappoint me.'

She takes the cup. The fumes are enough to make her head spin. *Just get it down.*

Terrible idea. The worst idea. She gags, making it shoot back up her throat, burning behind her nose. She clenches – *Don't vomit, please don't vomit* – shakily forcing it down. Not for long, though. It comes up in a torrent, like she's turning inside out. She can't breathe, she can't see, she hasn't a clue where she is or who she's with. It feels like she's breaking into fragments; the remains of her brain are strewn by her feet, bobbing in the sick like chunks of carrot.

There's talking, laughter. She can feel her body lying on the cold kitchen floor but can't move; she's completely detached. The smell of bleach. Her face being wiped with a wet cloth.

Maybe a few minutes or a few millennia later she's being hoisted up. She's outside, groggy, swaying. There's a cigarette in her hand, but when she takes a drag it nearly makes her throw up again. A car, warm. She curls against the door.

The thrum of the road against her head. Then they stop and she's outside again, Seth helping her. A familiar door sound, a familiar smell. Staggering upstairs. Flopping onto a bed.

Is she home? The lining of her throat feels shredded. She's face down and wants to turn around, see where she is, but her muscles are too floppy. Her will is not strong enough to get them to move. Her middle is lifted, and there's a tugging around her waist. *My skirt.* She tries to think back to what happened, the party, kissing, dancing, then what? The kitchen? It hurts her head just trying to remember.

Thankfully, she's with Seth. He's getting her undressed for bed. There's a *click-clack* she recognises but not from where; he's shuffling with something around his waist. The warmth of his skin presses to hers, until it's too much, too heavy, suffocating. He parts her legs, touches her. She wants to tell him to stop, she's not ready for this, but then he's holding her down. She pushes back, moaning. He doesn't understand and goes harder. She flails behind, but he grabs her arm and holds it behind her back, shoving it higher until she stops bucking and waits for him to finish.

The weight of him lifts, but she can't move. Her head hazes. Her thoughts are manic but slippery; each one seems vital, but the next instant is forgotten. She's aware of time passing, her bare bum getting colder, the sound of a woman screaming on the television. Seth must have put on a film.

Eventually the rawness of her throat is too much. She manages to push herself onto her elbows.

'She's alive,' Seth says. He's sitting up in bed, still in his jeans and black polo shirt, watching a film and smoking a cigarette. He offers her the packet, but the heavy smell of the tobacco makes her stomach lurch. When she shakes her head he takes a long drag. 'There was me thinking you were hardcore.'

She struggles to her feet, to the sink. Slumps onto the rim. 'I don't feel so good.'

'You'll be all right.' On the screen a woman is tied to a chair, her face bloodied and desperate as a garrotte is gently, almost tenderly, slipped around her neck.

Celine fills a cup from the tap, her hand shaking. She remembers his weight on her and her throat becomes paralysed; water spills from her lips when she drinks. *Don't say anything. It's your fault for getting so wasted. You were going to come back and do that anyway.* Her glittery silver top on the floor now looks cheap and common. Throwaway. Trash.

'I didn't like that,' she says, and covers her mouth.

They spoke about this when they first got together. Seth

89

hates women who *spoil the mood*. He'd told her at the time, 'If you've got a problem, let's talk about it later. Don't bring it up while we're having a good time.'

She doesn't look at him; she's hoping he's too lost in the film to have heard.

'What didn't you like?' he says.

'Nothing. It doesn't matter.'

He pauses the film. 'I want to know.'

'Please, Seth—'

'Was it the bit where I had to mop up your sick? Or the bit where I had to apologise to your friends for—'

'No, no, not that.'

'Was it when I all but carried you into a taxi?'

'Doesn't matter,' she says, taking a long sip of water, holding it in her mouth, her heart thumping so hard it makes the cup clatter against her teeth.

He's up and moving towards her. It might still be the drugs, but his face is unreadable. He takes hold of her chin, locking onto her eyes, his tone making her shrivel inside. 'Are you going to tell me what's wrong? Or am I going to force it out of you?'

'I— I wasn't ready when we got home.' *Stupid little girl.* She wants to cry.

'Ready for what?'

'For sex,' she mumbles, and bites her lip.

He lets go and steps back, chuckling. '*You* weren't ready for sex? The way I saw it tonight you're up for anything with anyone.'

'What? I don't—'

'Is that how you normally are with your friends?' Seth's smirk is cruel and cuts her to the core. 'Letting them touch you like that. Do you get off on it? That one of your fantasies?'

She feels herself flush. 'What fantasies?'

'That bloke, the scummy one with the pills. He was all over you and you were loving it.'

Did he mean Flynn? She sees a flash of something from earlier, when they were dancing, but it sinks back into the mud. 'He's a mate.'

'He was sleazing all over you in the pub.' Seth mimes the shoulder rub Flynn gave her, just as she was coming up.

'It's a massage, that's all. It's what people do.'

'What people? Swingers?'

'He's with Ren.'

'That munter? Yeah, right. He'd shag you in a second once her eyes were turned. I saw him when you were dancing, rubbing himself against you. And you couldn't get enough.'

It comes back to her now. 'He was a bit mashed, that's all.'

'What about when I'm not there? What happens then?'

She says it before she can stop herself. 'What about your phone?'

He gives her a sharp look. 'What about it?'

'You said it was out of battery, but I saw you using it.'

'Are you serious?'

She shrinks back. 'I just—'

'I've had enough of this. Fuck you, Celine.' He grabs his jacket and heads for the door.

'Please, Seth.' She reaches for him, sobbing, but he pushes her away. '*Please.*'

'I want you out of my life, you psycho bitch.'

'I'm sorry, I'm sorry. I don't know what I was thinking.'

'Never heard of a phone charger?'

'I didn't know—'

'You were too off your head to know anything.'

He lets her grab onto his jacket. She stands there, holding his sleeve, crying. Finally, he puts his arm around her and brings her in close and she melts into his warmth, still apologising, happy to apologise for ever. Fucking Flynn. She remembers that second pill, in the pub, the way he put it in her mouth. Fucking sleaze.

'I'm sorry,' she says, bringing his face down to hers, desperate for him. 'You're the only person I want. You and no one else.'

His eyes are soft again as he kisses her. She wants to fold up into him. *Never again. Never, ever again.*

From now on nothing will stand in the way of their love.

13

BRYAN

Bryan stares at the threatening Facebook messages. They were all sent last week, some on Wednesday afternoon – the same day he found her confused outside – some on Thursday, and the last one on Friday night.

Time's up bitch

The name of the profile sending them is Lee Connor, chosen no doubt to be too common to investigate. His profile picture, some young ripped bloke tearing off a denim shirt, has clearly been downloaded from the web. He's got one hundred and twenty friends, but all the names look Eastern European and Indian, and it's enough to click into a couple of them to see they have as much in common with Lee Connor from Slough – the only information he's entered – as Bryan does with Detective Inspector Coffee Stain.

It must be Niall.

I'm watching you, that's the first message from Wednesday.

93

It matches one of her journal entries, where she saw a shadowy figure in the trees. Was that why she went outside? If she was drinking in Manchester that time after seeing the figure, perhaps it was the same after the sighting last week? She had her afternoon meds, mixed them with alcohol, and thought she'd investigate. It would definitely explain why she blacked out.

But why didn't she say something?

It seems impossible that his wife could have been going through all this, being followed, threatened online – again – and yet not think it worthy of a mention. Bryan tries to remember their breakfast tray chats from last week, their dinner conversations. She'd been subdued, but that's not surprising, she's often a bit spaced out. Nothing suspicious, though. Either that or he's been too caught up in his own stuff to notice. He presses the heels of his palms into his tired eyes. *So fucking stupid.*

He calls it in to Ronson. The police need to see this.

Some four hours later, the detective deigns to arrive.

'You would not believe the day we're having,' he says at the door, clasping his hands in front of his chest. 'The kind that makes you want to give it all up. Look who I'm talking to. You get it, right?'

Bryan wants to tell him that no, he doesn't 'get' how it's taken Ronson half a day to investigate what in no doubt is crucial evidence. Furthermore, he did not 'give up' his job because he had a lousy morning – he served his twenty-five years and chose to do something new.

'Please come in,' he says. 'Let me make you a drink.'

'You're going to think I'm an absolute pain.' Ronson squeezes his forehead as he comes into the hallway. 'This headache won't quit.'

'Paracetamol okay?'

Bryan leads him through to the computer nook and excuses himself to the kitchen. He grabs the painkillers from the cupboard, shoves a glass under the tap. What the hell is Ronson's deal? Whoever heard of a detective showing up at the house of the victim's family and moaning about a headache, not once but twice. Go buy a bloody pack of Nurofen! Or better yet, pass the case on to someone in better physical shape than you.

When he comes back, Ronson's frowning at the screen. 'I don't know what to make of this.'

'It's got to be Niall, right?'

'Usually with harassment it's more personal,' Ronson says, taking the paracetamol and drinking the whole glass. 'Especially when there's history.'

'They were sent directly to Astrid. How much more personal do you want?'

'How's your wife meant to react to these?'

'Fear?'

'Would you be scared? "I'm watching you, you'll pay for what you've done." These are lines from a bad film.'

'You're complaining he's not more original?'

'She's not blocked him.' He clicks onto Lee Connor's profile. 'That's the first thing you do when you get a message like that, right? If she blocks him, she can't see his profile, but it's right there.'

'I really don't use any of these websites, so I don't—'

'Forgive me, but didn't you say you helped your wife compile her notes last time? I think you also mentioned that Niall Turton created multiple identities on Facebook.'

Bryan feels himself flush. Even though Ronson's not outright accusing him of anything, he's trying to catch him out. 'That's a long way from knowing what you can and you can't see when you block someone.'

'I don't mean to upset you.' The detective ruffles his hair, looks thoughtful. 'Let me show you something.'

They go through to the front room. It's drizzling outside the window, the grey clouds of Lancashire stretching into the distance, but it's still ten times better than looking out and seeing the endless concrete of the city. Bryan imagines Astrid out in the forest in this weather, gloomy to the bones – and last night too, down to five or six degrees. How could she survive that?

He goes to sit on the armchair, but Ronson invites him onto the sofa, where he takes a folder from his rucksack and holds it out.

'What's this?' Bryan takes it. Inside are photocopied sheets of writing.

'They're pages from your wife's journal.'

The first seems to be some dream she had, but the sentences are fragmented – something about a ship, a lost cat, sinking into deep black water – and it's hard to see how it relates to her disappearance. 'I'm not a psychiatrist,' he says, 'if you're looking for me to tell you what it all means.'

'See her handwriting?' Ronson says, pointing to where the letters are particularly slanted. 'Go to the next page.'

On it is what Bryan remembers from her journal last night, the columns containing the details of her recent harassment.

'See how neat her handwriting is,' Ronson says. 'No fear. No urgency.'

Bryan tries to read the detective's expression, but his face is fixed with that same tired smile as always. 'Maybe she thought she should keep it neat in case she needed to show it to the police.'

'Take a look at the next page. That's from Wednesday the first of November, in the evening.'

There's not much to it. A few paragraphs, the writing scruffy, some tired musings on the nature of the self that Bryan is sure she wasn't expecting to be printed and passed around the police. 'What am I looking for?'

'According to her log, she saw him that day, in the trees behind the house. Why didn't she mention it? In fact, she doesn't mention any of the sightings in her personal writing – only where they're recorded at the back. Don't you think that's a bit strange?'

Bryan notices the atmosphere has shifted in the room, the spot-light swinging towards him again, and throws his hands in the air. 'Why are you asking as if I would know? I don't look at her jour-nal, I didn't know about the stalker. All of this is news to me.'

'I'm just trying to make sense of it all.'

'Perhaps if you put this much effort into tracking down Niall Turton then you might be able to check with my wife yourself.'

'Are you sure there's nothing you can tell us about her behaviour at this time? Anything usual?'

Again, Bryan's mind goes back to that night, last Wednesday, when he got home late from the office and found the house empty, Astrid confused and practically naked out the back. Should he tell Ronson about that? But what would be the point? Would it help find her now? Or would it make him seem like more of a negligent husband than the detective clearly already believes – because in what kind of decent marriage does your wife not tell you when she's being stalked?

'I'm as confused by all this as you are,' Bryan says, handing back the sheets. 'But I'm not seeing any answers here.'

Ronson takes them, shaking his head. 'I must apologise, Mr Webb. You're right, of course. I just thought we had something interesting. A lead.'

'This is your idea of a lead?'

'Perhaps.'

Bryan bites down on his lip, swallows hard. He doesn't want to fall out with the detective, get on his bad side, make himself more of a target than he already is. Why else would Ronson show him these printouts if not to see his reaction?

'Have you even managed to find Niall yet?' Bryan asks.

'Unfortunately I'm not able to discuss that.'

'You can't tell me if you have any information on the person who's most likely kidnapped my wife?'

Ronson creaks to his feet, his knees popping. He glances at Bryan like they're both in on the same joke. 'Need to get some oil on these old joints.'

'Do you have anything at all for me?'

'We're doing our best, Mr Webb,' he says, not unkindly. 'As soon as we have something we can share, we'll be in touch.'

They go through to the hallway. Ronson turns by the door. 'I'll send a constable soon to get the computer, but for now please don't touch it any more.' His look turns serious. 'Don't delete anything. Okay?'

'Why would I delete anything?' Is this another indication that he's a suspect? The sooner Hoop gets back to him with what's in that case file, the better.

'We can retrieve it from the hard drive anyway, but you know some people get funny. Start clearing out stuff before the police see it. I'm suggesting it's best if you don't.'

'You're wrong about me. I haven't done anything to my wife.'

'No one's accusing you, Mr Webb.'

'What do I have to say to get through to you?'

Ronson gives Bryan a serious look. 'If there is a case to answer, that'll be for the CPS to decide.'

Does that mean they're already building a case against him?

'Perhaps if you stopped wasting your time trying to analyse my wife's handwriting you may have already found her by now.'

'Try to stay calm, Mr Webb. We'll be in touch.'

Once the detective has gone, Bryan spins away from the door, fists clenched. What is happening here? The longer this goes on, the less sense it's making. Ronson has a good point – why *didn't* Astrid mention being stalked again in her journal? You'd think the pages would be filled with fears and theories. Just like you'd think the first thing she'd do would be to tell her husband.

He rushes back to the computer nook, looks at the messages again, clicks into and out of Lee Connor's profile. Why didn't she block him after she received the first one?

None of this makes any sense.

Unless . . .

Bryan pushes away from the computer, his eyes widening. *Oh my God.* It can't be possible, but what other explanation fits everything that's happened – her disappearance, these messages, the fact that she neither mentioned being followed or wrote about it in her journal?

A ping from the screen. Another tab in the browser starts to flash. Bryan opens it and finds a message from Meera.

Are you free Bryan? It's URGENT. Can I come over to see you?

14

ASTRID

WEDNESDAY 1 NOVEMBER, 9.23 A.M., THREE DAYS BEFORE THE CRASH

Astrid turns to the side in front of the full-length bedroom mirror. Bryan would not approve of her outfit. He thinks off-the-shoulder tops look weird, knee-high boots are slutty, and don't get him started on women who wear them *outside* their jeans. When they go on a date, he prefers her in long dresses, sky blue or sunflower yellow.

This isn't an outfit, it's a statement. *Sod you.*

Sod you, Bryan. Sod you, Dinckley.

Sod her life so far.

She's scared, of course. Any normal person in her position would be shaking in their (slutty) boots. But she feels stronger than she has in years, focused and aware, closer to the woman she was before this nightmare began. The last few weeks have reinvigorated a way of thinking that she nourished at school (as a coping mechanism, but still): *everything happens for a reason.* Surely this journey isn't destined to end with her husband finding out, not unless fate is a sadist. Although she hasn't quite ruled that out.

The crunch of wheels outside. She checks the window and sees his navy-blue car coming to a stop. Hopefully that old busybody at the top of the road isn't twitching her curtains as they drive away.

The sun is out. They have the whole day. Astrid skips down the stairs, twirls and grabs her jacket from the hook, feeling lithe as a ballerina. Bryan always works late at the office on Wednesday, often not coming home until after six, so they have the whole day. The freedom feels glorious.

'Wow,' he says when she slides into the passenger seat. 'You look amazing.'

She flashes him a smile. 'You clearly have a low threshold for being amazed.'

They laugh, and then they're off. At the top of the lane, she sticks her tongue out at Meera's cottage. *You can have him. He's all yours.*

Blackpool was her idea.

For those who hate the place, they'll point to the fact that the beach is more mud than sand. They'll mention the rusty tower, like Eiffel's stunted cousin, the stink of chip grease and stag party vomit, the constant clanging of the slot machines on the strip. She doesn't see it that way. Yes, it's a bit garish. Yes, it's a bit grotty. But it's *fun*.

She grew up expecting to hate it there. The kids at her school used it as a punchline for jokes about scummy holiday destinations. It took Vivien quite a bit of persuading to get Astrid to go at first, but they had such a great time that it became a tradition. They'd get a big group together and go for a weekend in June, hitting the rollercoasters, something naff like Madame Tussauds, then rolling around the bars on the strip, before finally stumbling into Trilogy at midnight. That was where she started her first big romance, with Lucas, a Swiss design student. He said that he wanted to marry her, that he'd stay in England for her, that they'd have a whole family of Alpine-haired babies. It lasted the two months until he returned home at the end of summer.

That's the Astrid she's doing this for. The version of herself she's desperate to get back.

The drive takes less than an hour on the quiet motorway. They park a few streets off the coast, getting out to a cold, grey, windy morning. Where did the sun go? Is this some kind of sign, or maybe a metaphor? Home was sunny, here is gloomy. *Are you taking the hint?*

Then he's beside her, sliding his arm around her, guiding her towards the sea. 'Any day's a beautiful day when I'm with you,' he says in reply to her grumbling. She can't help but be swept along by him. *Stop doubting!*

They walk to the north pier, the longest, her favourite. You can stand at the end with the waves crashing below and believe you're in the middle of the ocean, thousands of miles from your problems. On your way already to a new life.

'Thanks for bringing me here,' she says. They're leaning on the rail, looking out at the dark swells.

'I can't believe the change in you,' he says.

'Thanks to you.'

He glances at her sideways, his look enigmatic. The wind has made his tanned cheeks pink. 'You've changed me too.'

A part of her is still holding back. Despite everything, she has doubts. Does she really understand what's going on? What does she actually know about the man standing beside her, beyond her attraction to him? If this were a film, would the audience be rooting for their romance, or screaming at the screen for her to run away?

'I just want you to know,' he says, turning to her. She follows his lead so they're face to face. 'I'm here for the long haul. Whatever it takes, I'm here.'

Her heart is beating so hard she's worried he can see the pound of her pulse in her throat (stupid off-the-shoulder top!). Has he always been this handsome?

He takes her chin in his fingers and brings her face forward to his lips. Thinking about this moment, once or twice or two hundred times, she'd pictured it rough with passion, but instead the kiss is gentle, tender. Something softens in her gut, and she melts into him. He holds her tight and they stay that way as the wind picks up, and the waves crash louder, and she thinks maybe this will work, maybe this will happen. Maybe they can start a new life together.

The seafront is quiet. They stroll along, hand in hand. When she suggests they get fish and chips and sit on the deckchairs, he laughs and says they can do a bit better than that. He leads her through a maze of small streets near the town centre to a boutique Italian called Sapori, where they share bruschetta and sautéed chicken livers along with a half bottle of red wine. Afterwards they grab some candyfloss and spend some fun but fruitless hours trying to win her a prize at the stalls. When he finally scores her a penguin soft toy at the coconut shy, she offers it to a young girl watching them – she can hardly take it home to Bryan.

'You'd make a wonderful mother,' he says on the way back to the car.

'I think that ship has sunk,' she replies.

He squeezes her hand. 'My parents were older when they had me.'

'One step at a time,' she says, a little too brusquely. That same doubt, bursting to the surface like a diver desperate for air.

'Of course,' he replies, but his voice sounds terse, and his grip loosens on hers. 'Let's just get you home.'

Once in the car the moment of tension seems to have passed. It's still only three o'clock, so they have plenty of time until Bryan gets home. They drive back in amiable silence, Heart FM on the radio, her eyelids slipping shut as the opening bars of Cream's 'I Feel Free' comes on.

So easy to fall asleep these days. These last few years, with her illness, it's been like trying to smile with her lips in a vice. No one can understand the prison of pain unless you've spent a few years behind its bars. Not days, like if you bang your head. Or weeks with a bruised rib, months with a broken leg. *Years.* Now all she has to do to fall asleep is close her eyes and clear her mind and . . .

She comes awake to the car jerking to a halt. Through the windscreen the traffic stretches over the hill and round the bend. All three lanes are jammed.

'I was hoping it would clear,' he says, apologetic.

If this is a trial, then it's a cruel one. Always catching her when she's most off guard. *Hubris.* She looks to the satnav, but the solid red line stretching off the screen is no comfort. 'Can we make it?'

'I want to say yes.'

Which obviously means no. 'Can you just tell me what's happened?'

He drags the map on his phone, taps at a tiny exclamation mark, sucks the air through his bottom teeth. 'Accident. Two lanes shut.'

'That sounds bad.'

'Could be worse.'

'How could this be worse?'

He cocks an eyebrow. 'The whole motorway could be closed.'

He's playing with her, trying to tease a smile, but he doesn't realise what he's done. She didn't tell him everything that she's found out. If she had, he wouldn't be so cocky now. He'd be just as scared as her.

This jeopardises everything.

Six has long gone when they finally speed past the sign for Dinckley. 'Stop here,' Astrid says, still half a mile from the cottage. They kiss before she gets out, but it's rushed, their breath stale, and leaning over the handbrake on a layby lacks the power and grandeur of the wave-lashed pier.

She takes the back way to the cottage. How's she going to explain where she's been? She didn't tell Bryan she was going out. She didn't take her car. Even if she wasn't dressed in a skimpy top and (let's be honest) fuck-me boots, he's hardly likely to believe she decided to go for a late-afternoon ramble.

It's already close to seven by the time she gets home. Lights are on in the hallway. No way she'll be able to get in the house without him noticing. What if he's called the police? The longer she's away, the harder it'll be to explain.

She pauses in the trees opposite the front door, then skirts round the side of the cottage. It's already dark, but the moon is full, and it would be easy enough for him to look through a window, see a flitting shape, and come charging out. She stays low as she goes past the back garden and into the deeper wood, finding the air-raid shelter by instinct.

Astrid strips down to her underwear. At the last second, she pulls off her bra (too lacy), and throws the lot inside the shelter. Shivering in the sudden cold, she wipes herself with dirt and dunks her hair in a muddy puddle, wringing the excess water with her hands.

By the time she gets to the cottage there's no need to act; her body temperature has plummeted. Bryan is on the phone by the sink, lips pursed, rubbing his forehead. She must look quite the sight when she slaps the kitchen window.

He glances up, confused. Then he throws his phone onto the counter and rushes to the back door.

'Oh my God,' he says, bringing her inside. 'What are you doing out there?'

'I—I don't know. I came out of the shower, and I went into the bedroom, and . . . I blacked out. I don't know what happened next.'

'What time was this?'

'I don't know. I'm not sure.'

'How long have you been outside?'

'I'm so cold,' she wails.

Bryan rushes to the utility room and comes back with towels. He still seems hesitant, until the first sob bursts from her, and she buries her face in his chest. A moment later he wraps her in the towel, holding her close.

'It's okay,' he says. 'You're safe now. You're with me.'

A shiver goes through her. That's what she's most afraid of.

15

BRYAN

Bryan opens the door to Meera, holding a sealed Pyrex of her masala chicken. She hands it to him and steers him inside.

'I did not have a wink of sleep last night,' she says, 'worrying about your dear wife.'

'Thanks.' The warmth of the glass is comforting against his chest. He realises he's not eaten since the couple of rounds of cold toast he forced down at lunch. Meera goes to take off her coat, but pauses, glancing at him. 'Please, come through,' he says. 'Can I get you a drink?'

Now the coat comes off, revealing a purple cashmere sweater so short it would lift above her midriff if she raised her arms. There's a definite strut to her step as she leads the way to the kitchen. Does she always wear perfume? By the time he's followed her, she's already filling the kettle.

She clicks it on and turns to him, leaning against the counter. 'But how are you, Bryan? This is so terrible.'

'Well, yes,' he says, and puts the Pyrex on the table. 'About as well as can be expected, which is not well at all.'

'And the police? Have you heard?'

If she's just come for a gossip, she's out of luck. His patience for her usual prattling is limited. 'You mentioned something urgent?'

'Sorry, sorry, I don't mean to be nosy! I just want you to know that I am here for you, Bryan. I pray to God that she is okay, but if . . . the worst.' She closes her eyes and shudders her upper body. 'I cannot bear to think of it.'

'I didn't get much sleep either.'

She nods, her face sympathetic, then makes the tea. Behind her Bryan shifts his weight from foot to foot. Would it be too rude to shake this supposedly urgent information out of her?

'Do you remember my doorbell?' she says as they sit at the table. She takes a sip of her tea. 'You asked me to see if there was any video from yesterday morning, when Astrid drove past.'

'You told me your son fixed it.'

'Yes, yes, he fixed it, but it keeps the videos for three months.'

Bryan sits forward in his chair. 'And?'

'Well, last night, when I was awake, I begin thinking maybe I could look through them to see if . . . well, I don't know what I was looking for.'

He wants to scream at her to hurry up, get to the bloody point. Instead, he grips the side of the table and says, 'You must have found something, then.'

'I have to say, Bryan, you don't get many visitors.'

'Please Meera. Can you get to the point.'

She slaps her cheeks. 'Oh my God, listen to me. I'm so sorry. My son always tells me I talk too much, but I'm nervous.'

'Of me?'

'No, no! It's just . . .'

'Just what?'

'Did I ever tell you about my husband?'

He knows she's divorced, but little of the backstory. Nor is he particularly interested now. 'You mentioned your doorbell?'

'Listen to me, Bryan,' she says, laying a hand on his arm. 'When I found out the truth about Suresh, it hurt me almost like he died. More, I think, because he was still alive! I could have killed him so much.'

'He left you?'

'He cheated on me, and then he left me.'

'I'm sorry to hear that,' Bryan says. His face feels hot, his stomach clenched. 'Why don't you show me what you've found.'

With a deep sigh, Meera takes out her phone. She taps at the screen with her long red nails. 'Maybe I am wrong,' she says.

She hands the phone to Bryan at the start of a video. It's from last week, Wednesday, at nine thirty in the morning, half an hour after he left for work. The same day he found Astrid outside.

He presses play. Across the street is the narrow lane leading to their cottage, and turning into it is a navy-blue car. It stops out of view and the video ends. He winds it back, enlarges the screen, but the camera isn't sharp enough to see the licence plate number.

'That's it?' he asks.

'Go to the next video.'

Bryan swipes across and presses play. It's six minutes later, 9.37 a.m. The same car turns out of their lane. He can't see the faces of the people in the car, the sun is reflecting off the windscreen, but he can see the number – when it arrived there was one, when it leaves there's two. You don't need to be a paid-up member of Mensa to work out who the second person must be.

He thinks back to when he got home from work that night. He *knew* there was something suspicious about it, he felt it in his sergeant's soul, but she looked so distraught, and it was hardly the first time she'd had one of those episodes, the kind of drugs she's on. Was she out with another man that day?

Where does that leave the threatening messages from 'Lee Connor'? Or the details in her journal about being stalked? Are those real, or have they been planted – but to cover up what?

One thing is for sure: his wife is not as innocent in this as he had presumed.

16

RONSON

The front of Greenbank police station in Blackburn looks smart, with its modern lines and glass everywhere, the see-through lift to the third floor, but once you drive through the gates and past the line of highway patrol cars, it's the same groaning hulk of steel and brick as when it was first expanded back in the seventies. Some parts inside are as cold and damp as back then too. Grim for coppers and crims alike.

Detective Sergeant Jessica Maxwell slots their car next to an armoured van. 'Well?'

'I'm afraid you may have to take me behind the sheds and put me out of my misery,' Ronson replies, eyes closed, head leaning back against the rest.

'You need to take a break, boss.'

Ronson cracks an eyelid. 'We can't all be radiant after thirty hours straight.'

'Aren't you exhausted?'

'I could say the same to you.'

'Go home, Gabriel.'

He grabs the door handle and sighs. 'Let's head upstairs.'

After leaving Webb's cottage, he'd gone back to the crash site to get an update, but it was still the same. The forest stretching for miles, vast enough to be searched for decades and still keep its secrets. The case is slipping away. He can sense it. Over the years many people have disappeared into those dark trees, never to be seen again. Will Astrid Webb simply be the latest?

The offices are quiet at this time on a Sunday night. Cleaners mill around the desks, wiping the surfaces, emptying bins. Further along there's the sound of vacuuming. They take the lift to the third floor, where some of the team are still staring at their screens.

Unlike the front of the building, the canteen is very much of a vintage era – an echoing space jammed with mismatched tables and rickety chairs, with photocopied notices so old the tape sticking them to the walls has gone brown, the ceiling stained the colour of mustard from when you could smoke inside. Thankfully the prices match the decor. It's possibly the only place in the North where you can still buy a chip butty for a pound.

Maxwell gets them coffees from the machine and brings them to the table, now spread with pages from the case file.

'You don't want to gather the troops?' she asks.

'As much as I can't wait to hear what they have to grumble about, let's get our heads together first.'

'Nothing more from the car,' Maxwell says, lifting the forensics report they received a couple of hours ago. 'Her prints on the wheel, her blood on the windscreen. Nowt from the passenger side.'

Ronson sifts through the papers for the blood splatter report.

'She crashed, we've got that much. No airbag, fine, it's an old car so it's probably used already. But look here.' He shows her the photos from driver's side. 'Acceptable pattern on the glass, and here on the dash, but the first contact has surely got to be the wheel – and nothing. Watch this.' He mimes a crash in slow motion, his body straining against the seat belt, his head slamming forward then jerking back, using his fingers to show the direction of the spray. 'If she doesn't bust at least her nose on impact, where's the spray coming from?'

'Maybe he's got a knife, and that's why there's blood.'

'We're back with her mystery assailant.'

'The cottage?'

Ronson takes a sip of his coffee. Everyone moans about it, that it's thin and bitter, but over the years he's gotten so used to the taste he can't stand anything else. 'Look at this,' he says, finding the photo of the back door. 'Someone goes to the trouble to smash it in, but then avoids the glass on the floor? To get inside they've either got to step on the glass – which would leave impact marks – or jump over it. And why bother doing that?'

'No footprints inside, no sign of a scuffle.'

'Exactly.'

Maxwell sweeps her hands over her face, takes out and reties her ponytail. 'You think it's a set-up?'

'I don't know what to think.'

'How was the husband when you saw him?'

'Tense.'

'Wouldn't you be with your wife missing?'

'He's hiding something.'

She gives him a sarcastic smile. 'Let me guess, his wife's body.'

'It's the obvious conclusion.'

'Don't like him much, do you?'

Ronson waves her away. 'You know better than that, Jess.'

'Sure, boss.'

He can see she's not convinced. 'There's plenty willing to vouch for Bryan Webb, what a good bloke he is, but you don't run a station in Manchester for over ten years without knowing how to come down hard when you need to.'

'Oh, right,' she says, her expression firmly implying *here we go again*. 'I was wondering when this would come up.'

'Webb has a rep, if you ask the right people. My way or the highway.'

'Policing by gossip, are we now?'

Ronson presses his hands to his chest. 'You wound me.'

It may not seem like it to look at him, with his grey hair and comfy shoes, but in his prime Ronson had a reputation as a maverick. Sticklers like Webb have always rubbed him up the wrong way, with their shelves of *Blackstone's* manuals. When the crackdown on rogue officers started in the noughties, surprise surprise, who were the first to have their dirty little secrets uncovered: the by-the-book bobbies who liked to beat everyone over the head with the rulebook.

Maxwell looks over the pages spread out on the table. 'You really think Webb killed his wife and staged the crash?'

'You want to rule it out?'

'No insurance payout. No sign she was having an affair. No motive.'

'You know what else Webb doesn't have? An alibi.'

That's the crux of it. Those two-and-three-quarter hours from when Bryan Webb says he left the house to when he got back. They've scoured the traffic cameras from Dinckley to Longridge Fell but can't see any sign of him cycling past. Nor have any witnesses come forward to validate him being up there on Saturday morning.

All that is in marked contrast to Niall Turton.

Since his harassment of Astrid Webb, Turton has been done twice for indecent exposure and outraging public decency, the latter offence landing him a ten-year sexual harm prevention order. Nowadays he's living with his uncle near St Helens, on the way out to Liverpool.

They paid him a visit yesterday afternoon, six hours after the discovery of the crash. He seemed stoned when they came in – not at all like someone who'd just come back from kidnapping and possibly killing someone – but perked up fast when they mentioned Mrs Webb. Didn't deny what happened in the past but made it very clear he'd not seen her for years, had no inter-est in seeing her, and would they kindly leave him alone. His uncle said they were at home together all morning.

'He's still the obvious suspect,' Maxwell says.

Ronson finishes his coffee. 'A repeat offender.'

Turton had agreed to a search, but it hadn't uncovered much besides some borderline pornography.

Maxwell finds the write-up of the visit. 'How reputable is the uncle?'

'With your sex pest nephew living with you, smoking pot and looking at pictures of possibly underage girls? I'd say maybe not much.'

'It's hardly the same as murder.'

Ronson takes a long breath through his nose. It seems so obvi-ous that it must be Turton. He's stalked Astrid Webb before, he's continued to rack up the charges – and he certainly seemed shifty enough during their chat – but when Ronson pictures him sneaking round the side of the Webb's cottage, smashing the back door, forcing her probably at knifepoint, it doesn't match up to the sad case they'd interrupted at his pre-dinner bong.

'If we're calling a debrief,' Maxwell says, 'better do it now. By eight you might be on your own.'

'Part-timers.'

'Some of us like going home.' She catches his eye. 'Sorry.'

'Don't be, Jess. You head off, I'll carry on for a bit.'

'I wasn't hinting for that.'

'Go on, I've got this.'

Maxwell comes round the table and crouches beside him. She rests her hand on his arm. 'You've got to take a break.'

Her smile is sad, and the one he returns probably isn't much better. 'You know what they say. Plenty of time to rest when you're dead.'

'Go home, Gabriel. Please.'

Ronson pats the back of her hand. Go home to what? An empty house. It's not the same since Cath passed, all those cold rooms. 'I'm just going to check something, then I'm off. I promise.'

'All right,' Maxwell says, and sighs. She stands and gives him a hard look he can't quite meet. 'If I don't hear from you, I'll be back at six.'

Ronson watches her go. They've only been working together a few years, but already she's the best sergeant he's ever had. Smart, always so in control, but with that extra bit of empathy the best detectives have. It's good to know that when he does finally flame out there's an able deputy to step into the role.

Aside from the hum of the strip lights, it's quiet in the canteen. He leans back in his chair, hands behind his head, and stares out of the window into the darkness. What if it's neither of those two men? What if it's something else entirely – like Mrs Webb doing a runner? But they have her medical records. A woman in her condition is in no fit state to up sticks and vanish. Presumably she'll go through her medication, and what then? How's she going to fill a prescription if she's supposed to be dead?

He hunts through the papers again, finding her mobile phone records. They've already been analysed by one of the team. Most calls are to her husband, and the rest have checked out. No provable evidence of an affair, or that she staged an escape with a lover. And yet, someone as sick as Astrid Webb, would they really have it in them to be sleeping around?

Someone else is involved. Ronson knows it, he can feel it.

But who could that someone be?

17

CELINE

Celine's in her flat, leaning into the bathroom mirror. She's focused as she smooths blusher on her cheeks, as she glosses her lips, as she rubs styling mousse into her fair hair. A pause to take a drag on the spliff smouldering in the ashtray, laced with enough of the good stuff to lightly float her mind, then up close to sweep mascara along her lashes.

'I'm intrigued by you,' Seth said, the first night they met. 'And I'm rarely intrigued by anyone.'

That had been June. She'd been in town for a few drinks, sitting outside the Old Welly in Shambles Square. One of the other girls clocked him first, the hot guy staring at their table, like he thought they might be people he knew. They were all clucking for him; tanned and rugged, strong arms, thick black hair like something from a Jane Austen remake on the telly, but in jeans and a Diesel T. When at last Seth strolled up to them, he ignored the rest of the girls and came straight for her.

Come eleven that night she'd sacked off her mates and gone with him to a bar called Prohibition. Sat among the fancy crowd and glittery lights, they drank fizz, dug deep into their lives, and pashed so hard the couple next to them had to move away.

He got them a room at the Radisson on Deansgate. His place

was being done up, and she could hardly take him back to the squat. They stayed awake until dawn making love, finally falling sleep in an embrace, waking nose to nose.

That night, he said the Celine she was pretending to be didn't exist; she'd explained what had happened with her family, why she'd run away. He kissed the scars hidden on her inner thighs and said she was never allowed to hurt herself again, that if she hurt herself she was hurting him now.

'I've never felt this way before,' he'd said. 'I think I might be falling in love.'

During the summer they made plans almost every night, but since the end of September he's been distant. Not like he was at the start, talking on the phone three or four times a day, plus messages. When she mentioned it, he got snappy, something else he didn't used to do, but said he had a day off coming up. They'd spend it together.

This is that day, and she can't wait to be with him.

She gets the 192 to St Peter's Square and hurries the rest of the way down Deansgate. It's sunny in town and the streets are busy with the lunchtime rush, shoppers raiding the end-of-season sales, office drones snatching a drab sandwich. She spots a couple of the staff who work in a pub she knows smoking out the back and gives them a wave, swaying her hips when one of them wolf-whistles.

They're meeting at a pub first where Seth's having a sesh with his mates. Only for a bit, he assured her, someone's leaving do, then they'll be out on their own. He's promised her a fine day. A posh lunch, a mooch through the shop, then on to the bars, wherever she wants to go. He didn't need to tell her how the day was going end. It makes her spine quiver just thinking about it.

She doesn't actually mind meeting his friends. Sometimes their relationship seems like a fantasy, almost a fairy tale. She worries that that he'll get bored of her, that he'll want to find someone who's thirty like him, even though he's said that he finds women his own age boring because they just want to sit at home and watch romcoms. Introducing her to his friends makes it feel a bit more legit. She'll gets to see a different side to her man; she wants to know everything about him.

The Moon Under Water tries to look smart with its gold-painted rails and all those dangling lights but it's really just a big Wetherspoons. She finds them in a booth at the back, a large group of boisterous blokes, some around Seth's age, others much older, in their fifties even, she finds it hard to judge. They all cheer when she arrives, and she goes to squeeze in next to Seth, but instead he clambers over them and says they're heading straight off. It's disappointing, it looks like they were having a laugh, but she doesn't let it show on her face; no chance is she going to ruin today.

On their own, her anxiety fades. They stroll towards Castlefield pressed close to each other, Seth whispering in her ear how stunning she is, how jealous his mates looked when she arrived. As soon as they get to San Carlos, a swish Spanish tapas place where everyone's attractive and the staff wear little black bow ties, he orders her a double vodka cranberry. When the waiter goes to get their drinks, they sneak keys of coke, ducked close to the table. Seth's told her he has to be careful with drugs, they get tested occasionally at work, but today's different, it's special, she's special, and, holding her hands, looking in her eyes, like he's seeing right into her beating heart, he tells her that no one in his life has ever, *ever*, been as special as her.

They don't really bother with the food when it comes, not now they've got a buzz. It's the same with shopping, although they still do the rounds, Harvey Nics, Selfridges, the little boutiques on Old Bank Street. Seth sneaks into the dressing room where they go at it until the middle-aged woman from behind the counter bursts in, ranting about calling the police.

'It's called sex,' Seth tells her. 'Try it. Might loosen you up.'

More keys. A bottle of Prosecco in a dimly lit bar. Kissing Seth on a dance floor, eyes closed and swaying to funky Latin house. He tells her to stay put while he nips to the loo. The dance floor isn't busy, just couples and stragglers. A bunch of youngish lads are watching her from the sides trying to force one of their mates up to speak to her. She's not interested in any of that so she drifts closer to the DJ, still moving to the beat, but she can feel their gaze on her. Perhaps they hadn't seen her with Seth.

She forgets about them but a moment later she hears, 'All right, beautiful.'

One of the lads is behind her; he lays a hand on her waist, and she slaps it off.

'What'cho doing here with your dad,' he says.

She can tell from his drooping eyelids and the beer spill down his shiny shirt that he's had a skinful. 'Do one, dickhead.'

He tries to reach around to grab her arse, grinning like he's the man – then he's moving backwards at great speed. Seth's got him by the neck; he's pushing the lad to the floor, pummelling him. The music's still going, security isn't interested. Seth grabs the lad's collar, fist cocked, waiting for him to say something, but he's out of it already, his head rocking side to side like it's loose on his neck. All his mates are cowering behind a table.

Now security come forward. Seth says something to them she can't hear, and they all laugh. He comes to her, hand out, face saying, *Sorry about all that.*

They kiss, and he whispers in her ear. 'Anyone wants you, they've got to come through me first.'

18

CELINE

It's hard to know when Seth's asleep, he doesn't snore much, so she gives it a good hour after they turn off the light before slipping out of bed. Celine began searching his things a few weeks ago, after lying awake, heart thumping, desperate to know why it felt as though they were drifting apart.

So far, she's found nothing concrete to worry about, but there are hints. A receipt for what looks like a romantic dinner at the Menagerie. A crumpled tissue with a hint of a smudge of mauve lipstick. She moves methodically through the pockets, jeans first, front and back, and the little one for a condom. Next, his jacket, easing the zips and buttons open a millimetre at a time. She finds his wallet and feels through it; Seth doesn't carry much in it, just cards, bit of cash.

His phone is plugged in beside the bed. She smothers it in a jumper as she eases it from the charger, knowing the screen will light up, and tiptoes to the bathroom. She hates doing this. What if he gets up for a piss? Her fingers are shaking as she unlocks it with his passcode – he's never careful about hiding it.

She checks his messages, hoping to see to the same stuff as last time. Just banter with his mates, football, dirty jokes, taking the mickey out of people she doesn't know. Her chest seizes when she sees a number not saved as a contact. Inside the message is an address. It ends with, *see you tomorrow at 2 xx*

Celine checks the date he received it; this afternoon while they were out shopping. He's not replied.

She'd asked him what he was doing tomorrow, whether she could see him again as he wasn't in work. *I wish I could,* he'd said, *but I promised a mate I'd help him move house.* What kind of mate signs off with a couple of kisses?

That and the coke from before means she spends the night staring at the ceiling. When Seth wakes and says, 'Hello beautiful,' she plays up her hangover to cover her dismay. He has a wash, swills a quick coffee. One more snatched kiss and he's out the door, calling behind, 'No rest for the wicked!'

Celine is supposed to be working the afternoon shift at the Three Bells, but calls in sick. All morning she can barely swallow as she tries to load directions to the address on her phone, but the handset's crap, and her signal's crap, and eventually she gives up and finds an internet cafe in town where she's able to print a map. Then she sits in Piccadilly Gardens chain-smoking rollies until it's time to go.

Why does it have to be another woman? Maybe they're having a poker game or something. The kisses could easily be a joke, loads of his texts have that kind of bantz, although she's never really understood why blokes find it so funny to pretend to be gay but then get really aggro if someone calls them that for real. But if it's innocent, why not tell her? Is she so pushy, so demanding of his time, that he has to lie to her otherwise he won't hear the end of it? He's probably thinking he already spent all of yesterday with her; he knew she'd get the hump if he didn't drop all his plans today. You can't blame him for lying when he's got to deal with that shit.

When she gets off the train the sky's clouded over. The station's not much, not even a shop, and she doesn't have to show her ticket when she leaves. She comes out to a residential street of semi-detached houses, and follows the route carefully with her map, until she gets to a proper country road where she has to walk on the grass verge as cars terrifyingly whoosh past. It hadn't seemed that far when she'd been looking at it earlier, but after an hour she's still walking. What if she's taken the wrong turn? What if she's heading down to the motorway? It's already after one. She'll never get there for two if she has to double back.

It's so like where she grew up, round here. Boring fields as far as the eye can see. At least until she was twelve, when her mum met Derek and they moved to his massive house in Chester; five bedrooms, even though he lived on his own, and tall gates at the entrance to the drive. Celine always thought there was something a bit skeezy about the gold rings squeezed onto his fat fingers, and the way he walked around with the top three buttons of his shirt open to show the sweaty rug beneath.

For years he never bothered much with her. The house was big enough for them to avoid each other, and she wasn't there much anyway. One night she got in late, like two o'clock in the morning; he must have been out as well, because he was in the kitchen, drinking a brandy in one of his crystal glasses, and started having a go at her. *Why you always so bloody miserable? You know it costs nothing to smile.*

She might have mumbled at him to fuck off and leave her alone, she can't quite remember her exact words, but it was enough to get Derek off his big arse and round the counter. *Who do you think you are? How dare you disrespect me? This is my house, and now you're sixteen things are going to change if you expect to stay here.*

He was blocking her path to the door. She should've taken the long way round the counter, but she was drunk, feeling bolshy, and who was he to tell her what to do? As she pushed past him, she muttered a few choice words about him not being her dad.

'If I was your dad,' he said, grabbing the hem of her miniskirt and yanking it up, 'I wouldn't let out you dressed like a slut.'

Celine spun around, grabbed a vegetable knife from the draining board. 'Touch me like that again.'

Derek backed off, hands up, chins wobbling beneath his shocked mouth. She threw the knife in the sink and ran upstairs. Wedged a chair under the door handle.

You've always been difficult, is what her mum said the next morning, when it all came out. *You just like to cause trouble.*

Derek, of course, denied it all, saying that Celine came home pissed and looking for a fight, while he was doing nothing more than having a quiet nightcap before bed.

That was almost a year and a half ago. She hasn't spoken to her mum since.

Finally, pavement, houses. A street sign. Celine compares it the map and wants to fall to her knees because it's correct, she's gone the right way.

The address is hard to find as it's for a cottage that's set back on its own little road. It's long and old-looking, one of those where you can see the wooden beams, the smooth outside walls painted white. Now the sun's gone behind clouds it's chilly; she should have brought a hoodie or something.

Ten to two. She kneels in the bushes, shivering, the damp soaking through to her knees. What's she doing here? Cold, knackered, hiding outside what's probably his grandma's place like a stalker. What's she going to do if Seth sees her? That's their relationship done and it'll be all her fault.

Footsteps, whistling. Someone's approaching the cottage. She peers from behind the leaves – it's Seth, swaggering down the lane with a bottle of wine. Her breath stops as his gaze sweeps past her. He knocks on the front door, and pushes his arms out, stretching. She's quaking so hard she has to press her hands into the dirt to stop herself toppling over.

The door opens. Seth says something and laughs; he's in the way, so she can't quite see who's on the other side; a woman's voice tells him to come on in. Celine cranes her neck, but she overbalances and has to move her foot to stabilise. Something cracks beneath her heel. She freezes.

'You hear that?' the woman asks. Seth turns and scans again, slower this time; Celine shrinks down, praying he doesn't catch a glimpse of her clothing through the bush. He moves to the side and the woman comes out. She's as old as Seth, if not older. Thin, blonde hair, face all made-up, wearing a dark V-neck playsuit. Not stunning, but they could be a couple. Celine can see they'd look good together.

'Just a fox,' Seth says, placing his hand on her back, surely too far down for them simply to be friends.

The slam of the door reverberates through the air.

Celine waits for a bit, but it's too depressing to stay for long. What does she expect to see anyway? Him coming out looking satisfied? No thanks.

The walk back to the station is hellish. She's crying too hard to focus on her feet, and often strays onto the road, only jumping out of the way of an oncoming car at the last second. She keeps hearing the woman's voice, seeing her face and the hang of her clothes. Seth's hand resting on her lower back as he guided her inside.

But on the train, a new resolution grows inside her. A new voice demanding to be heard. It's saying, *What would Seth do in this situation?* It's reminding her of their date last night, the way he grabbed that lad.

'Anyone wants you,' Celine says to herself, trying the words out in her mouth. 'They've got to come through me first.'

19

ASTRID

Astrid should have left by now. She should have been far from her husband, far from Dinckley. But Bryan won't leave her on her own. For days he's remained steadfast in his sentry duty in case she takes 'another little wander', working upstairs instead of at the office, popping his head into whatever room she happens to be in, just to 'check she's okay'. Every time he appears in the doorway, she expects it to be with a knife in his hand, the strings from *Psycho* starting up, the final act to this madness playing out in a pool of blood. Her blood, or maybe his. Who knows any more?

She's not slept much (or maybe at all) for the last few days. Although it's different to when she was ill, the passing hours not so onerous. Or it could simply be that there is an end in sight, a curtain call for this stage of her life. Finally, she hears Bryan's door open, the *clomp-clomp-clomp* of his old brown Birkenstocks heading down the stairs. From the kitchen comes the sound of water filling the kettle, the clatter of crockery on the counter, his morning throat clear like an old car trying and failing to start.

It's only fair, Astrid supposes, for Bryan to be concerned about what happened on Wednesday night. A few weeks ago, before she even had an inkling of the truth, she would've been terrified to black out and 'go for a wander' in the forest. She'd be worried about brain tumours, demanding appointments for an MRI scan. Instead, she's been playing it down so he'll stop worrying. How can he not find that suspicious?

Back he comes up the stairs. At eight forty-five to the minute the door creeps open, and he edges into the room with her tray. Oat biscuits, slices of apple and grapefruit, and there beside her tea, the Lilac Monster of her nightmares. The sight is enough to send a shiver through her sternum.

He sets the tray down then takes his mug and falls back into his chair by the bed. Their same routine. For now and for ever if he had his way. 'Status report?'

'Some light showers,' she replies, her drowsy expression at odds with her thumping pulse. 'Otherwise, calm.'

'It's such a fresh morning, why don't we go for a walk? You can even keep your clothes on this time.'

She manages to match his laugh, while inside her heart drops through a chute. For days she's been waiting for him to go out long enough that they can go ahead with the plan. The only thing keeping her sane has been the assumption that he'd never miss his Saturday morning bike ride.

'Maybe tomorrow,' she says, wincing at an (imaginary) ache in her back. 'Still want to take it a bit easy.'

'It's really brightening up outside.'

'You should definitely go for your bike ride then.'

'If anything happened while I was out—'

'You've been stuck in this house for days.'

'Nothing is more important to me than you,' he says, leaning forward. It's all she can do not to pull away when he plants a kiss on her forehead. The moisture from his lips feels revolting on her skin.

'And nothing is more important to me', she says, 'than you doing the things you love, like taking the bike out after a long and very stressful week.' She nods towards the window, where the sun is edging out of the clouds. 'Better catch it while you can.'

He frowns, eyes narrowing. 'Are you trying to get rid of me?'

'Only so you won't moan to me later about being cooped up all day.' She squeezes her eyes shut, touching her temple, their recognised signal for a looming migraine. 'Sorry. That's come from nowhere.'

'You poor thing,' he says. 'Rest up. I'll come check on you soon.'

Astrid waits for the door handle to rise back up before allowing her pained smile to fade. She covers her face with shaking hands. *Oh my God.* What's she going to do now? What if the others think sod this, sod waiting around, and walk away, leaving her here, trapped in Dinckley?

She burrows under the covers, lying on her side as though sleeping, and starts her burner phone. With Bryan roaming, she needs to be careful. What would she say if he came in and caught her using it? *I blacked out and ended up in a Vodaphone shop.* That excuse isn't going to work a second time.

She opens her messages, sends:

He's not going on the bike ride x

Every moment of the five minutes until his reply appears is agony.

All her doubts come flooding back. *You're making a mistake. You're being tricked. You're suffering psychosis brought on by the reckless abandoning of your medication.* Has she actually gone mad? Is this all a delusion brought on by her broken mind? Sometimes it feels that way.

What evidence does she really have for any of this? Practically none. Every second smarter people than her fall for scams. But why her? For money? Ha! Revenge?

Maybe.

Especially after what she's been told.

The phone vibrates in her closed fist. She checks the messages, relief flooding through her limbs at his reply: *It's happening. Be ready.*

No kisses this time. His tone feels pushier. That sensation again, like she's reading this wrong, seeing what she wants to see. Not noticing the real truth lingering behind the lie, which is that she's a woman in her early thirties who's not had a real job for five years. Who has lost touch with all of her family and friends. Who doesn't even have her own personal bank account, let alone cash to put in it. Zero. Nothing. What if this goes wrong? She can hardly expect to skulk back here.

What if she finds herself on the streets?

Every minute that passes, staring at the screen, waiting in hope for him to send a follow-on message with her forgotten kisses, the doubting voice is growing louder. She has a bed here. She has warmth and comfort and food. She was cared for when she was sick, and who's to say that life wouldn't be better now she's free from her constant pain? She could tell Bryan about the miracle of giving up her medication, and he may exult in it, twirling her round and kissing her, the relationship back to where it was at the beginning, when she thought he was a hero.

Bryan thuds up the stairs. She jams the phone up her pyjama top, curls around it. Bites down on her panicked breath. He goes into his bedroom, then silence. *What's going on?*

The door to her room opens. She clenches her body, eyes squeezed shut, hoping he'll think she's either in pain or asleep. Her pills! She hasn't taken them. The last couple of weeks, since going cold turkey, she's wrapped them in toilet paper and flushed them down the loo. If he sees they're still in their Saturday morning compartment he'll get suspicious for sure.

'Sorry to disturb you, love,' he says. 'I think I will take that ride after all.'

Should she reply? Should she moan in acknowledgement? To her surprise, he doesn't wait, instead easing the door closed. Then he's back downstairs. The front door slams shut. She bolts forward to look out of the curtains in time to him swerving round the potholes as he races to the main road.

Is it happening? Is she really doing this? What if she gets caught? What if Bryan comes back early? What if, what if, what if. She forces herself to imagine how she will feel if she's still here when he gets home. That's enough to override her fear, to replace it with a singular voice saying, *Move – go!*

She sends a message. *Leaving NOW.* Preparation takes less than ten minutes. She's long memorised what she's going to take, what she has to do. Then she's out of the door. Out of this life.

Into the unknown.

20

CELINE

Celine rouses to the sound of someone screaming. She's not sure where she is or what's going on, but then it starts coming back; she hasn't seen Seth for over a week, not since she tried to make him that nice dinner. They've spoken once, a snatched call yesterday; he said it's hard to talk as he's working away from home and there's no signal. *Be patient,* he said, *remember I love you. I won't be this busy for ever.* But she thinks he's lying. That the woman in the cottage is stealing him away.

How long has she been holed up in her flat, getting wrecked? She claws the sleep from her eyes and squints at the TV screen. A Japanese horror called *New Global Death* is playing, and even after seeing it numerous times she still has no idea what it's supposed to be about; it's just two sadistic serial killers trying to outdo each other by taking it in turns to murder people in the most outlandish manner.

Right now, the one with the bad dye job is trying to remove the skin from a trussed-up young woman. Celine remembers the first time they'd watched it together, still sweaty from sex, the tough feel of his body beside her, her mind blowing in all different directions. Before he introduced her to Asian extreme cinema, she didn't even know films like this existed. All she'd seen were dumb horror flicks like *A Nightmare on Elm Street*, with fantasy villains no more authentic than the tooth fairy. But this felt real; it was scary in a way that silly baddies in bad prosthetics never could be.

Head woozy, she grabs the remote. Her hand is slick with blood. She pulls back the sheet and sees the carnage at the top of her left thigh; two new slashes amid the skin-churn of scars. *Oh no. No, no, no.* Seth is going to be furious.

She has to get up. Clean herself and the bed. Thankfully the stain hasn't soaked through the sheets to the mattress. She shuffles into the bathroom, dabs the area with damp tissue paper, sprays it with a stinging blast of perfume to kill any bacteria, gritting through the pain as it jolts down her leg.

Celine hobbles back, removes the sheet and puts down a towel. On the screen a terrified man is begging for his life behind the counter of what she thinks is a grocery store, it's hard to tell with all the signs in Japanese. She checks her phone. Not even five in the morning; middle of the fucking night.

Still nothing from Seth.

She's supposed to be starting at the pub at nine, but there's no way she can face it. The thought of spending the day bored stupid behind the bar, listening to the old soaks on the stools moan about the government or their dodgy hips or how life used to be better when you could smoke inside is enough to make her want to jump into the screen and plead with the killer to murder her as well. Paddy the manager won't be happy; she's already cried in sick a couple of times this week. She sends the text anyway. Dodgy tummy, been up all night. Promise will be back for her next shift. The only thing that could make her situation more unbearable would be if she lost this job.

Her shoulders slump at the thought. What would she do

then? *Don't think about it.* She opens the drawer and takes some bumps from the baggie; she ran out of Seth's good stuff days ago, so had to call Flynn to score. All he had was some scuzzy speed that's rank on its own, but you have a couple of drinks and it's a different story.

Celine gags as it goes does down the back of her throat, and takes a sip of the vodka Coke on the nightstand to clear it. As she's flipping through the photo album she takes more bumps, more sips, carrying on until her heart is thundering, her synapses are in flames, and she finds herself staring at Seth's picture, jaw clenched so tight it could crush rocks, thoughts jamming her mind.

IwantyoudonʼtleavemepleaseSethIʼllkillherifthatʼswhatitakes Iʼlldoanythingsolong—

The buzzer pulls Celine back to reality. Panting, drenched in sweat, she looks around. Who could that be? Not Seth, he has keys. Another time with the buzzer, their finger held down, the sound ripping into her skull like a power drill.

Shouting from outside. 'Cel? *Celly!* You alive in there? I can see your light on.'

She drags herself from the bed. Everything's in slow motion, the movement of her arms leaving trails. At the window she rests her forehead on the cold glass.

'I see you!' Renata hollers from the front gate. Under the streetlights her cheeks are flushed, and all she's got on is purple leggings and the feathery yellow coat they all call Big Bird. Clearly, she's come straight from clubbing. 'It's fucking Baltic out here.'

Celine holds up a finger to tell her to wait. She staggers around the flat, vision weird, legs wonky, trying to make the place presentable. Off goes the film; shove the knife under the pillow; pull on her joggers to hide the tissues. *That'll do.* She releases the door then sits on the bed to make a rollie.

Ren bustles into the flat. 'Bomb go off in here?'

'It's not that bad,' Celine says, trying to light the cigarette, but she's made it terribly and bits of tobacco fall out the bottom.

'You been sat here on your own all night?'

'I do live here, you know.'

Ren's chewing on her lips, wasted herself. 'What's going on with you? You were such a beautiful little thing.'

'Gee, thanks.'

'Stinks in here and all.'

'It's too cold to open the windows.' Celine takes a bump and offers up the bag. 'You want?'

Ren takes it and jogs the powder, her bracelets clattering. 'Go have a shower. Alf's will be open soon, we can get brekkie.'

'You're all right.' Celine takes a sip of her vodka Coke.

'Go easy, love,' Ren says, eying the bottle on the floor. 'It's first thing.'

'You always have a drink when you're on it.'

'Only if I've been out, not sitting there on my tod. This ain't right, Cel.'

'Have you come over just to have a go at me?'

'You can't fester here like this.'

Celine breathes out long and slow through her lips, fingers tingling. 'Already got one mum, thanks very much.'

'Have you had a row, you and—'

'We're *fine*, thank you.'

'You've not been in work, I've not seen you out. I come round and the place is a tip—'

'Have you seen your place? Not exactly spotless, is it?' Seth was right about her. *Just a fucking busybody sticking her beak into everyone's business.* Celine had defended Ren at the time, but now she sees it, so clearly.

'I'll let you off that,' Ren says, hands on her hips, bracelets falling over her fingers. Her lips are pulled back to show her still grinding teeth. ''Cos I can see you're twisted. But if that bloke gave a shit about you then he wouldn't let you be here like this.'

'Least my boyfriend's not a sleaze.'

'What d'you say?'

'The party. He was all over me when we were dancing. Seth saw it.'

'*My* Flynn? Over you?'

How big were those bumps? It's coursing through her; she can feel her right hand quivering. She closes her eyes and leans her head back. Ren is going on, calling her ungrateful, telling her where she can get off, but Celine feels no compulsion to pay attention. When she opens her eyes, the room is empty.

Ren's right about one thing, though. She can't fester here all day. Something has been building inside her, something terrible and deadly, the dark core she always knew was in her heart, desperate to be let free. She senses it now as a physical presence, pushing her to the boundaries of her body. There's a soft *pop*, and then it's out. She's an observer now, watching as she dresses in work jeans and a ratty Argyle wool jumper one of the lads at the squat gave her; she needs to fade into the background, so no one will notice or remember her. With her duffle coat on, her hood up and shadowing her face, she looks invisible. As though she's not even there.

Outside, the dark world is sparkling, the edges sharp as

sheared glass. Lyrics from a long-forgotten song are wrapping round her mind: *nothing . . . can keep us apart. I said, nothing can keep us apart.* Hood up, head down, marching to the station. Her hands roam endlessly over her pockets, checking money, stash, knife, money, stash, knife. In her mind the scenes are soaked in blood.

She gets on the train as it's growing light, wondering why it's so quiet, before realising it's Saturday. *Perfect.* Into the toilet for a bump, a big one, and another for good luck, then back to her seat to grip the armrests and strap in for ride. *Whoosh!* She's pressed back into her chair by a kind of g-force, unblinking, jaw locked, trapped in the machine-gun fire of her thoughts *What if she calls the police? What if you get arrested? What if Seth's there? What if they both start laughing at you? Whatifwhatifwhatifwhatif—*

What if you kill her?

At the other end, Celine knows the way. This time the walk seems to last seconds. Some cars going past, a cyclist, but there's no need to look at her. No need to remember her.

Knife in her hand, she creeps towards the cottage. Her nerves feel stretched tight. She's been compulsively licking her lips; they're raw when she wipes her mouth. What's she going to do? Ring the doorbell? Break in?

On the way here it had felt as though she wasn't in control, that her body was being guided by the dark forces inside her; once she arrived she thought those same dark forces would know what to do. Now she's here, that's not the case. The crest of the buzz from the bumps on the train have gone past their peak, and Celine is suddenly and wholly back at the levers of her mind.

In the still morning, the only sounds are the birds, her breath, and the *pow-pow-pow* of her pulse.

If she turns back now, what's waiting for her at home? The same misery as when she left.

What would Seth do if he found out she was seeing another bloke? What would he do to keep that bloke away from her?

The front door opens, and the blonde woman steps out.

Anyone wants him, they've got to come through me first.

21

RONSON

Ronson wakes with a start on the sofa in the rec room. He grabs his phone, scans his messages. No new discoveries, but already some fallout from his decision yesterday evening to move the search east towards Bleasdale, including a 4 a.m. missive from Superintendent Zamora, enquiring if he's perhaps lost his bloody marbles. Right at this moment, trying to peer through the newly waking brain fog, Ronson is wondering the same thing.

He had to do something to shake it up though. Wait any longer and the case will get away. You get a sense for these things, whether the leads are going anywhere, and here they were all heading to dead ends. When that happens you've just got to trust your gut.

Besides, Zamora is always looking for an excuse to have a go at him. Since coming to the station last year, he's made it clear his first priority is *clearing out the dead wood*. Ronson knew he was on that pile from the moment he shook hands with the super, but it'll be a long time yet before he agrees to being pushed out to pasture.

147

He drags himself up from the sofa, feeling every one of his fifty-eight years. It's murder on his back, sleeping here, but at least he bagged a few hours. Back home he probably wouldn't have got that – it's too strange to sleep in their bed without Cath. He prefers being here, at the station. Ready for the break-through when it comes.

The canteen is still quiet when he gets his first coffee, but it's starting to fill by the time he's finished it. Maxwell joins him at the table with a refill.

'Don't tell me you slept here,' she says.

'Fine, I won't.'

She gives him an exasperated look. 'One day I'll come in and find you keeled over this table.'

Ronson laughs. 'Stop trying to cheer me up.'

'I take it', she says, lowering her voice, glancing round to make sure no one's close enough to hear, 'last night's move was your doing.'

'I'm still the SIO, if that's what you're asking.'

'Quite a few unhappy voices on the ground.'

'You know the best way to handle a mutiny?'

'Go on,' Maxwell says, lifting an eyebrow.

Ronson pats her arm. 'Have an able deputy to sort it out.'

'Speaking of which, shift is changing soon. Should we have a briefing?'

'Gather the troops,' Ronson says, twirling his finger in the air. 'I'll be along in a minute.'

Maybe he should have left it last night. Maybe if he'd let the search team get on with their jobs, Astrid Webb would have been found. Ronson rubs his face and gets up to go. You can dine for ever on maybes and never be full. When you're the senior investigating officer, you're never going to be right all the time.

The more important thing is to be decisive.

When he gets to the briefing room, Maxwell is addressing the smattering of grey-faced detectives. She's beside the illuminated map of the Forest of Bowland AONB projected on the wall, laser pointer directed at the search area, her expression only one step below seething. Clearly, it's not going well.

'I don't care if you're pissed off,' she's saying to Detective Sergeant Faisal Kapoor, one of the other old hands at the station. He's been a sergeant at Greenbank longer than many of the constables in the room have been alive. 'I tell you who's more pissed off. Astrid Webb's family. Astrid Webb's friends—'

'Do me a favour, Jess,' Kapoor says. 'Go throw yourself in the Ribble.'

There's a couple of chuckles, soon silenced when Maxwell looks round. 'Anyone else got something to contribute?'

'I've not finished, thank you,' Kapoor says. 'You've got a job lot of officers out there, searching through the night, for what?' He glances round at Ronson, who's perched on the edge of a desk at the back. 'Do you even know what we're looking for?'

'We're looking for Mrs Webb,' Ronson replies.

Kapoor waves him away like he's heard it all before. 'Do you realise how many people we get reported as missing round here?'

Ronson shrugs. 'You suggesting we shouldn't look for her?'

'What I'm suggesting,' Kapoor says, and gestures to the rest of the room, 'what a few of us were thinking, is that what we have here is a tragic incident where a woman with severe health issues decided to take a drive on her medication. She zoned out, crashed her car, and stumbled into the forest.'

'She wasn't driving on medication,' Ronson says. 'Her pills for that morning are still in the . . . holder. Whatever you call it.'

'If it's an accident,' Maxwell says, 'why's there a break-in?'

'She's done it herself,' Kapoor replies. 'Paranoia, or psychosis – she's on heavy meds. Her husband's gone out and she's had a panic attack.'

Detective Constable Samia Fletcher pipes up. 'Or she's done a runner.'

'She needs to get her medication,' Maxwell says.

'Maybe she's found another way to get them,' Fletcher says. 'Like on the web.'

'Could be that,' Kapoor says. 'Either way, we shouldn't be putting half the bloody police force into finding her.'

'We do what we have to,' Ronson says. 'Until we know the truth.'

Kapoor throws up his arms. 'You're just going to keep sending people here, there and everywhere, then? Doesn't matter about someone else getting mugged, or their house robbed?'

'That's enough,' Maxwell says, then to Ronson: 'I'm with you, boss. We all are.'

'I'm bloody not,' Kapoor says, on his feet. 'And I know plenty on the ground who feel the same.'

Maxwell steps towards him. 'Sit down, Faz.'

'Looking here, looking there,' Kapoor says. 'Looking like we haven't got a bloody clue.'

'That was my decision,' Ronson says.

Kapoor shakes his head. 'You're the one without a bloody clue then.'

'I warned you,' Maxwell says. 'I'm writing you up.'

'Does that mean I get to go home?'

'Quiet,' Ronson says. His phone's ringing – it's the search site. 'What you got?'

Detective Sergeant Stanton's at the other end. Everyone in the room must see the change in Ronson's face because when he hangs up they're all alert, the tiredness and the frustration from a few minutes ago gone.

'Get a car ready, Jess,' he says. 'We've found a body.'

22

BRYAN

Bryan isn't one to look back on life. He doesn't pore over old photos, or scan through past emails, or search for people he's lost touch with on social media just to remember them, and in doing so remember something of himself, the person he used to be. More than once he's commented that those who spend too much time locked in nostalgia forget there's still a life to lead.

The more you cling to the past, he remembers saying to Astrid, *the more you let it define you, the harder it is to move on.*

What a pompous twat. There will be no 'letting go' if his wife doesn't come home. There will be no 'moving on'. One path will remain: to sit here mentally slapping himself for smugly believing that nothing like this could ever happen to him. He perceives this keenly, awake for the second night in a row, staring out of the kitchen window as another cup of tea goes cold in his hand, staring into the darkness, going over and over what happened in the lead-up to her disappearance.

That video, on Meera's doorbell. He took a copy and scoured it for information, moving it along frame by frame, but the blue car is on the other side of the road, and the reflection of the

153

clouds obscures much of the windscreen. At nine thirty-one it turns onto their lane, and six minutes later the same car comes out. In the three frames before it turns it's clear there's *someone* in the passenger seat. The number plate unfortunately is too grainy to read.

Who was she with? Another man? It seems inconceivable. Astrid barely has any interest in sex – an effect of her medication – although their relationship has never been about that, at least not for him. They have plenty of tender moments, a kiss when he brings her breakfast, a hug in the kitchen when she's preparing dinner, and perhaps, when her back isn't too bad, a slow dance to something good on the radio. As for making love, they've not attempted that since their aborted effort in Paris last year, when she had to rush away to the loo while they were undressing for a very unsexy bout of diarrhoea. By the time she returned the moment had passed.

Could she really be having sex with someone else? Especially the kind of passionate stuff you get in affairs – the snatched shags in the backseat, the hurried rutting against a hotel wall. No chance. Astrid would be moaning, and not in a good way, before her lover had even lifted her leg.

Bryan had such high hopes for their life together once they were married. A life like his parents had. Calm and peaceful, wholly without drama. His dad managed a pharmacy in the nearby town, and his mum taught art at the local school, until her repeated throat infections became so bad she was unable to lead a class. Bryan's upbringing, at least in his memory, was made up of roast dinners and walks in the forest and helping in the shop on the weekend. He can't imagine his mum so much as flirting with someone, let alone cheating.

Astrid wasn't happy, he knows that. He just never thought her way of finding that happiness might be with someone else.

Did he really miss all the signs?

He drags himself from the chair and boils the kettle. He's so knackered his thoughts are sliding around like someone has soaped the floor of his mind. At some point in the early hours, if only to knock himself out, he thought it would be a good idea to crack into the brandy again. One turned into two, two turned into three, and after that he stopped counting. So much for his rule of a single measure before bed.

It almost worked. He remembers sitting on the sofa, his eyes shut, the glass slipping from his hand, the world falling away, thinking, *Oh, thank God, thank Christ*, until he was jerked back from the darkness again by the sound of someone banging on the front door. He'd lurched to his feet, to the hallway. Of course no one was there. After that, he was awake again.

As he's pouring his tea, he realises that his meeting with the Minister for the Department of Crime and Policing is supposed to be today – they're at the final stages of signing a partnership to provide services for the government's new national stalking hub. A huge opportunity for the Foundation. All those months of preparation, all those endless Zoom calls buttering up civil service bores, but what does any of it mean if Astrid is gone?

Not much.

His phone vibrates on the counter. A WhatsApp message, but not from an existing contact. He examines the tiny face in the picture to see if it's someone he recognises. Probably a con – you get a lot of that these days, people trying to get close to victims only to accuse them of being crisis actors who've staged the whole thing for attention. Scum they are, and he shouldn't engage, but he has to know.

Hi Bryan, the police have been in touch about Astrid, and I feel so bad. She messaged me recently for the first time in years and I ignored her. I guess I was still annoyed at what happened but now I wish I'd replied. Please let me know if you hear anything at all. Vivien xx

Vivien? Who the— *Vivien!* The loud girl with green hair and the bottom lip ring Astrid used to live with. She was heartbroken when they fell out. Nearly twenty years of friendship gone because of a comment posted online.

She got in touch with me recently and I ignored her.

Bryan takes a sharp breath. If Astrid got in touch with Vivien, then maybe . . .

That's been the problem with this idea of Astrid having an affair. Where would she meet someone to do that? Not in Dinckley, that's for sure – she can't stand most of the people in the village. Maybe online, she is on self-help forums sometimes, but it's a big leap from that to having an in-person fling.

But what if it's someone she already knows? Someone that wouldn't balk at her illness, but who might try to use it to their advantage?

Zack. One of her other friends from back then. He always had a thing for Astrid. Bryan will never forget the first night he met him, out in some pub in Chorlton, one of those hipster places where every staff member has tattoos on their hands and they only serve craft beer that tastes like it's been brewed in a someone's gym sock. Zack was mooning at her the whole evening, always trying to sit next to her, pawing her arm as they spoke. Never said two words to Bryan.

He'd asked Astrid, and she didn't deny it. *It nearly happened,* she said, *but we were never single at the same time.* Bryan wasn't sad when she and Zack drifted apart. Same as when he didn't bother to show up at their wedding. Good riddance.

Could she have contacted Zack, like she did Vivien? Could he have used that to sneak back into Astrid's life? It might explain why she didn't mention what's been going on. Perhaps they became friends again, but she turned him down? He starts stalking her, sending her nasty messages. Until what? He *kidnaps* her?

Bryan sits on the stairs, jogging the phone in his hand. He's still not heard back from Hoop about the case file, and the big man won't appreciate being called again about something else, but this is life and death.

'I need another favour,' Bryan says, when Hoop answers. 'Can you run a check for me against the DVLA database?'

Hoop puts up some resistance – *I can't keep doing this* – until Bryan reminds him he's done the square root of sod all so far for someone who he's known for over twenty-five years. Someone who went through academy training with him. Someone who knows everything there is to know about Chief Constable Douglas Hooper, which he may not want other people—

'All right, all right,' Hoop says. 'You've made your point.'

Bryan tells him he needs the model and colour of any cars registered to someone called Zack Cookson. 'And you've still got to get me that case file. I need to see what the fuck's going on.'

Hoop sighs and says to give him a few hours.

When Bryan hangs up, his heart's thudding. Could this really be a lead? Energised, he races upstairs for a shower. His phone rings while he's undressing.

He jams it to his ear, thinking it's Hoop. 'That was quick!'

'Mr Webb? It's Detective Inspector Ronson.'

'Sorry, I thought you were—'

'Is there any chance we could send a car to pick you up?'

Now he has this hunch he wants to dig further into it. That won't happen if he's sitting at the station for the next six hours just so Ronson can give him an update.

'I've had a terrible night,' Bryan says. 'Why don't you drop round here when you can? Or if you're too busy, send that family liaison officer who's probably sat around scratching their bum.'

The detective's sigh is so long and tired that Bryan feels the hope draining from his body.

'Mr Webb,' Ronson says. 'We need to get you right now.'

23

BRYAN

An hour later the car shows up. On the way, Bryan has to tell the constable driving to pull over so he can be sick. There's not much to come up: the banana he forced down while waiting for the lift, last night's brandy, which not only burns as it comes back up, but seems to coat every part of his mouth in a rancid taste.

When he closes the door, the constable carries on driving without a word. She's dumpy, snark-faced, and completely lacking in the social graces needed to become an officer. If he were her sergeant, he'd send her on a course on how to crack a smile. Instead he opens the window and settles for some deep breaths.

Oh, Astrid. Oh, bloody hell.

He's expecting to go to the hospital to identify the body, and is surprised when they arrive at Greenbank police station, driving through the gates to the main car park. Getting out, he feels woozy, still weak from throwing up, and nearly stumbles over his own feet. The only way to stay upright is by holding onto the car roof.

'Need a hand?' asks Police Constable Kindness.

159

Bryan tells her he's fine, then focuses his attention on moving his legs in the same manner as he's been doing for nearly fifty years now. He can't believe they've found her. It seems impossible. Perhaps it's a mistake, or someone else entirely. *Please don't let it be her.*

The constable scans her pass at a side door. Inside, she leads him through several corridors of magnolia hell to an interview room. It's a nice one – padded chairs, table not bolted to the floor. The constable doesn't bother asking if he wants a drink, confirming she really has had a personality bypass, just says the detective will be in soon and leaves him to it. He makes a mental note of her shoulder number. One more line to add to the list of grievances in his official complaint once all this is done.

At least he's not being detained – otherwise he wouldn't be left unattended. It's ridiculous to think that he would be, but he knows Ronson has got it in for him. Detective Inspector Coffee Stain made that much clear when he came round to check those messages on Astrid's Facebook account.

There's a recording machine on the table. Bryan lifts the corner of the machine to see if it's attached, but it comes away. Was this brought in here specifically for him? Is he going to be interviewed as a suspect? The thought of it is enough get the sweat popping on his scalp – it's easy to come across as guilty, especially when someone's trying to catch you out.

Ronson comes in looking like he's not been to bed. Greying hair in whorls, cheeks pouchy, the top button of his shirt undone and tie skewed below. He dumps his rucksack and slumps in the chair opposite. Blows out his cheeks as though he's just got home from a long commute.

'My humble apologies for keeping you waiting, Mr Webb,' he

says, taking a brown folder from his rucksack and dumping it on the table. 'Has anyone got you a drink?'

'Are you going to tell me why I've been dragged here?'

'You'll appreciate we're all very tired, Mr Webb. We're doing our best.'

'Sorry.' Bryan wipes his forehead with a sleeve before the sweat can get his eyes. The detective's taking it in, no doubt wondering if his agitation is guilt. 'This has been a very stressful few days.'

Ronson opens the folder, takes out some ten-by-eight stills, places them face down on the desk. 'I promise you, we're going to find out what's been happening here.'

Bryan covers his mouth and moans. 'Is that . . .'

'Do you mind if we quickly check one thing?' Ronson asks, pulling out his dog-eared notebook and unhooking the elastic. 'Remind me what time you left the house on Saturday morning?'

Bryan can't take his eyes off the photos. 'Are you going to bloody well tell me if you've found my wife?'

'Truly, I'm sorry Mr Webb. It's for the super, he's on my case about this. We've got to get that time confirmed first. Please.'

'I told you. I left about nine.'

'Was that before or after nine?'

'What the bloody hell does it matter?'

'It's just that we have a record of you receiving a phone call at 9.03 on Saturday morning. Do you recall that?'

'Am I being interviewed?'

'If you could just help us out by answering the question.'

Bryan slams his hand on the table. 'You're an absolute disgrace, you know that? You've got me sat here, worked up, holding out on showing me the pictures of someone who might be *my wife*. Show me the damn pictures, man! What kind of person are you to leave me here like this? If that's my wife I want to see her.'

'You're right – *you're right.*' Ronson is shaking his head as though he can't believe how thoughtless he's being, but Bryan's not buying it, not any more. His whole shtick, the messy clothes, the careless air, it's all a load of bull. 'You get so far into a case,' Ronson says, 'you stop thinking straight. There's no excuse.' He hands over the photos. 'Here you go. Please, take your time.'

The pictures show selected body parts of a woman in a forest – a section of forearm, a foot and ankle, part of a thigh and the hem of a long dress, each one against a backdrop of leaves and twigs. Her muscles are stiffened, her skin tainted a pale purple. The final one is a close-up of her ear. A sweep of fair hair runs behind it.

Bryan lets go a long breath. 'That's not my wife.'

'I figured that out already,' Ronson says, eyes sharp. 'I'm hoping you might be able to tell us who she is.'

24

BRYAN

The air in the interview room has gone still. Bryan's aware that not only is Ronson watching him, but also any number of detectives in the back office crowded round a screen. All of them scrutinising how he's sitting, how he's breathing, how often he's swallowing. All of them wondering whether he killed this other woman who is not his wife.

It's all Bryan can do to keep his voice calm. 'I'm very sorry that someone else has been hurt, but I can't tell you anything except, thankfully, it's not Astrid.'

'She very much matches the description of your wife though, doesn't she?'

'How am I meant to know that from these photos?'

'Same build, similar hair. We're putting her at mid-thirties, which is about the same age.'

'Just her and few hundred thousand women in the North of England.'

'Still strange that she should show up in the same area, around the same day.'

'Has someone reported her missing?'

163

Ronson leans back, regarding him. 'We'll have to wait for the post-mortem results, but it looks to me like a bolt-cutter was used to remove the fingers. Her face is so badly damaged I couldn't bring myself to show you the photo.' He grimaces, neck tight, like he's seeing it again. 'To destroy the chance of a dental identification, no doubt. This is someone who knew what they were doing.'

'Or they've watched too much *CSI*.'

'Watching it is one thing. Doing it is something else.'

Bryan wipes his forehead again. 'Is this even a proper interview?' He flings a hand towards the recording device. 'Why's that not on?'

'We're just having a chat for now, but you're welcome to have a duty solicitor here if you want. It might take a while. We can pause this until then.'

Even at big stations like this there are never enough solicitors around, especially on Monday morning – and Bryan has no intention of spending the rest of the day stewing here while they dig one up.

'It's terrible what's been done to that woman,' he says. 'And I hope to God you find out who she is so her family aren't in the same hell as me. But from what I can see, from the bits of her in the photos, I honestly don't believe I know her.'

Ronson opens his pad again. 'Let's go back to the morning of the crash. At three minutes past nine you received a phone call that lasted forty-two seconds. Do you recall that?'

Bryan drags his phone from his pocket, unlocks it and scrolls through his call log. 'Sorry, I completely forgot about that. I answered but no one was there. I thought maybe it was one of those automated machines.'

'No one said anything?'

'Not a word.'

'How did your wife seem before you left? Nervous?'

'You don't think I've been over this myself a hundred times?'

'Could your wife have known this woman?'

'Honestly, I don't know, but I doubt it. We have a very quiet life.'

Ronson closes his notebook. 'Two blonde women, similar height, similar build, similar age, are involved in incidents at around the same time, within fifteen miles of each other. One of them has been found murdered. Do you believe in coincidences, Mr Webb?'

Bryan lifts his hands, ready to respond, but Ronson pulls out his phone. He checks the screen, finger raised.

'I'm so sorry about this,' he says, sliding out of the chair. 'I'll be back in a moment.'

This time Bryan's not fooled. He knows the detective's tactics by now – leaving the photos on the table, no doubt going into the room next door to watch him on the cameras. What will he do? Look at them again, or ignore them? It works too, because suddenly he doesn't know how to act. If he sits still, it may appear sociopathic. If he fidgets, it may appear incriminating. He's not being detained, so he supposes he could walk out, although he probably wouldn't make it past the gates before being stopped. He settles for leaning on the table, face in his hands.

When Ronson comes back it's with a cup of water. 'You didn't tell me you were sick in the car,' he says. 'We should have got you a drink.'

'I think you were too busy accusing me of being a murderer.'

Bryan takes the cup, pleased to finally be able to wash away the harsh aftertaste from before.

Ronson squeezes his forehead and sighs. 'I'm fighting for your wife here. You know we can't rule anything out.'

'What about the stalker? Niall Turton.'

'Investigations are still under way.'

'If you've found him, bloody well tell me.'

'You know I can't discuss it, sorry.'

'Look at this,' Bryan says, showing him the video from Meera. The blue car arriving, then six minutes later leaving – he explains what happened that evening, how he found her confused outside.

'Why haven't you mentioned this before?' Ronson asks.

'It's her medication, it spins her out sometimes. At least that's what I thought.'

'And what do you think now?'

'Obviously, I'm concerned.'

Should he mention Zack? The hunch that it's his car? Or would it be better to wait until he's heard back from Hoop to be sure?

Ronson swipes the video back to the start. 'Do you know where your wife might have been going?'

'I wish I did.'

'You were out for the whole day?'

'I work a bit late on Wednesdays – I don't get back until after six.'

'We tried to contact Astrid's mother in Norway, but she wasn't particularly helpful. Same with the teachers she used to work with. Seems she's drifted away from a lot of people.'

Could they have spoken to Zack already? 'Who else have you been in touch with?'

Ronson goes *hmmm* and rubs his stubble. 'Are you in a rush, Mr Webb?' He waits for Bryan to shake his head, then goes on: 'The national media are sniffing around this story, and we need to get ahead of it. We're giving a press briefing at one about your wife. How would you feel about going in front of the camera, making an appeal for her to come home? We haven't ruled out that she might be missing of her own accord.'

Bryan's gut reaction is to balk at the idea. You go to the media, you get the circus. There'll be rubberneckers all over the area within hours. He'll have amateur sleuths camped outside the front door, wanting to put their theories to him, or worse joining up with Ronson in thinking he was involved. And what if Astrid is being held against her will? What if the scumbag who's got her, Turton or whoever, thinks the net is closing and decides to cut his losses, finish her off fast?

'What do you say?' Ronson asks.

'Of course,' Bryan replies. No way is he having the detective think he's being any way obstructive or unwilling to help. 'I'll do anything to get my wife back safely. *Anything.*'

Sergeant Maxwell drives them to the Greater Manchester Police Headquarters, where there is a dedicated media room. Bryan knows the building well and recognises some faces as they're heading to the fourth floor. Considering why he's here, the welcoming smiles are muted, but appreciated all the same.

It's strange being back. Unlike Astrid, he doesn't pine to return to the city. These days he finds it too loud, too dirty, too smelly. When chatting to old mates he's always saying he'll come in for a visit, grab a pint, make a day of it and go to the cricket like they used to, but despite his best intentions he's always too busy. Never did he dream he'd be coming back in these circumstances.

When he first started on the force, speaking to the press involved someone shoving a microphone in your face and asking you a question, but you could probably film a BBC drama with all the kit they've got in their new media room. There's one of those big cameras with a frame that you can sit in, lights positioned all around the walls. The long table like something from a panel show is lined with thin microphones, bent to point towards the person in front of it.

Superintendent Peters greets Bryan like an old friend, clasping his hand in both of his own, even though they've only met a couple of times. Guiding Bryan to the coffee station – the machine looks nicer than the one he treated himself to last Christmas, a lesson about keeping the press on side – Peters expresses his commitment to doing whatever it takes to find his wife. By the time they're sitting in front of the GMP decals, ready to go on, Bryan's wondering whether there's any way he can pull some strings, get the investigation moved here. The whole set-up seems much more professional.

There's less than half a dozen journos in, but both the *Manchester Evening News* and the BBC are here. Ronson gives the introduction to the case, explaining when and where Astrid disappeared. No mention of the body found this morning – obviously trying to control the narrative. Whether it's the lack of sleep and food, or the overload of stress and anxiety, Bryan starts to spin out. He suddenly sees himself how the public's going to see him. They're going to be wondering the same question as the detective: *did he do it?*

He wants to reach for the glass of water, but he's too worried his hand will shake. Same goes for wiping the perspiration from his forehead before it forms the flop sweat everyone will interpret as a hint that he's involved. Too soon, Ronson is introducing him.

Bryan stares down the eye of the camera, mind blank.

People under pressure are capable of things they never imagine possible. That's the only way he can explain what happens next. He knows what he's supposed to say, he's seen a thousand of these missing-person appeals, the pleas to come home, the reminder of all the love waiting there. But before he can even get Astrid's name out, he feels the tightness in his throat, the air catching in his chest, the intense pressure behind his eyes. He can't hold it back even if he wants to. Soon he's there, sobbing on live television.

He can't ever remember crying, even as a kid, even when his parents passed away, but now he's started he can't stop. Thankfully he's still able to squeeze out a few words about how much he loves her and wants her to come home.

Afterwards, he's embarrassed. He knows he shouldn't be, but you can't help how you feel. Everyone's nice about it, though, and a couple of officers he used to knock about with come down to say hello, have a quick catch up. It's almost pleasant, seeing those old friends – at least until he sees Ronson at the back of the room.

The detective's leaning against the wall, arms folded, watching him. The cold look on his face tells Bryan everything.

As far as Ronson's concerned, he's a murderer.

PART II

PART II

25

ASTRID

Astrid stares at the email that will change her life.

Dear Mrs Webb,

We are writing to you regarding your recent order of the following items:

1kg loose leaf chamomile tea
1kg loose leaf peppermint tea
500g Ayurvedic Ginger Boost mix
500g Blood Orange Rooibos
200 biodegradable tea temples

Due to a mix-up in our packing, we believe we may have sent you the wrong blend. Astrid, this is not the tea company. Please don't panic, I'm your friend. I have contacted you this way in case Bryan sees you opening this email. If he is there, close and delete it. I will know and contact you a different way. If he is not there, then click the return shipping link at the bottom to find out the truth. Your husband is not who you think he is. We hope you continue to order from the Tea Network, and our sincerest apologies for this confusion.

Return shipping label

Kind regards
Tom Shearman

Please don't panic? Whoever this person is, they don't know her too well. Already she can feel her skin flushing, her lungs going tight, a tingling feeling in her fingertips. Is she hallucinating? It wouldn't be such a big surprise, considering the morning raid on her painkiller stash, but it doesn't feel that way. Quite the opposite. She's all too aware, all too tuned in to reality, the drip, drip of her second-by-second countdown to her one o'clock medication passing like water torture.

Where does the Tea Network fit into all this? Is someone who works there spying on her? What would happen if she replied to this email? Or called Tom Shearman at the Tea Network (if he exists)?

Astrid checks the email address it came from again – customer.service@theteanetwork.net – but that means nothing. Everyone these days knows an email can be made to look like it's come from a real address, or the address could be slightly different from the real one, like .net instead of .com. They'd watched a *Panorama* about it. Spoofing it's called, or something. The program told you how to check if it's authentic, but she remembers being baffled by all the talk of email headers and

IP addresses. It's not likely to make much more sense now.

And yet, what was she thinking only moments ago? How she can't take it any more, how she can't go on like this. Is it crazy (yes) to imagine this is the universe reaching out to her? She doesn't know what she has done to deserve these years of nausea, migraines, the chronic back pain, but perhaps she has paid her penance. To karma, or fate, or the whims of the gods. Or perhaps some interplanetary alignment has simply shifted in her favour?

Whatever has happened, could this be the chance she wanted to change her life?

Before she can stop herself, Astrid clicks the link.

A new webpage opens called chatyou.io. It's not much more than a left and right window, a flashing cursor at the top of each. She waits. What now? She glances at the clock in the corner. Only twelve minutes to go. She'll give it until one o'clock, and if nothing happens she'll shut down the window, delete the email, pretend—

The cursor in the right-hand window starts to move.

I wasn't sure you were going to click the link.

It feels as though she's being watched, or set up for a prank show. *Your husband is not who you think he is.* Surely it's not possible to use someone's marriage that way? She should close the chat window, shut the computer. It's not too late. But once again, something inside her seems to be controlling her hands.

Who are you?

A friend.

Tell me who you are.

I don't suppose you have many of those left. Correct me if I'm wrong.

Astrid sits back, hand to her mouth. She longs to check all the curtains in the cottage are closed, the windows locked, that there's no shadowy figure lurking in the trees. Hands trembling, she types, *What do you want?*

I want you to see the truth about your life.

What truth?

About your husband, Bryan.

What about him?

He's not as nice as he makes out. He's a mean, manipulative bastard. You're miserable because of him.

Her husband. *Her husband.* The one who spends his days raising relief money for victims of harassment. The one everyone in the village greets as though he had been shearing sheep on the local farm as a boy. The one who served for twenty-five years in the police, and only gave that up to care for her. Sure, that makes sense. If they'd said he was having an affair, or had some love children lingering in his closet, she might have bought it. But this is clearly bullshit.

What if this is someone with a grudge against the Foundation? A jilted ex trying to cause trouble for a victim they've helped? What if it's one of Bryan's exes? He's never said much about his previous relationships, except that none of them went very far, at least not to engagement or marriage. The job always came first, he'd said. At least until he met her. *What if it's Niall?* She tenses. Could he really be back to terrorise her again?

Leave me alone, she types, wincing through the fast-descending headache. *I don't believe you.*

Do you find yourself anxious around him? Too eager to please?

Enough. This charade is getting dangerous. No doubt she's being scammed, of course. It's probably some young lads in a dusty country far away who've hacked into the Tea Network. They probably sent that same email, that same link, to a hundred different women. It wouldn't be too hard to scour the net and find her husband's name to tie into the narrative. Next it'll be offers of a secret long-distance relationship, then exhortations for money. If it comes off once it's hugely profitable.

I'm calling the police, Astrid types.

If you left him, where could you go? Name one person you could stay with.

I'm not telling you anything.

Are you worried what he'll do if you step out of line?

Is this person accusing her husband of abuse? She knows all about that from the women they've helped with the Foundation. As irritating as Bryan can be at times (unfair but true), he's never so much as pointed at her in violence. They row, all couples do. Although the stress causes everything to flare up afterwards, so they try to avoid it.

I'm not falling for this, she writes.

> How much money do you personally have? How much could you get?

Here we go. Revealed at last. Astrid allows herself a knowing smirk, but it brings her no satisfaction, just a touch of anguish she tries to pretend isn't there. Five past one. Time to soften the edges on this cruel world for a few more hours.

More typing appears on the right, faster now.

> I don't want your money. I don't want anything except for you to understand that you are a PRISONER.

This is now officially crazy. A prisoner, with no guard, and her own getaway car parked out front.

> Do not contact me again.

> If you are on drugs, stop taking them!!

Astrid closes the chat window. She's not on *drugs*. She's not getting high on them (well, not often). The medication makes her life bearable, and then only just.

Someone is clearly out to interfere in her marriage, to turn her against her husband, either to smear his name or to extract cash from her, and she's not going to fall for it. Grimacing, she hobbles to the kitchen, and tips the 1 p.m. compartment of pills and capsules from the Lilac Monster into her hand. She's about to press her palm to her mouth and duck her head to the tap, but instead stares at them.

How has her life turned into this? Taking so many pills she could probably bottle her blood and sell it in Boots. And they're right, whoever's on that chat – where could she go if she ever did decide to leave Bryan? Her mother in Norway? Ever unsupportive, she couldn't distance herself quick enough when Niall did his meddling. He emailed her saying he lent Astrid ten thousand pounds, which she's refusing to pay back, so he's coming after her for the debt. A fractious call followed between Astrid and her mother, in which she made it clear she didn't believe any of this 'stalker ruining my life' rubbish. They haven't spoken since.

Is it Bryan's fault her mother is a paranoid nutcase? (Like mother, like daughter.) What about her other friends? Is it his fault she got blitzed on red wine and painkillers and hate-posted on Vivien's Instagram? Or that friends like Zack drifted away once she was married?

Astrid takes the pills with a swig from the tap. The water's so cold it sends a chill deep into her jaw. Why's she even thinking about this? Most days she can barely bring herself to leave the house, let alone plan on sofa-surfing her way to a happier life. Being ill makes you reclusive. It's hard to get out and make new friends when you're in pain. Your smile looks like a pretence, which people can read, and then they ask you about it, and then you tell them about it, and (what do you know?) you never hear from them again. You scare them off. Damaged souls aren't readily taken on as new pals. It's nobody's fault but that of her own pathetic body that she's so alone in the world.

Twenty minutes later she feels her mind soften, the migraine receding. She has so much still to do before Bryan gets home. For once she's pleased for the monotony of the domestic drudge. Clothes are sorted into whites and darks and the first batch goes in. Then she's straightening the beds, wiping down the bathroom, the toilet, trying to ignore the motormouths in her mind, one side insisting she go to the police, another laughing at her for even falling for it and clicking the link, yet another voicing its disappointment that it's *not* true, like a petulant child denied sweets at the checkout.

She's in the kitchen, absently rolling raw chicken breasts in a Mediterranean marinade, when the front door slams shut. From the hallway comes the sound of Bryan wrestling his bike into the house, followed by his usual cheery, 'Hello, love.'

'Got to jump on a call at half four,' he says, clattering into the kitchen in his cycling shoes. He moves behind her, squeezes her as gently as if she's a balloon about to pop, and plants a tender kiss on the back of her head.

'I'd hug you,' she says, 'but I've got chicken hands.'

'Status report?'

'Clear day, even a bit sunny.'

'Wonderful,' he says, patting her bottom and clicking on the kettle. Even when it's cold, he rides in Lycra. One of the things she's always liked about him is when he moves around in his cycling gear, the lean muscles in his chest and legs flexing beneath the second skin. He nods to her tea mug. 'Want a refresher?'

If you left him, where could you go?

'I'm fine, thanks,' she says, but when she looks down she sees she's throttling the strips of oily chicken.

No one is responsible for her being miserable, least of all her husband. It's no one's fault but hers that she's so alone.

How much money do you personally have? How much could you get?

Again, how is he to blame for her empty purse? He's always pushing her to start businesses, earn money. It may not be teaching, although she's not sure how she'd manage a class in her state, but if she pulled her weight they'd be more than comfortable.

Bryan pours his tea and heads for the computer nook. 'I'm just going to check my mail.'

The email. She didn't delete it. The web page will go to her account first, and it'll be there at the top. When he sees that it's from the Tea Network, a problem with the order, he'll be right on it. That's what he does. Getting involved, solving problems. That's what he lives for.

'Wait,' she says, washing her hands, drying them on a tea towel as she comes after him.

He pauses. 'What's up?'

'You've only just got home from work. Why don't you relax for a bit? Take a bath.'

'I'm got that Zoom in a minute.'

She turns him away. 'At least go and get changed—'

'I just need to check—'

'You're all sweaty and you're going to get the chair wet and—'

'Okay! Okay! I'm going.' He hands her his mug, wafting with orange and fennel, his expression bemused. 'Put this down for me will you.'

She waits for his footsteps on the stairs, then darts to the computer, opens the web browser, loads her email. It's still there, right at the top. During the afternoon she tried to trick herself that she'd imagined it, or dreamt it, as though it were an extension to her zoned-out session on the sofa that morning. She fights the urge to read it again and deletes it. *Phew.*

No more doubts. No more getting scammed. No more pointless questions about her life.

Except perhaps one: why was she so worried about Bryan seeing it?

26

ASTRID

Astrid knows she should be relieved she saw through the scam. She knows she should tell Bryan about the email, in case they target him. Instead, while they eat their chicken and chargrilled vegetables, while he rambles about the comings and goings of the Foundation today, a meeting with Blackburn football club about a corporate donation, further talks with the government about a possible role in their new national stalking hub, she grips the side of the chair with her free hand and holds down the words that feel to her as hot and terrible as acid reflux thrusting up her throat.

'Lovely dinner, by the way,' he says, holding aloft a length of asparagus, before crunching down on it. 'Dee-licious, my darling wife.'

Astrid manages to force out, 'I'm so glad you like it,' and lunges for her glass of water, knocking it.

'Steady,' Bryan says, grabbing the glass before it spills. He hands it to her, and she takes a long sip, watching him over the top.

When they first got together, he cooked her lavish meals,

183

flambéing and sautéing, as good as the stuff they made on *MasterChef*. If it weren't for Bryan, she'd no doubt still be surviving on ham sandwiches and packets of egg fried rice. On one of their first dates, she'd quipped that no matter how fancy it looks going in, it all looks the same coming out, and he'd roared with laughter. Cupping her cheeks, he'd said, *You'll do for me.*

What would Bryan say if she brought home a loaf of white bread? Or a packet of supermarket ham, the cheap salty kind with the slight texture of rubber? Would he object? Would he throw it straight in the bin, barring her from eating *that processed muck*, and hand her a piece of grilled sea bream in its place?

This is ridiculous. More than that, it's exactly what the person who sent her that email was hoping for. They've smeared Bryan, to his own wife, and she's falling for it!

'I've been thinking,' she says, and covers her mouth.

Without looking up from his plate, Bryan makes a noise for her to go on.

Why cause a fuss, a possible row, and the stress (and aches) that will surely follow? But same as on the chat it feels as though she's not in control of her body, except this time it's her mouth instead of her hands teaming up with her brain.

'I was wondering,' she says. 'Well, I was thinking, about money.'

He tips his head to the side, amused (confused?). 'Yes please, if you're offering.'

She tries to laugh at this old joke, but it sounds too flat to be convincing. 'Do you remember when you put a limit on my debit card?'

'*We* put a hundred pounds daily limit on it, after *you* blew nearly a thousand quid in a night on Candy Crush.'

That was in her darkest days, before they moved to Dinckley, back when she'd sink a bottle of red wine a night. The same period that accounted for the destruction of her friendship with Vivien. Things are different now.

'That was over two years ago,' she says.

'And it's not happened since.'

'Don't you trust me?'

His eyes narrow. 'What do you want to buy?'

'Just as a matter of principal.'

'If there's something you need—'

'That's not the point.'

'Has someone asked you for money?'

'Nothing like that.' Her face has gone hot, the muscles in her neck stiff. 'Forget it.'

She wants him to drop it, but she can see that he's not going to from the way he's sitting up, arms crossed, staring at her with those old sergeant's eyes, a look that always shoots stress through her body.

Do you find yourself anxious around him? Too eager to please?

'I'd like to know where this has come from, Astrid,' he asks.

'It's nothing.'

'You can go to the bank any time and take out a hundred pounds.'

'Per day,' she says, before she can stop her lips from moving.

Why is she doing this? Clearly some kind of scheming, self-sabotaging lunatic must be at the controls. How else can she explain her desperate need to make her already miserable life worse by angering probably the only person in the world who cares even a shred for her. She knows he's funny about money – he's explained about their budget now they're mostly living off his police pension. The morning after the Candy Crush fiasco was the closest they ever came to breaking up. Yet here she is, prodding away.

'How much do you think we've got to live on?' He gets up, storms his half-finished plate to the sink, scrubs it under the water like he wishes it was her face. 'Everything's going up, food, heating, and now you're saying you want to go out spending—'

'That's not—'

'If you're so keen for more money, get a job. No one's stopping you!'

Her voice is so quiet she can barely hear it herself. 'I want to teach.'

'We've got a couple of hundred pounds' worth of tea in there,' he says, gesturing towards the Palace of Failure. 'So how about you sell some of that? Or if you can't be bothered, there's couple of crates of rope you *had to have*, because macramé therapy was the next big thing.'

That's not quite how she remembers it – he's the one always pushing her to start a business whenever she mentions something she even mildly enjoys – but she needs to put the brakes on this row before her back spasms and she's awake all night in an agony that not even her painkillers can touch.

'Forget I said anything,' she says. 'Forget it all.'

'You know, Astrid.' He turns his head to the side, as though he can't bring himself to look at her. 'I try my best. I honestly do. I work hard, I'm upbeat, optimistic, I'd do anything for you. Now you're making me feel like I'm *stingy* for not letting you go crazy with the debit card, or whatever you want to do. We're barely covering the bills.'

Again, from nowhere. From a place that's able to bypass her conscious mind, because otherwise she would veto the thought before it became words: 'You bought your bike.'

A beat. His lower lip falls a touch. 'I bought that with my own money.'

'I thought your money was our money.' (*What are you doing? Stop! Stop!*)

'Don't you want me to stay fit? Don't you want me to exercise? I'm busting a gut every bloody day for other people, and the *one thing* I get for myself, and you can't give me it. All the time, it's bike this—'

'That's not true!'

'You can have a bike too, you know. If you could ever be bothered to get off your—'

'Please, Bryan! Stop!'

A shake of the head, a sad snort, and he's gone. Out of the kitchen, clomping up the stairs to his office. The slam seems to shake the whole cottage.

The rest of the evening is spent tensed and stressed, waiting for the inevitable backlash from her body. She wishes he'd come downstairs so she can explain about the email, but then he'll know their row was because of it, and he'll think she doesn't trust him, that she's been wondering whether what she was told is true (hasn't she?), which will no doubt end in more rows, more feeling like her spine is on fire, an abysmal night tonight.

To grind through the time, she scrolls Instagram. She doesn't use social media much. What could she post? *Feeling rotten today, time for my meds ;-)* Sometimes she lurks, but that's even worse, seeing all the happy, productive people while she rots away in the countryside, long forgotten by those who knew her, destined to be fleetingly recalled during a moment of what-are-they-doing-now reverie, then lost to their memory for ever. How depressing.

For maybe the fifth time today she clicks on Vivien's profile, to see if she's responded to the friend request. Earlier in the afternoon, hazed from her one o'clock meds and obsessing over what was said in that mystery chat (*If you left him, where could you go? Name one person you could stay with*), Astrid had reached out to Vivien and a couple of others, even digging out Zack's old email address (he doesn't use social media) and sending him a quick message. *Hey stranger, how's life?*

So far, no one has replied.

Vivien's children are older now, two and four, and her profile picture is of the three of them in a park, all clustered around the same swing, their faces pressed together. The account is private so that's all Astrid can see.

Would Vivien have forgiven her by now? The comment Astrid posted when Vivien uploaded a picture of her second baby was inexcusable. Blame a depressed mental state (she still hadn't come to terms with her illness), a despondency at her and Bryan's failed attempts to get pregnant (probably for the best), and a bad mix of intoxicants for what she managed to post beneath the small pink bundle:

I know you're not supposed to say this, but that is one ugly baby!

What could have gotten into her? Jealously, perhaps, a sour note of bitterness, even though on the surface she never felt either of those things. She has no memory of writing those words, but something must have been formulating them beneath her conscious mind, waiting for a chance to set them free. Same as today with Bryan. There really must be a toxic stew boiling away beneath her scalp.

The living-room door opens and her husband comes in, holding his nightly glass of brandy. 'Hey love,' he says, looking unsure. 'Sorry for before. I didn't mean to lose my rag.'

The clench holding her rigid for hours finally softens. 'I'm sorry as well. You know I go a bit crazy here sometimes.'

He approaches her, smiling. 'Crazy and beautiful, a deadly combination.'

'Don't you know it.' She tips her head up as he leans down to kiss her.

'It's nearly nine, do you want me to bring everything in?'

'Yes please,' she says.

Half an hour later, as they're watching *Countryfile* (which she hates, but is hardly going to complain about now), her head goes hazy and relief like warm liquid spreads through her limbs. *At last . . .*

Astrid allows herself to drift. The next thing she knows, Bryan is telling her it's time for bed. 'You coming up?'

She sways her head. 'I'll stay in the spare.'

'Would be nice for you to come to bed one day.'

'One day,' she says, and gives him a bleary smile. His lips are preciously warm when he kisses her goodnight.

She must be tired from the day's 'excitement', because she can barely focus. The next thing she knows her phone buzzes in her hand. She lifts it to her face and squints at the screen. Nearly midnight. A reply from Zack. She sits up, blinks, rubs her eyes.

Wow, Astrid. Blast from the past. I've actually been thinking about you a lot lately. Fancy meeting up?

27

CELINE

Celine comes to staring at her blood-crusted hands. Tears drip onto them, softening the dark crimson. In her mind is a long, low drone, like at the end of a gig she went to when one of the band dropped their electric guitar too close the speaker. *Bzzzzzzzzzzzzzzzz.*

How long has she been in bed? Three days? Four? She pats around the mattress in the gloom, finding her phone buried in the sheets. No missed calls from Seth. No messages either.

She tosses it aside and reaches for the baggie, even though she knows already it's empty; more than that it's been ripped open, licked clean. A comedown is on the horizon. She can feel the rumble of it in the distance, approaching at a rapid rate. The lava flow of her bad decisions. Soon to bury her alive.

The flat is filthy. Heaps of clothes and wads of bloodied tissues and something sticky covering the floor that might be a spilt bottle of Pepsi. In the sink are plates smeared with food that must be over a week old; the whole place stinks like the bins behind the pub. She goes to the window, wet with condensation, and wipes a patch with her sleeve. It comes away grimy. She starts to cry again.

How has their relationship gone so badly wrong? She's tried to catalogue the steps it has taken from the summer when Seth couldn't get enough of her to now, barely hearing from him.

Who can blame him though? She may not have gone through with threatening the blonde woman at the cottage, but what kind of person heads to someone's house, off their nut, packing a knife? When the woman came out of the front door, Celine's legs froze; she couldn't get them to move her from the trees, no matter how much she screamed at herself that she was weak, that she didn't deserve Seth's love. The woman just got in her car and drove away.

Celine wipes her eyes. And yet, didn't he text that afternoon? When she got back home from the cottage. Apologising for being distant, saying he had some personal things to sort out, which he'd explain when he saw her. *I love you*, he said at the end. *Can't wait to be back in your arms.*

If he's dumped her, how do you explain that?

She slopes to the table where she's been keeping the photo album clear of the carnage and flicks through it. Here they are on their first real date, dinner at Grand Pacific, drunkenly posing like models beneath an opulent chandelier, the whole place so romantic, like something from *Titanic*; here they are in towelling robes, arms entwined as they sip healthy drinks at the spa they went to in Alderley Edge; here's her favourite, a selfie of them in bed, their heads together, their shoulders bare, Seth's smile slightly dopey. It could be the cover for a film, one of those romcoms where it all goes wrong, but then at the lowest point it comes together. They always end happy. Why can't this be the same?

At the back are loose pictures she's not yet stuck in the album. She holds one of her and Seth at the party beside the photo of them in the spa. Look what she's become. In the spa she's so fresh, her skin clear, her hair glossy, and at the party she's bloated, spotty, bags beneath her eyes.

No wonder he's keeping his distance. She needs to clean herself up, clean this flat up; she's spent so much time trying to make this a nice place for them, and look at it. What would Seth think if he came through the door? That really would be it.

Her phone vibrates on the bed. She dives for it, fumbling to unlock the screen. It's only Paddy down the pub.

You coming in today? Supposed to have started at 2.

It's five past. Work have already been more than understanding; if she loses Seth *and* this job, what happens then? Back to the squat, if she's lucky. Otherwise it's Christmas on the streets.

She digs around for her black T-shirt, but can't find it in the mess. Forget it. Grab one from behind the bar. She drags on her jeans, feeling the toilet paper wrapped around the top of her thighs bunch and imagining the fresh cuts coming open, soaking the denim in blood. Worry about that if it happens. A swill of toothpaste then she's out the door.

It's gone half two by the time she bursts into the Three Bells. Out of breath, head spinning, sparks flashing in her eyes, wondering if she might find someone to spot her a line of wizz. That's the only way she's going to get through the next eight hours. She'd call Flynn again but she already owes him money.

Paddy comes up from the cellar as she's crouching in the hall, looking through the crate for a spare black T.

'All right,' he says, not catching her eye. A massive difference from the usual *Hello my darling* and borderline handsy hug. Not that anyone minds; Paddy's old school, in his early sixties, with big gaps in his teeth from fighting. He's fiercely protective of the girls behind the bar.

She finds a T-shirt and doubles it over her own. The lunchtime rush is done, so she tries to look busy by wiping down the pumps; Paddy's at the other end, filling the washer; her heart's pounding right at the opening to her throat. Usually, when someone's late there's banter. One time someone turned up three hours into a four-hour shift and they all pissed themselves.

Why's Paddy freezing her out? She wants to get it going herself, make a joke about her oversleeping, even though it's an afternoon shift, but her mouth is dry and she doesn't trust the sound of her own voice. Ten minutes later Renata strolls in the door.

'Hey,' croaks Celine. Ren passes her on the way to the back without acknowledgement. Celine follows her though. 'I'm sorry about the other day. What I said about Flynn. I didn't mean it.'

'When you called him a sleaze,' Ren says, bracelets clattering as she hangs up her coat.

'I've been having a hard time.'

Ren pushes past her to get to the bar. 'Doesn't everyone know it, babe.'

'I said I'm sorry,' Celine says, following.

'You always did think you were better than us. Fancy yourself so special.'

'Please don't be mean to me.' She can't cry again; it's impossible that she has enough tears.

'Flynn told me how you've been badgering him, offering him all sorts to get free drugs.'

'That's not true!'

'Although I don't know why anyone would bother. Look at you, like you've just crawled out a skip – and FYI, people have showers for a reason.'

Paddy comes over from the washer and gives Ren a hug, 'Hello my darling,' he says, his hand roaming to the top of her bum. 'Thanks for coming in at short notice.'

Celine feels herself sway and has to grab onto the bar. If Ren's here . . .

'Go on,' Paddy says to Celine, tipping his head towards the door. 'I think you're done here.'

'I'm done?'

'You can't show up for work like that. You'll scare the punters away.'

'I'll go upstairs, have a shower.'

'It's not just today.' Paddy's face is stone. 'You let us down last week and all.'

'But I was ill.'

He glances at Ren. 'Disco fever don't last a whole week. Go on now.'

Celine knows she can't return to the flat. She can't be alone in there, alone for the rest of the day. Who can she call? All her friends in Manchester are either through Ren or the pub.

'I'll work for free,' she says.

Paddy tuts, irritated. 'You're embarrassing yourself.'

'Can I at least stay here for a bit?'

'If you're buying a drink, you can do whatever you want.'

Celine gets her coat and stuffs the spare T-shirt back in

the crate. Around the front of the bar, she perches on a stool, presses a napkin to her eyes.

'What do you want, then?' Ren asks.

'Just a pint of lager.' A mistake, probably. Should have got a Coke, or a water, even. This is only going one way once she starts drinking. *Good*.

Ren dumps the pint on the bar, slopping it over the sides. Celine's card is declined; thankfully, she has a fiver. How can she be out of money? She sips her pint, but the bubbles rub against her raw throat, her stomach twisting against the cold, and she's not even a quarter of the way through when her head starts to spin. Ren stays at the other end of the bar, even after being told to keep the change.

Celine calls Seth, but his phone is still off. She promised herself she wouldn't message him again, but she can't help it.

Need to talk it's URGENT xxx

She gives up after half the pint. It's not sitting well; she thinks she might be sick. As she heads to the door, Ren comes round the bar at last, smiling, until she's close. Then the smile drops.

'You think you're so dark and mysterious,' she says. 'With your poncy boyfriend. But all I see is a pretentious bitch who's finally getting found out.' She pushes Celine through the door before she can respond.

Outside, a drizzle picks up. Celine's sobbing too hard to see where she's going. How's she going to make it to the end of the day, let alone through the rest of her life?

Not far away is the thrum of the M56, getting busy, people

heading home from work. How easy it would be. Close her eyes, walk a few steps. She takes out her phone; one more chance.

This time, this final time, when she calls Seth he answers. As though it's meant to be.

28

CELINE

Celine hurries home, the rain picking up, the wind whipping. She barely feels it. All she's aware of is her quick feet, the rushing in her chest, the sound of Seth's voice apologising for not being in touch – family issues; he'll explain soon – and telling her he'll swing by a bit later. She didn't dare ask if that means he's staying the night. Once she has him in her arms, she'll work some magic; he isn't going anywhere.

She bursts through the door. He didn't say what time he'd be over, he sounded tired and harassed to be fair, but when he arrives the place will be spotless. She grabs a shopping bag and scoops tissues and Rizla packets and roach-jammed beer bottles; clothes are folded, mouldy mugs cleared, the mattress is flipped to hide the blood stains; she does the washing up with the radio on, singing along to a remix of 'Firestarter'. Finally, she scrubs herself beneath the lukewarm dribble which is about the best you ever get out of her shower. He won't be happy with the new cuts on her legs, but she can't do anything about them now. He'll understand. She's his dark star, after all.

The tidy turns up goodies, including some Blue Skys wrapped in cling film she vaguely remembers Flynn stuffing in her hand at the party. Best not go down that route, not yet. But she grabs a mug from beside the sink and helps herself to a vodka, just a single, splash of Pepsi, to go with a ciggie. She doesn't want to get too wasted though.

Three mugs and a couple of lines of who knows what later, she's dancing, the radio blasting. Is it too early for a pill? Seth likes it when she's all loved up and ready for anything. The fan heater's on full, she's working up a sweat; she strips off her dress, still moving her body, eyes closed. A metal scraping sound from the door. Seth's key – he's here!

He comes in with his black coat dripping, a kit bag slung over his shoulder. 'What the fuck is going on, eh?'

'You've been working so hard,' Celine says, twirling towards him, hoping to land in his arms. Instead, she bumps off his wet chest, and staggers back two steps. She sees his face in the light and her heart crumples; she feels ridiculous in her underwear, not the sex kitten she'd been picturing. 'I thought I could help you to wind down a little.'

'You told me it was urgent,' he says, throwing the bag down with a thud.

'It is. It is. I needed you *urgently*.' There's a strange outdoors smell on him. A bit like mud, but richer and deeper, not altogether pleasant. She tries to lead him further into the flat. 'Why don't you come in and have a wash. I showered, and I feel lovely.'

He shrugs her off. 'You sounded suicidal.'

'I haven't seen you for ages.'

'I'm up to my neck in work, and all the rest going on – which I told you about – and you're giving me this shit.'

She feels frozen before his anger. It feels so unfair that she's missed him so much and he's not even bothered to give her a kiss hello. She doesn't want to fight back because she doesn't want him to leave; she needs sympathy and fast.

'I got fired today,' she moans. Tears seal it; his expression softens. He takes her in his arms. She doesn't care if his coat is cold and wet, or that the metal buttons are pressing into her skin, she'd stay in this moment for ever if she could.

'Smart girl like you,' he says. 'You'll always land on your feet.'

'It's fine now you're here.' She moves back and starts on the buttons, but he stops her hand.

'I can't.'

'Have a drink.' She tries to pull him to the bed. 'Stay a for a little bit at least.'

Seth laughs and takes her cheeks in his hands. The smile he gives her is the one she knows and loves. He kisses her hard, one arm pressing her close, the other hand on her neck, her back, cupping her behind.

He pulls away, rocking his head. 'Give me a couple of hours, okay?'

He's lying. She can sense it. He's going to leave here and go back to *hers* and she'll be left alone, sitting in her pants, getting wasted. The dooms are staring at her from deep in the hills, waiting for her to lock eyes. She can't let that happen. *She won't.*

'Don't go to her,' she says.

He snaps to attention. 'What was that?'

The noise in her ears is loud, a siren, blocking the sound of her voice as though someone inside doesn't want her to know what's being said. 'You don't need her.'

'Not this again! You were the one giving it out to that bloke at the party. Not me.'

'Just don't go to her, this one time. Please.'

'What the fuck are you talking about?'

Her blood's beating too fast. There's a surge from deep in her, as though she's about to be sick. 'I've seen you.'

His face goes still. 'What?'

'I— I followed you. To the countryside.'

'You did *what*?'

'I'm sorry. I'm so sorry.' She crosses her arms over her chest, waiting – *hoping* – for him to explode, anything to show her she hasn't gone too far, that he still cares. Anything but him leaving and not coming back.

He gives a little laugh. A sigh that's part amused, part exasperated, part something else she can't read.

'Celine,' he says, 'you are a wally. That's my sister. And yes, I am supposed to be heading back there.' He pauses and pushes his hair back, his brow creasing, biting his lips like he's about to cry himself. 'I didn't want to tell you about it, because . . . well, you hadn't met her yet, and it's personal. But she's not well at the moment. It's really bad. Between checking up on her and work I've been flat out. But you're right – I've not been paying you enough attention, and I'm sorry. That changes now.'

His eyes are sparkling like they've got tears in them. He places a finger on her chin, and glides it down her throat, using it to uncross her arms, bringing it to rest on the bow at the top of her silky knickers.

She wants to believe him. She *does* believe him. But she remembers the shifty way he approached the blonde woman's cottage, her tone when she greeted him at the door. Did they look anything like each other?

'You know what,' Seth says, unbuttoning his coat. 'I think I will have that shower.' He slips it off, and now when he holds her she can feel his body warmth, the steady beat of his heart.

'What's her name,' she says. 'Your sister.'

'Wendy. Would you like to meet her?'

She hugs him tighter. 'I'd love that.'

'As soon as she's better, we'll go on a day out together. You and her will get on so well.' They kiss again, slow and deep. 'I know you'll be great friends.'

He gives her bum another squeeze then goes to clean up. She's so dumb, accusing him like that, so childish. Paranoid is what it is. If anyone's going to destroy this relationship, it's her.

Seth comes out barefoot in smart jeans and a burgundy polo neck, black hair slicked, and joins her on the bed. 'Here, try some of this,' he says, taking a pristine baggie of beige powder from his back pocket and tipping some onto the nightstand. 'This stuff is the bomb. Might even join you for once.'

He grinds it with his gold card, cuts the pile into two healthy lines, and rolls her a twenty; they kiss above the lines as she takes the note from him. She bends her head over the tray, and he holds her hair.

Celine springs back, grabbing her nose, retching at the paint-stripper taste in the back of her throat and flailing for the water. Serves her right for being so greedy; she knew the line was too big. The rush in her chest is powerful, but so's the sudden flying kick of a headache. She lies back, trying to control it, but her eyes are rolling. She wants to say, *Are you not having yours?* but her mouth has gone slack. It's as though she's being dragged backward very fast into somewhere very dark, and she's holding on by her fingertips. *Clinging.*

Seth strokes her cheek with the back of his fingers. 'Don't worry, it's just a bit of ket.' He leans down to kiss her forehead, his face breaking apart. 'All right,' he whispers, close to her ear. 'It's a lot of ket.'

Celine tries to sit up but her body's not working. Seth's on the phone. Is he calling for help? She vanishes into a mental vortex. At some point she's aware of more people in her flat, voices, music, a party. She's desperate to cover herself up, she's practically naked on the bed, but the link in her brain between wanting to move and doing so is broken. Someone lifts her face, slaps her cheek, tells her, *Say cheese!* The laughter that follows stays inside her head, amplifying louder, until she wants to scream just so she doesn't have to hear it any more.

The party's getting rowdier. Finally, she's able to move a bit and crawls to the corner of the bed, but the covers are gone. Her flat is trashed, her beautiful gilt-edged mirror broken on the floor, her clothes rail kicked over and the fairy lights that had been strung round it ripped to pieces. Seth is leaning into a woman by the kitchen table, kissing her neck. Celine brings her knees up and wraps her arms around them.

A lifetime later, it's over.

She stays curled on the mattress as she hears people leave. Her head is dragged up by the hair. She forces an eye open.

'I catch you spying on me again,' Seth says, 'and I'll cut your fucking eyes out.'

He drops her head, and she curls up tighter. His footsteps recede towards the door, then stop.

'You were such a little cutie,' he says. 'But look at you now. Didn't anyone tell you drugs were bad?'

29

BRYAN

Bryan stares out of the windscreen as the water outside goes from murky green to grimy blue to total black. He feels the drag on the chassis, the slight rocking motion, as the car sinks. What was he thinking? Did anyone see him drive in? He presses the window button, but the electrics must be fried. The door won't open from the pressure outside. Oh God, what has he done? *You fucking idiot!* He scabbles at his pockets for his phone, can't find it, twists desperately in his seat then sees it in the cradle on the dash. His fingers must be sweaty because he has no purchase on the screen. How much air is in here? What a stupid way to die! How deep is he sinking? Outside is so devoid of light the darkness seems to stretch for ever. He gazes into it, breath quivering. *Don't panic.* He's safe as long as he's in the car.

Bang.

He turns in his seat. Something hits the back window. A web of cracks appears, dense at the point of impact then spread out. What kind of creature could cause that damage?

Bang. Bang, Bang.

More cracks appear. Water trickles in. *No, no, no.* Something dark swirls behind the car. One of the cracks collapses and the trickle becomes a torrent. Stiff grey fingers work into the hole, pulling away chunks of glass. An arm shoots through the gap as he's about to scream and grabs him by the—

Bryan wakes, drenched in sweat, panting, grabbing his neck where the hand was.

He's still in the car. Still parked close to Zack Cookson's house.

His place is a double-fronted redbrick terrace in Chorlton that looks like it's been around for a long time, but has been done up to a high standard. Fresh pointing, painted iron railings. Doing well for himself.

It doesn't surprise him that Zack is still living in this hipster part of town, still trying to be cool, despite being in his thirties. Probably still with his full roster of girlfriends. *I like keeping it casual*, he explained to Bryan the first time they met. *I prefer just having some fun.* Thankfully that roster had never included Astrid.

What if Zack regretted not making a move on her? Has he wormed his way into her life – and what? Seduced her? Kidnapped her? Or what if it's something else? He was always a little bit flash, with his sunbed tan and greasy stuff in his hair, paying for everything with a gold card. What if he's out of money? What if he can't afford to cover the mortgage on this fancy place? An article about the Foundation was in the *Manchester Evening News* only a few months ago, talking about all the funds they've raised.

What if Zack saw that and thought he'd try to get his hands on it?

Bryan rubs his face, takes a sip from his water bottle. Late last night, Hoop finally called with the details of the car – a blue Honda, the same one as in the video. The same one parked outside Zack's address. Bryan wrestled with telling Ronson, but it was already past ten, and how would he explain where he got the information? Instead he drove to Zack's house and sat outside all night. Partly to catch him first thing in the morning, partly because Bryan couldn't spend another night roaming the cottage and waiting for dawn. Maybe somewhere different he could trick his body into grabbing a few hours' rest. He shudders as his mind replays the highlights of the nightmare – the dread, the dark water, the dead hand coming through the glass.

There's nothing else to do now but wait. Each minute feels as long as an ice age. Six o'clock, six thirty, the darkness fading to charcoal grey. Should he ring the bell now? Get him out of bed, throw him off guard? The last thing Bryan needs is a scene. Best wait for him to be up already. Play it innocent, the worried husband looking for his wife, wait for him to slip up. Don't go barging in full of accusations.

A bloke's coming up the street. Thick coat, hood up – can't see his face. A bag slung over his shoulder. Could that be Zack? He looks around the right height, but Bryan's not sure, and nor is he in the mood to grab a random and pull down their hood. This street might be pleasant, but Moss Side is only a mile away. Grab the wrong random and you'll be waving goodbye with a knife sticking out your gut.

The bloke goes to the correct address and lets himself in with a key.

That's got to be Zack. Where's he been all night? Unless it's not him. All because your car's registered somewhere doesn't mean you live there – he could easily have moved out.

Bryan shoves open the car door. Sod it, he's got to find out.

He stalks up the street to the house, coat wrapped tight to the cold, and ducks inside the gate. At the front door, he pauses – all the lights are off. It can't have been more than five minutes since that bloke let himself in. Obviously gone straight to bed.

The bell doesn't seem to work, so he knocks. No answer. Zack can't be asleep already. Another knock, louder.

Footsteps in the hallway. Bryan stands to the side, out of view of the spyhole, adrenaline pumping, ready to jam his foot in if Zack goes for the quick slam. A shape appears behind the pebbled glass. The door opens.

It's not him. Rather there's a pissed-off woman about Bryan's age, wrapped in a pink housecoat that's as shapeless as a tea cosy, blocking the hallway light. She's holding onto the lock with one hand, and gripping a metal travel mug that looks capable of causing a serious case of concussion with the other.

'Who are you, then?' she asks.

She must live here, but Bryan can't see her and Zack being together. Is he a lodger? 'I'm looking for an old friend. Zack?'

'What time d'you call this to come round, banging on the door—'

'I just got into town. I tried calling him, but his phone's off, and he said—'

'All right, all right.' She turns away. 'I don't need your frigging life story. Go on up, last door on the left. Quiet, mind. Other people will be asleep.'

Bryan pads up the stairs. Must be a guest house. Inside isn't quite as nice as the front, the paisley carpets worn on the treads, the cream-coloured walls dulled with age. He goes to knock on the door, but remembers the warning about being quiet. What the hell is he doing here? Zack's not going to like him barging into his room. Should he just leave? No doubt that busybody downstairs will ask Zack about it when he gets up – *Who was that mate of yours coming round before dawn?* It won't take much for him to work out who it was, especially if he's involved in this.

Bryan eases down the handle. Better to catch him unprepared, before he can think up a story. The light in the room is faint, but enough to see it's practically empty – only a desk, a dresser, a wardrobe, and in the corner a double bed. The dickhead's spark out, still with that thick head of black hair, the duvet halfway down his body. Hands up around the pillow like he's surrendering in his dream. His coat and bag are still by the door. Bryan crouches and feels the cold of the morning on the material.

Where would he have been, all night on a Monday? What if he's keeping Astrid somewhere?

Bryan sneaks his hand into the coat pockets, recoiling at a crumpled tissue. Bag might be a better idea. It's long and thin, like a holdall. He creeps the zip open, and reaches inside, feeling clothes, what may be a coil of cable, metal objects – tools? Or maybe handcuffs? He knocks something and there's a heavy *clunk.*

Zack turns over. 'Who's that?'

'It's Bryan Webb. Astrid's husband.'

He scrabbles back, clutching the duvet to his chest. 'What you doing here?'

'The woman downstairs let me in.'

'Get out.'

'I didn't mean to startle you.'

'Get. The fuck—'

'*Please*. Astrid's missing.'

'Are you deaf? Get out of here!'

'Have you seen her?'

'Get the fuck out or I'm calling the police.'

This is exactly what Bryan wanted to avoid, but they're here now. Let the police show up and take them both in together.

He folds his arms. 'Be my guest.'

Zack pauses like he's about to lose his rag again, but instead sighs and reaches for his cigarettes. 'You've not changed,' he says, lighting from a Zippo. He leans back and puts an arm behind his head in a way that even in the gloom Bryan can see flexes his biceps. He's bulked out in the last few years. 'Still throwing your weight around.'

'I just want to find my wife.'

'What's happened to her?'

'There was a car crash, an accident – it's been in the news.'

Zack takes a long drag. 'I'm sorry to hear that, I hope she's okay.'

'We can't find her. Have you heard anything from her? Anything at all?'

'You sure she hasn't seen sense and done a runner?'

'She's been in touch with Vivien.'

Zack glances off to the side, like he's thinking. He looks back at Bryan and shakes his head. 'Can't help you, I'm afraid. Not heard from Astrid since you two skipped town.'

'Bullshit.'

'I've answered your questions,' Zack says, 'Now do one and let me get some kip.'

'Late night? Who were you with?'

He barks a laugh. 'Who the fuck do you think you are?'

'I know you've been with her.'

'Just get out.'

'I've got it on video.'

Zack stubs out his cigarette and gets out of bed in his boxers. 'You remember last time I saw you,' he says, approaching. He looks solid, strong. 'You said it's easy to get a search warrant for someone's place – even easier to turn up a couple of kilos of coke and a set of scales in the cupboard. So why would I ever risk even speaking to your wife, let alone see her?'

They're close now. Lunging distance.

Bryan steps back, tensing. He used to be handy in his heyday, but he's not had a proper ruck for years. Zack, however, looks primed.

'The police know you were with her last week,' Bryan says.

'I don't give a donkey's bollocks what the police know.'

'You're telling me you've not seen my wife.'

'Get out of my room, or I'm going to make you.'

'If you've hurt her—'

Zack's lifts his fists like a boxer. He feints right and Bryan dodges left, clattering into the bin by his feet.

'Come on, Grandad,' Zack says, doing a dodge-and-weave move. 'Have a pop.'

'I don't want to fight,' Bryan says – at least, not on Zack's home turf.

'You'd best fuck off then.'

'Listen, we've never got on. I can't change the past. Astrid is missing *now*. She's been gone for three days already – don't you care? You were friends for years.'

'You sneak into my room like the fucking Stasi, wake me up after I've been grafting all night, accuse me—'

'I haven't accused you of anything. I just—'

'I've not seen her. I've not heard from her. So if it's okay with you, *officer*, I'd kindly like you to go.'

'If you've done something to her, I'll find out. I swear to God I will.'

'You're not a copper any more. You're nothing. You're no one. I'm going to tell you one last time before I hand you out a proper lesson. Get. The fuck. Out of my room.'

Bryan wants to smash that smirk off his face, even if it means getting punched in the process, but what will that achieve? Nothing but a headache from Ronson, and maybe a criminal charge. He leaves to the sound of Zack's jeering.

Back in the car Bryan beats the steering wheel. He was never a detective, but even he can work out that Zack's attitude is odd, to say the least. They never got on, and things were said, that's fair enough – and it's feasible he missed her disappearance in the news. But now he knows she's missing, surely he'd be worried? They were good friends. As annoyed as he had every right to be, waking up and finding someone in his room, if Zack really is innocent then he'd understand that Bryan is just desperate to find her.

Zack would want her to be safe. No innocent person in that situation would try to start a fight. Bryan's done messing about with this – he calls Hoop on repeat until he picks up the phone.

This time when Bryan tells him what he needs, he also tells him what will happen if it's not forthcoming.

30

ASTRID

Astrid forces down an apple slice as though she's ravenous.

'Honestly,' she says. 'I'm feeling much better.'

This despite the last week being one of the worst of her life so far. She's been as sick as she can remember, too nauseous to eat, practically bed-bound with the spasms in her spine, her constant migraine so bad it's as though someone keeps slamming her with a sledgehammer when she's not looking. All of it triggered no doubt by that stupid email messing with her head, her even more stupid row with Bryan about money, her cataclysmically stupid (possibly marriage-ending) decision to lie about sneaking to town today to meet Zack. She knows Bryan would try to talk her out of it, that he and Zack never got on, but the thought of seeing an old friend again, and perhaps catching a glimpse of the person she used to be, is worth more than all the agonies her crappy body can heap on her.

'You still look peaky,' Bryan replies. The frown hasn't left his forehead since she announced she was heading to Manchester this morning.

213

'I've got to get out. I'm going barmy lying here.'

'Come on a walk with me, then.' He does a preparatory knee-bend. 'I can show you these old ruins I found.'

'I can look in the mirror for that.'

He misses their old joke in his keenness to find a solution. 'If you're up for some fresh air, let's take a drive. We can go to—'

'Or come out with me,' Astrid says, clenching her toes so hard the muscles cramp. 'I know how much you like browsing round the shops.' She catches the glint in his eye. 'I'm not buying anything.'

His smile goes tight. 'You can buy yourself something if you like.'

'I just want to look.'

'You've been so ill this week.'

She eats another apple slice. It fizzes in her stomach as though coated in sherbet. 'I'll come straight back if I start to feel bad. Promise.'

Bryan's frown becomes a furrow. 'Maybe I should go with you.'

(*No, no, no.*) 'Great! You can sit in the dressing room and tell me if—'

'I thought you weren't buying anything.'

'If I do it'll be under a hundred pounds,' she says, a little too quickly. He returns his sergeant's stare (*look innocent, look innocent*) to her attempted smile.

'All right,' he says, sighing hard enough to let her know it's really not. 'Let me at least give you a lift to the station. And keep your phone on, so I can check you're okay.'

Hiding her pained wince, her vertebrae like hot slicing blades when she moves, she leans forward to give Bryan a kiss on the cheek. 'Of course, my dear husband.'

Five years ago, her illness started with a stomach ache. As simple as that. A hard ball at the top of her intestine that wouldn't go away no matter what she tried from the chemist. This was at the height of Niall's torment, with all his lies and gossip and fake email accounts, when she and Bryan were working overtime trying to collate the information to get the restraining order. Not an easy task when the person you're trying to restrain is nowhere to be seen.

She assumed it was stress. She assumed that once Niall had been purged from her life she would begin to feel better. Instead, her symptoms multiplied. Migraines, vomiting, not to mention the dreaded back spasms. She'd wake up with her body feeling like it had been twisted the wrong way during the night, and spend the first ten minutes of the day retching into the toilet bowl.

Bryan said he'd seen this kind of thing before, with victims. *Give it time,* he said, *you need to heal.* But even after Niall finally left her alone her symptoms persisted. If anything, they got worse, accelerating to the point where she struggled to get dressed or brush her teeth.

She wasn't getting anywhere with the NHS – her own doctor seemed sure much of her pain was psychosomatic – so Bryan paid for her to go private. At the smart clinic they visited in Hale, she was told that although her symptoms implied an unusual autoimmune disease the diagnosis was not clear-cut; she was put on methotrexate, plus sumatriptan for her immobilising migraines. That gave her chronic diarrhoea (sexy), so it was changed, and changed again, the different combinations tried until she was at least able function. Her symptoms were managed but not improving.

Next, a psychiatrist, who determined her to be depressed and anxious (no shit) and added various SSRIs to her script. Another, more expensive, doctor moved her onto something called a T-cell costimulatory blocking agent, along with a prescription for OxyContin (hello oblivion!). Add in something she can never remember the name of to stop her vomiting, and something else with an even bigger name to stop her hands from going red and itchy (a side effect of the medication further up the chain), and that's the four-times-a-day routine making her life bearable.

For anything better, there is her secret Oxy stash. Today it's the only thing that's going to get her to Manchester.

Astrid waits to board the 10.45 to Piccadilly before taking two Oxy halves (no messing about), crunching them with her teeth so they get in her blood quicker. Anything to stop the invisible hands playing her spine like an accordion.

As the train rocks, the pain recedes. It's so strange how different she is from when she used to hang out with Zack. Back then she was such a square you could have used her to draw right angles. Sure, on weekends in Blackpool, or a night out at the Boardwalk, she'd get blasted on vodka Red Bulls (usually two would be enough), but Vivien and most of their mates were into proper drugs. Ecstasy and cocaine mostly, with the occasional sunny mushroom afternoon.

Astrid wasn't against them doing it. Everyone was funny and loving when high, but she could never imagine relinquishing control like that. She couldn't picture herself with those space-alien pupils, her jaw weaving from side to side as though remote-controlled by a toddler. Yet here she is, her eyelids half-mast and twitching as the Oxy takes hold, her mouth slack and what feels like droplet of dribble clinging to the edge of her lip. She's aware of a young man in the seats nearby watching her, but she can't move because around her feet are many hundreds of snakes that will wake and slither up her body if she does. They're twisting and writhing over her feet, wrapping themselves around her ankles. It would be disconcerting, if it wasn't for the fact the pain is fading, its molten fingers withdrawing its grip. So let the drool fall. Who cares?

Someone touching her shoulder. Astrid opens her eyes and sees a kindly looking old woman, like a fairy tale. 'You're here,' she says.

Astrid climbs from the chair, limbs stiff. She's so dazed she has to use the backs of the seats to get to the door. The cold air shocks her face when she steps onto the platform, into the flurry of people, the stench of diesel and the yelling of the brakes, the echoing speaker system announcing that the eleven fifty to Euston has arrived on platform eight. She stagger-weaves to the barriers, aware she's banging into people, they probably think she's drunk, catching her feet in the wheels of someone's luggage, tripping and crunching down on her knee. The shock of the impact up her back bursts through the Oxy bubble. Tears fill her eyes, and she lets out a breathless moan. She crawls to the closest bench, feeling humiliated, and sits with her head in her hands, trying to breathe through it. Was that a sign?

Turn back now before it's too late?

Half an hour and half an Oxy later, she's able to move.

Thankfully, she isn't meeting Zack until one. Her plan had been to have a stroll, revel in her old stomping ground, but now the excess time will be taken just getting there.

She makes her way through the busy town centre, holding onto railings where she can, shuffling like someone twice her age. It takes for ever to get through Piccadilly Gardens to the post-box red pagoda in the centre of Chinatown, their once upon a go-to place to hang out after clubbing. Zack is already there, smoking and reading the *Metro*. He looks up as she stumps towards him.

'Jesus,' he says, throwing down his cigarette. He goes to help her. 'You get in a fight on the way over?'

She returns his hug, burying her head in his neck. 'I tripped. The floor won.'

'Oh, sweetheart.' Zack gets his arm under hers and all but carries her to the pagoda.

Close up, the red paint is flaking, the wood beneath damp and starting to rot. 'This place looks like how I feel,' she says.

He replies with a grin. 'Getting old, babe.'

'Happens to the best of us.'

'And the worst,' he says, lifting an eyebrow in that way of his – how much she's missed seeing that!

'What happened to us?' She squeezes her eyes shut, shakes her head. 'Sorry. Debbie Downer here.'

'No, no, I'm sorry. It's my fault.'

Bryan's voice: *Where was he while you were sick? How many times has he been to visit?*

'Why didn't you come to the wedding?' she asks.

Zack looks down, makes a sound as though he's just been handed a very heavy weight. 'I kind of got the feeling I wouldn't be welcome.'

218

'From who?'

'You know who.'

'Come on, he's not that bad.'

'He's never liked me.'

'I remember the first night you met you were sending daggers at each other.'

'Well, whatever. I wanted to come to the wedding, I should have come. I made a mistake.'

Astrid gives a long sigh, bumps his shoulder. 'You're not the only one.'

He bumps her back, then stays leaned in, touching. 'You mean about the old man?'

'Don't call him that,' she says, but doesn't move away.

'Sorry. How is *Bryan*?'

'I'll tell you all about it. But you'll have to buy me a drink first.'

On the walk to All Bar One, another old hang, her back feels almost pain-free. She takes languid steps like a normal person (*thank you little Oxy friends!*). Zack's telling her about his work – something in construction, or engineering, she's never quite got it – how he's really thrown himself into it these days.

'Sounds exciting,' she says.

'Only if you like bunking in a portacabin with four other blokes.'

'Depends how fit they are.'

'These are middle-aged blokes with bad farts and beer guts.'

'I think you're supposed to be beer gut positive these days.'

Zack laughs so hard they have to stop walking until he gets his breath. How she's missed this. The only friends she has now are the other hopeless cases hiding behind their avatars on the self-help forums. There's little chance of a fun chat with them. Weepy support, yes. Bantz, not so much. It's ten times worse with Bryan. Every day the same dull discussions about the shopping list, or the towel rotation, or the website for the tea-making business she can't get her head around, no matter how many YouTube tutorials on WordPress she slogs through. But this (*this!*), just having a laugh. How has she done without this for so long?

Zack opens the door for her at the bar. They're reminiscing about a messy night out (when was it not?), which ended with her keeping him company in the emergency room with a broken nose. Nothing malicious. A wayward elbow from the bloke next to him on the dance floor.

'You remember how the doctor was looking at you,' he says. 'Like you'd been slapping me around.' He puts on an officious voice: '*Would you like to speak to me in private, Mr Cookson?*'

They get a booth towards the back. She's laughing so much she collapses onto her side as soon as she sits down. 'All the nurses were staring at me on the way out.'

He motions a drink by his mouth. 'Still on the g and ts?'

Of course, she shouldn't. She's still recovering from being ill all week, having barely eaten, plus the Oxys. Alcohol will most likely mess her up, almost certainly spin her out, but as of now, as of this second, this is the best she's felt since the day they packed up and left Manchester. Take it slow, small sips, plenty of water. She'll be fine.

'Great memory,' she says.

He taps the side of his head. 'Up here for thinking.'

Astrid's phone buzzes. She fishes it from her pocket, squinting at the message because her eyes won't focus.

Bryan.

Blah, blah, whatever. She tosses her phone onto the table. Just cram it for once. *You don't own me.*

The email last week, those chat messages.

Do you find yourself anxious around him? Too eager to please?

Not now, not when she's enjoying herself. Leave all the headaches for back home.

Zack comes back with a pint for him, a high-ball glass that looks suspiciously like a double for her, and a couple of bags of salt and vinegar. He puts the drinks down, splits open the crisps to share, then sees her face. 'What happened?'

'It's nothing.'

'I leave you laughing. I come back and it looks like you just watched a kitten being beheaded.'

Right then, as if by fate, her phone buzzes with an incoming call. Bryan's name flashes on the screen.

'You not going to get that?' Zack asks.

She watches her phone until it goes quiet. When she glances up, his expression is amused, complicit.

What are friends for, if not for something like this?

'Zack,' she says, 'I think I need your help.'

31

ASTRID

The alcohol is a good idea, a bad idea, a good bad idea, if that's possible. It's the first she's had in what must be three months, since the little glass of red with her spaghetti Bolognese on their anniversary. What fun! Until she vomited half an hour later, and for the whole night.

Not today, though. Today she is soaring. She's so high it's hard to keep track of what Zack's saying, though she knows it's funny, it must be funny, because she can't stop giggling. When she sips her drink the top of it glitters like a tiny crystal lake.

'It's some kind of meta-stalking,' Zack's saying. 'Trying to warn you like that.' They're back to this again, her mystery emailer. He's sure it's Niall, crawled back from the slime, looking to screw with her head once more. 'So creepy.'

'I don't know what to think.'

'You sure it's not Bryan, testing you?'

'Don't be silly.'

Zack takes a sip of his pint, his air playful. 'How old is he now? Sixty? Sixty-five?'

'He's not even fifty yet and you know it.'

It's getting harder to focus. The sounds of the bar echo and reverberate in her ears. Clanking glasses, other conversations, the low bass beat of the background lounge music, and above that, louder than the rest, the endless crashing of her pulse.

'If I give you my bank card,' Astrid says, 'can you go to the bar? Actually, no. Can you get another round, and I'll pay you back after?'

That eyebrow goes up again. 'Worried his nibs will see you've been blowing his cash?' She bites her bottom lip, and he waves her away. 'Don't worry about it. Drinks are on me today.'

She tells him to get her a single. He comes back with sambucas.

'Chin, chin,' he says, toasting his shot glass while she's still staring at hers. 'Don't tell me you've forgotten?'

She had, until he mentioned it. Their one dalliance together, as much you can count the two of them nailing most of a bottle of sambuca on a bored Wednesday night, then being interrupted by the doorbell while he was fumbling around her bra clasp. He was expecting a delivery so had to answer it, but by the time he'd got downstairs and back up again the moment had passed. It's not that she didn't find him attractive (everyone did), but she used to prefer arty types who knew their way around a Dostoevsky novel. Besides, she was hardly the party girl of his dreams. That was what made their friendship so workable: neither saw the other as a viable partner. At least back then.

'I'm already smashed,' she says. 'Any more and you'll be carrying me back to the station.' She goes to push it towards him, but something switches in her brain, and she brings it to her mouth. There's a split second to register the aniseed scent, the

224

oily motion of the liquor, a startled voice in her mind going, *Don't do—*, then it's down the hatch, the warmth rushing to her stomach.

Astrid grabs the side of the table. 'Hoooo, boy. That was a mistake.'

Zack says something she doesn't catch and she leans in, almost sending her new gin and tonic toppling.

'Woah now,' he says, grabbing it. 'Did you have a few before we met? You're looking pretty smashed for a couple of drinks.'

'*Weeeelll*,' she says.

He leans forward. 'Go on, do tell.'

If anyone will understand it's Zack. He was always getting drugs for people, even if he didn't do them much himself. How much of a relief will it be to finally unload about her life to someone who knew what she was like before?

'They're hardly meant for fun, but . . .' She unzips the inside pocket of her jacket, takes out her pink travel pill case, opens it to show him.

'Pills,' he says. 'Retro.'

She points to the two halves. 'OxyContin.'

'What are the rest for?'

'Depression, anxiety, nausea. And that's just the good stuff. It's so much fun being me.'

'Jesus, Astrid. What happened?'

She frets with the hinge of the case, the Oxy bubble evaporating once more. What would he say if she took another half now? Would he try to stop her, like Bryan would? Would he laugh and ask her to split it?

'You have no idea,' she says.

'I know you left the city because you thought the pollution

was making you sick, even though you already lived in Hale. Barely Manchester as it is.'

'I hate Dinckley so much.'

'Come on, I've seen pictures. Looks beautiful there.'

'It's boring.'

'Maybe that's more who you're with than where you are,' he says, his smile mischievous.

'Stop,' she says, but without conviction.

'Count yourself lucky. I've been stuck at this bloody guest house for months now while I make my new place liveable.' He stretches, rubs the back of his head, casual. 'You wouldn't believe this, but I bought somewhere not too far from you. Up by Clitheroe. It's an old farmhouse, a bit of a dump – could do with a woman's touch.'

'Everyone's always going on about how great the country-side is,' she says, 'but they don't have to live there. They don't have to listen to the deathly conversations about the size of someone's cabbages. Or the change in the bus schedule to Blackburn. Do you know there's a thing called muckspreading? Muck in this case being another word for *shit*. That's right, they spread shit everywhere. The whole place stinks of shit for months at a time.'

By the time she's finished her rant, most of which she can't remember now she's stopped, Zack is wheezing so hard he can't get his words out. 'Oh, Astrid,' he says. 'You crack me up.'

She takes a sip of her drink that becomes a glug that turns into most of the glass. How good is it to say how she really feels about that awful place, without having to check herself with Bryan, who straight away goes on the defensive.

'You're in the shit, As,' Zack says. 'Only a friend can tell you

226

that. This' – he points to the jacket pocket where she stuffed the pill holder – 'is bad news. You take that every day?'

The booze has hit her control panel like a wrecking ball. 'Four tmmm . . . day.'

'How do you know you're not making yourself sick with all this rubbish?'

'Mmmma ready sick.'

'With what?'

'Autoimmune. Thing.'

'In other words, they don't know.'

She gives a woozy shrug. 'S'what they say.'

'You've got to give this shit up. All of it. I'm being serious. I was on antidepressants for years—'

'*You?*'

Zack looks to the side. 'Tears of a clown, dontcha know. Made me want to kill myself. So they put me on antipsychotics instead.'

'Wha' happen?'

'Made me want to kill other people.'

Astrid snorts a laugh. She wafts a hand in the air. 'S'all fucked.'

'I'm serious. These doctors are in hock to big pharma, getting poor saps like you – no offence—'

'S'all right.'

'Repeat prescriptions. That's what it's all about. Mix and match those meds, load up on side effects. You and the government splitting the bill, of how much? Thousands a year, maybe tens of thousands for the more expensive stuff – bet they're branded drugs. No cheap generics. All of that is profit going into some Swiss billionaire's pension fund.'

He sees her gazing at him like she's brain-damaged and breaks into a laugh. 'The best thing you can do is come off them. Cold turkey.'

'Speakin' of . . .' she says, digging around for the pill box. Not had her one o'clock.

'You're aware that you've got another of those Oxys in your hand.'

Like she doesn't know. 'Got to take 'em together.'

'You're already wasted.'

She tosses them in and washes them down with the rest of her g and t. 'S'good. I'm good.'

'You look so unhappy,' he says, taking her hands, but she keeps her eyes fixed on the bar behind him, the staff busying to serve the lunchtime rush. He tries for a smile. 'Trust me, drugs are bad.'

'Need them.'

'Let me help you come off them.'

'Can't.'

'It's like if you've got an itch. You want to scratch it, right? What happens if you scratch it, then rub ten different lotions on it, then go at it with sandpaper? You're going to mess the whole thing up. Better to have the itch, try not to touch it, and more than likely it'll go on its own.'

Easy to say when it's not you crippled by a migraine or bent over from back spasms. When it's not you going from clinic to clinic desperate for answers. When you're not the one who's transformed from a healthy, active person to someone who struggles to get out of bed in the morning.

But . . . what if he's right?

'You're one of the most beautiful, intelligent people I've ever met,' he says. 'I can't stand seeing you this way.'

That's enough to break her. He holds her close as she sobs into his shoulder.

'It won't be easy,' he says, stroking her hair. 'Like jumping off a moving treadmill. But give it a week and you'll feel amazing – you'll be wondering how you ever got so addicted to that shit.'

After that is a haze. The Oxy kicks in and she's off somewhere, her body still down below, fixed to the reality of the booth, the bar, Zack telling her about some girl he's seeing, which part of her still finds disappointing despite her ethereal state.

Time vanishes down a sinkhole. They're in the bar, then she's retching in the bathroom, then they're outside. The streets are getting dark. He's leading her somewhere, which is good, because without him she would probably lie down on the pavement and pass out. They go into a shop and she watches a video of a dog running up to the camera on a huge phone screen for what seems like hours until she realises the whole thing – the dog, the screen, the phone – is all part of a poster. There is no video.

Outside, on the move, eyes half closed. Zack leading her. They arrive somewhere loud, echoing, busy. Pigeons are pecking around her feet.

He's shaking her arm. 'Hey? Hey? You in there?'

Piccadilly train station. How did they get here?

'I'm worried about leaving you,' he says. 'Do you need me to get you on the train?'

'Go,' she says. 'I'm okay.'

Zack doesn't look convinced, but she's suddenly feeling too sick to talk. She's crashing, her head spinning, a shuddering spasm twisting her at the waist. He can't see her like this.

At the barrier, he helps get her ticket ready. 'I'm here for you,' he says, as they hug goodbye. 'Call me any time, day or night. I love you, As. Remember that.'

She goes through the barrier. A man bashes into her arm, and she spins around. What's she doing here again? *Move out the fucking way, love.* A whistle shrieks close to her head. It's too busy. She can't breathe. She's got to get off the platform, but the crowd is too thick, it's pushing her back. Her feet get tangled. She grabs an arm, but is shoved off. Need to get clear. She's losing it. Someone grabs her round the waist. She sees the dark blue of police uniforms and throws back her elbows, howling at them to get off her. More officers grab her, holding her down. Where are they taking her? To Dinckley? To her husband? She bucks and scratches and screams for them to let her go, don't take her back there, please don't take her back. All that's waiting for her there is death and she doesn't want to die.

32

BRYAN

Bryan gets what he needs from a surveillance gear shop with no sign and boarded-up windows hidden beside a double-fronted porn place on Oldham Street. Then it's back for the tricky part – attaching the GPS tracker. He parks a bit away, lingers on the corner until the street is clear, then hurries with his hood up to Zack's blue car.

Thankfully it's parked beside a lamppost. Bryan goes behind it, drops down by the back wheel, pretending to tie his shoe-laces, and snakes his hand under the chassis. The tracker's magnet attaches to the metal with a satisfying suck. Then he's up and walking again. Job done.

He finds an egg-and-bacon cafe nearby, orders a coffee, and sets up on a table at the back. Two young girls are behind the counter. God knows what they must think of him – laptop and notepad open, clenching his fists and muttering curses as he tries to install the tracker software, the sweat sluicing off him like he's just had a shower. They keep glancing over and covering their mouths to talk.

Maybe they saw him on the news? Everyone else seems to have done. His phone is jammed with messages, mostly from old colleagues he's not spoken to since he left the force, too many for him to reply to them all. There's even one from Linda at the Department of Crime and Policing saying they're all praying for Astrid's swift return. They can reschedule the meeting then.

But what happens if she doesn't come back? What of the life they've built? It simply doesn't work without her. He checks the clock – over two hours since he called Hoop, more than enough time to get off his sizeable behind.

'I thought you'd have that case file for me by now,' Bryan says when Hoop answers.

'I'm telling you, Webb,' Hoop replies, voice firm, 'you've got to calm down. There's a lot of heat on this case now, since that body was found.'

'That's not my problem.'

'And I've told you, it's all digital access now. Audited.'

'You're a bloody chief constable.'

'All the more reason for them to ask why I'd be looking at the file.'

'Get someone else to look at it, then. At the very least, find out if they've spoken to either Niall Turton or Zack Cookson.'

'Can't you just let them get on with their job?'

He thought Hoop would be on his side. That he'd go out of his way to help, but he's barely wet his nib. Ask for the case file, can't have it. Ask for specific information from the case file, can't have it. Yes, he's got the details for Zack's car, but Bryan could have called someone lower down the food chain for that.

He's done messing about with this. Hoop thinks he doesn't

have to help, but he's wrong. Bryan reminds him what he said this morning. What will happen if Hoop doesn't get him what he wants.

The silence after Bryan's stopped speaking goes on for so long he wonders if they've been disconnected. Finally, Hoop says, 'You really want to go there, Webb?'

'I need to find my wife.'

Hoop swears and kicks something that sounds like the side of a desk. 'You know we're done now, right? I get what you need and you never call me again.'

'You'd do the same.'

'You're a fucking prick, Webb.'

'That mean you're getting me the case file?'

'I'll try my best.'

Bryan's about to tell him he'd better do more than try, but an alert pops up on the laptop from the tracker app. Zack's car appears on the screen as a glowing red dot. He's on the move.

So much for him going back to sleep. Time to see what he's really up to.

33

ZACK

Zack flops onto his back. He slaps for his cigarettes, lights up, grinds his eye with the heel of his hand. What has he got himself into?

Was it too bad, what he had before? Working hard, playing hard, but all under control. Easy to manage. No danger, no bother. No psycho ex-coppers sneaking into your bedroom at seven in the morning.

If it was anyone else but Astrid. His weakness, the one that got away. What shoulda, woulda, coulda been, but never was. Partly because of her – she was way too *nice* compared to his usual type – but mostly because of him. With Astrid, it would have been serious, and settling down with just one girl was never his sort of thing. He still didn't think it was, until he saw her again in Manchester. Something just clicked into place.

How much does the old man know? Not enough to go to the police, that's for sure. Or at least not enough for them to get in contact with him again. He'd called them himself on Sunday morning, once the news stories started to appear, and she'd been named as missing. The detectives didn't seem too interested in his account of them reconnecting as friends – especially as he had a solid alibi, having nipped down to have a long, memorable conversation with Elaine on Saturday morning. As far as Zack could find out, they didn't seem to know about Astrid's burner phone, the one he bought for her before getting her back to the train station.

Judging by this morning's events, neither does Bryan.

Zack sits up, stubs out his cigarette. Takes a long sip from the silver water bottle on the side table. So stupid to get drunk last night – he didn't need to get involved in any of that. How long is he going to let himself be ruled by his bad habits?

Maybe that's why the thought of being with Astrid is so appealing.

Downstairs, Elaine's stomping around the kitchen. Slamming down the kettle, slamming closed the fridge, the cupboard door, scraping the chair out from under the table. An elephant in jack boots has more grace than her. Bustling around in that house-coat like a big pink troll, smelling of old tea and misery. She'll be drilling him for details about Bryan later – who he is, how does Zack know him, what on earth was he doing showing up here before breakfast, and leaving just as fast. That's if she wasn't standing outside the room with a glass pressed to the door.

The sooner he's out of here, the better. It was only supposed to be for four months while he did up the new place, but work has been crazy busy, and the girl he was seeing hoovered up the rest of his spare time – although thankfully that should be done with now. He thought he was going mad when he bought the cottage in Clitheroe. Early-onset midlife crisis. But now, with Astrid, with what's going on, it could turn out to be a genius move.

Speaking of which. He's up, so he might as well get started. Lots to do today.

Twenty minutes later he's dressed and ducking down the hallway, getting out the door before Elaine can collar him. At the gate, he looks along the street. It wouldn't surprise him if the old man had been staking him out this morning and caught sight of him coming home. That would explain his appearance in the room literally fifteen minutes after he'd gone to bed.

Zack pulls the car from the kerb, checking all around to see if anyone's following. As an extra precaution he rags around the backstreets of Chorlton, taking corners at random and shooting out of the junction onto Wilbraham Road, causing the Range Rover behind to brake and honk.

First, he has pick up the bits he needs. He goes through the town centre, turning off at Manchester Fort and driving into Monsall, a nothing part of town too rough for anyone to be watching him.

The hardware store is dark inside, with caging on the windows and a hand-painted sign above the door saying *House Goods*. He buys nails, pliers, a new tarp, heavy-duty cleaning equipment; he pays in cash, his baseball cap pulled down low. Not that anyone would say something to the police, even if they did remember him. That's why he goes there.

He heads north out of the city, sticking to the B road he knows has no traffic cameras. The turn-off is easy to miss. The first time he went there he must have gone up and down the same stretch ten times before he clocked the cattle gate, the winding dirt path on the other side. He finds it this time with ease, following it all the way to the end, where it stops at a small, weathered cottage, the windows blacked out, the walls mottled with lichen. Abandoned is how it looks.

Probably for the best that Bryan backed down this morning. As fun as it would have been to drive his fist into the old man's nose, to feel the satisfying crack of the bone breaking beneath his knuckles – he's dreamed about it since that night in Chorlton when he did his bad cop routine, warning Zack away from being friends with Astrid – it's better to see him in mental torment instead. Anguished, harried, looking like he's been awake for years already.

Better to know that the nightmare, for him at least, is just getting started.

34

BRYAN

In the cafe, Bryan stares at the red glowing circle of Zack's car as it whizzes around the streets close to the guest house. Has someone taken it for a joy ride? How would that be for terrible luck – that crappy old Honda getting nicked by local hoods, who then drag Bryan in pursuit all over the city, until he finds its charred remains on the moors.

The car turns onto the main road, heading north. Clearly that performance was to flush out anyone following. So bloody innocent, eh? Bryan scoops his stuff and bolts for the door.

He keeps the laptop open on the passenger seat so he can track the red circle as he's driving, tailing it through the town centre, out the other side on Bury Old Road. After taking a right at Manchester Fort, he notices the circle hasn't moved, and drags the steering wheel to the side, mounting the kerb as he stops. There's a toggle button in the corner to change the map to street view. A parade of shops, most of them closed. He jams his foot on the accelerator again. What could Zack be buying there?

The shops are deep in Monsall. He knows this area well – it's

239

close to where he was stationed. For most of that time it was a grubby, druggy scumhole that dragged down the rest of the city. From what he can see, not much has changed.

Zack's long gone by the time Bryan gets there. Up close the shops are even scuzzier. A derelict laundrette with a smashed window, the sole remaining washing machine tipped on its side, a Chinese takeaway so grungy it's probably even too nasty for the local rats, and a general store with a hand-painted sign.

Got to be the store. He slips into sergeant mode and swaggers inside. *On the lookout for a dangerous criminal. Think he was here ten minutes ago. Man in his thirties, medium build, black hair.* The bored Asian woman behind the counter is not so easily duped.

'Sorry, sorry,' she says, 'no English.'

Thankfully he's not quite out of the habit of carrying emergency cash in his wallet. Fifty pounds in folded bills slid across the counter is enough to get her talking.

Bleach? Heavy-duty gloves? *Tarpaulin?*

Either Zack's planning on doing something very messy, or he's already cleaning up.

Bryan cuts back into the traffic. Zack's past the ring road, heading through Heywood. He's staying off the motorways – he'd get north quicker on the M66. Is that so he's not picked up by cameras? Clever.

Soon the council blocks and *Coronation Street* terraces give way to warehouses and industrial estates, then to boggy fields and wind farms, and finally those long, fabulous Lancashire vistas. He could stare for hours at that patchwork of farms and grassland, broken up by trees or bodies of water, going all the way to the pale purple of Pendle Hill, so far it seems to barely crest the horizon. Even on a mucky day like this, the grimy Manchester clouds stretching for ever, it's glorious.

How Astrid isn't interested in all this he'll never know. She liked it at first, when they'd come for a weekend, getting away from the pollution, those particulates in the air. Of course, she still feels grotty most of the time, but he tells her, where would you rather be feeling grotty? Back in the city with the noise and the traffic and the scallies all over the place, or here, with this right outside your door?

Near to Clitheroe, Zack comes to a stop. What's he doing all the way up here, twenty miles from where they live – close in countryside terms – with enough kit to put a serial killer to shame? Bryan puts his foot down.

The road goes narrow, tall hedges on each side, curving one way then the other. It's hard to keep an eye on the map and what's coming up at the same time. Round the next bend, and he should be seeing Zack's car, but it's nowhere. Then he's past the red circle.

Bryan screeches to a halt. What the hell is going on? He jags the car around in a five-point turn, fingers tingling, nearly spilling into a ditch, and races back.

This time he slows to five miles an hour. No car. It's just vanished.

How is that possible?

He goes lightheaded. Black spots appear at the side of his vision. Everything feels unreal, a delusion, a fever dream. Perhaps he's still in the cafe, staring at the wall, the girls behind the counter gossiping behind their hands about the weird bloke in the corner, while his frazzled sleep-deprived mind takes him on this elaborate fantasy.

Something slams into the windscreen – *BANG!* – and his legs shoot into an emergency stop.

A crack snakes from the top to the bottom of the glass. He gets out of the car, grasping the door, his whole body shaking. What is going on? Another fucking nightmare? Zack lobbing rocks from the bushes? Or maybe it's something altogether more apocalyptic? Cosmic hailstones to punish him for his multitude of sins. They were always attending church when he was a kid – the only time his dad closed the pharmacy was to go for the Sunday service. What if his parents were right all along? Heaven for the saintly, and hell for the rest of them.

At the front of the car, Bryan lets out a yelp of a laugh. It's only a bloody crow! Lying on the ground, neck broken. Dumb bird.

He leans back on the bonnet, hand to his chest, waiting for his breathing to calm. Drama over, but that doesn't answer the question of what happened to Zack – how could he disappear like that?

Bryan gets back in the car and checks the tracking app, zooming in as far as he can. The road, the hedges running either side, a gate a bit further back. He gets out and walks towards it. Tyre tracks. And there, on the other side of a cattle grid, the black tracking device. It must have come off going over the grid.

He drives through the gate. The track is thin and pitted, running first along the inside of the hedgerow, then cutting into the trees. His back wheel skids and he swings to the side. When he straightens up, he's not sure if he's heading the right way, but it's impossible to turn around so he keeps going, slowly crunching over twigs and fallen branches.

A cottage up ahead. Remote, rundown, impossible to find if you weren't looking for it. The kind of place you might bring someone if you didn't want to be disturbed.

Zack's car is parked outside.

Bryan's further up the ridge, on a slight plateau, having missed the path leading down there. A bit of luck. No one will ever see his car up here.

He gets out and skids down the slope. The place isn't as remote as it first appears. On the other side there's a private road going down the hill, leading to some large farm sheds. Zack probably came this way to avoid being seen.

Close up, the cottage is in even worse repair than it looked from a distance. Now Bryan's got one of his own, he knows how much you need to do to stay on top of the upkeep. Weatherproofing the wood, filling in masonry cracks – you don't get rain protection like you do in the city, and it's easy for water to get in and rot the beams. No one cares about this place, that much is clear from the swollen sills, the green-stained plaster. He presses his ear to the outside wall, listening for voices.

Silence.

What if he's got this all wrong? What if Zack isn't involved with his wife's disappearance at all, and Bryan's just shoved him into the position of prime suspect thanks to fairly flimsy presumptions – certainly not enough for the detectives to be interested – because he's stressed and knackered and desperate for a lead? Maybe Zack's doing up this place to sell? Or to rent? Surely that's more realistic than him keeping Astrid here? Except how much of a coincidence is it for Zack to be lurking around Astrid days before she vanishes? Too much of a bloody co—

A scream – a woman's scream. From inside the house.

Bryan races to the front. The door doesn't look much, but the last thing he wants is to put his foot through it, and be trapped like that when Zack finds him. He skirts to the window, cupping his eyes to peer inside. They're blacked out. He hears movement. A heavy thud. Should he call Ronson? What if Zack's hurting her in there?

He bangs on the window and darts round the corner. Should have grabbed a weapon first. He scrabbles by his feet to find a stone that fits his palm, then leans out to see the door. Nothing.

That decides it – definitely something dodgy going on in there. Otherwise, Zack would at least poke his head outside.

How long would it take the police to get here if he called them? Half an hour? Longer? Anything could happen in that time.

Bryan creeps along the side of the cottage. Both sets of windows are locked. He eases open the rusty gate leading to the garden, wincing at the squeal of the metal. The back is in just as much of a shoddy state. Knee-high grass, piles of broken ceramic pots, a shed listing thirty degrees to one side, only staying upright because of the tangle of vines growing over it. A warped back door, the wood mossy and peeling. He tries the handle, not expecting much, and is pleased to feel it give. Not locked.

Gently, he lifts and tugs at the door until it opens with only the faintest of scrapes. Bryan steps inside, stone ready to swing. He's more prepared for a scrap than he was this morning, but it's still been plenty of years since he had a serious punch-up.

The air is damp and musty. Bryan can smell the rot. It's going to need some serious work to get this place up to par – even more indication that it's not being done up to sell.

He tiptoes through the kitchen. There are no appliances, only chipped, discoloured cupboards, containing nothing but cobwebs and plastic container lids. What if he's got this wrong? How's he going to explain his presence away if he bursts in on Zack doing a spot of DIY?

Find Astrid first. Worry about everything else after.

A knocking sound from somewhere in the cottage. Maybe upstairs? That might explain why Zack didn't hear him banging on the window.

Bryan cracks open the door to the front room. It's been stripped back to the brickwork, the antique fireplace jutting out from the wall like a single rotten tooth. He slips inside and tenses as the first floorboard squeaks.

Another scream, louder this time. Bryan runs across the room, pulls open the door. The hallway is empty.

He steps into it, stone ready, approaching the stairs. A shadow by his feet – someone behind him. He spins around, but not fast enough.

The blow hits him above the ear. After that there's nothing.

35

RONSON

The afternoon is slipping away. Three days now since the crash and still nothing definite, only theories, suppositions, coincidences and inconsistencies. Nothing to build a case around.

Ronson returns to his office after another fractious briefing with the team. He leans back at his desk, hands behind his head, and once more sorts through the jumble of clues piled in his mind, trying to form them into a picture of what might have happened on Saturday morning. A murder and a disappearance this close together have to be linked, yet none of the suspects fit easily into the puzzle.

Could Astrid Webb be the culprit? Her car was crashed close to where the body was found, and now she's missing. It makes sense to think that she's done a runner. And yet, she's a sick woman, bed-bound some of the time by all accounts. Would she really have the ability to murder someone? Plus, it's *her* blood in the car, not that of the victim. Is it feasible for her to be so ill, possibly injured, and yet capable of not only leading someone hours away by foot, but then cutting off their fingers and smashing in their face with a rock?

It's common knowledge that people demonstrate surprising power under great duress; the story about mothers lifting a car to save their child has been witnessed many times. Hysterical strength, it's called. Could that really have happened here?

Now that a body has been revealed to the media – the press conference at 11 a.m. this morning had a substantially better turnout from the nation's papers than the one twenty-four hours earlier – the gossip among the journos is mainly about Astrid Webb being the murderer, perhaps because the full details of her medical condition haven't been released. Already he's seen headlines demanding the police treat her as a killer on the loose instead of a missing person.

Could they be right?

Maxwell's crisp rap on his office door. He calls for her to enter.

She backs into the room holding a couple of coffee mugs, placing his on the desk and leaning back against the bookcase. 'Let me guess,' she says, taking a sip. 'You've solved the case and we can all go home.'

'Insightful as always,' Ronson says, smiling. 'I'm promoting you to inspector.'

'Come with a raise, does it?'

'The bad news is there's extra work, but the good news is that there's plenty of it.'

'I'll pass.' She scans the papers spread over the desk and sighs, her shoulders sagging. 'This is giving me a headache.'

'Join the club,' he says, his eyes gliding to where she's just been looking. Did he leave the report out? No, the investigations from Chen and Goldstone this morning are face down on the table. Still, he needs to be more careful. Not of Jess, at least he hopes not, but there are eyes prying into this case. Eyes that have no right to be prying.

Ronson has little doubt who's been directing them.

If Bryan Webb is truly innocent, why is he getting people to check the case file? How else to explain the access by officers outside the department? Ronson's request for more detailed audit records has, so far, been greeted with apologetic responses about the glitchy software and brush offs citing a backlog of service requests, but he's been around long enough to figure out what's really going on. The strings being tugged, the favours being cashed.

Does that make Webb complicit in his wife's disappearance?

Not necessarily – but that doesn't make him innocent either. Could he and his wife be working together? From the moment Ronson met him at the crash site on Saturday morning, he got the feeling Webb was holding out on him, that he was lying about what he knew. Ronson had followed that feeling all the way to turning up the body. What else would it uncover if he carried on the same route?

'There's a piece missing,' Ronson says. 'Right from the middle of this mess. We get that, we get it all.'

'What do you think about Niall Turton? Did we give up too easy?'

'What's there to think? He has an alibi.'

'Sitting around with his uncle smoking pot.'

'It's more than Webb.'

'Turton's got previous with Astrid Webb, and he's been done twice since then for indecent exposure.'

'He's on a ten-year sexual harm prevention order.'

'Exactly.'

'How does he get to her, though? He can't drive. There's no CCTV of him taking a train. It's a fair way to Dinckley from St Helens.'

'And there's zero evidence that he's been in contact with her again.' Maxwell tugs out her ponytail and reties it, tighter than ever, as though it might help keep her eyes open. 'We're circling the drain with this one.'

'Don't get downbeat, Jess.'

'It's hard not to.'

Ronson glances again at the written statements he received from Chen and Goldstone less than an hour ago. It's circumstantial evidence, of course, but it's compelling. It breaks through the surface of the Webbs' supposedly perfect marriage.

It shows that what's inside is not a pretty sight.

'What about Zack Cookson?' Maxwell asks. 'We matched the car in the video Bryan Webb showed you.'

'Cookson was upfront about his reconnecting with Astrid Webb.'

'He didn't mention seeing her three days before she disappeared.'

'You think that's suspicious enough to bring him in for a chat?'

'It might be when the all the records we have of them being in touch end with their meeting in Manchester on Saturday the twenty-first of October.'

That's true. Astrid and Zack shared a flurry of texts and phone calls before that meeting, then nothing afterwards. It could be that they moved to email, or some other messaging service – or burner phones, perhaps, if they were sneaking around. A possibility that makes Bryan Webb's involvement all the more likely.

In what though? Kidnapping? Murder?

Or is he just the poor cuckold in a sorry situation?

That's before they try to tie in the body they found – the other woman who seems to bear too much of a resemblance to Astrid Webb's description for him to call it a coincidence.

Forget about a single missing piece. They're still searching for half the damn puzzle.

Ronson's phone vibrates on the desk, playing a frantic violin version of 'Flight of the Bumblebee'. The super's ringtone. As high-strung and irritating as the man himself.

When he answers, he can tell from Zamora's curt greeting this isn't a social call. The super wants him up in his office, pronto.

Abraham Zamora moved to the North West from the Midlands, where he dragged two forces out of special measures. He came with a reputation for being sour, uncompromising, liable to blow up at any unfortunate constable that happened to catch him in a mood. By all accounts, one of the first things Zamora did in the Midlands was clear out the old guard, hinting in the strongest fashion to the over sixties they might want to consider putting their feet up for good. So far, he'd left Ronson alone – results are results, after all – but the super has left Ronson in no doubt that he is not a fan.

'Take a seat,' Zamora says. Even behind a desk he's an imposing figure, tall and lean, his beard well-groomed, his stare unyielding. 'You need to explain why you're dragging your feet with the Webb case.'

'We're working hard,' Ronson says, hands resting on his lap.

The best way to deal with bullies is to keep calm, don't escalate – that's what gives them power. 'Making a lot of progress now.'

'You're all over the place.'

'That's not fair—'

'Your team are sick of it.'

'We had a briefing an hour ago. Smiles all round.'

Zamora stabs a finger at him. 'Don't bullshit me. I've been hearing complaints for days.'

'You can't please everyone.'

'Cut back on the search, redeploy the bodies into investigating Astrid Webb's network—'

'With respect,' Ronson says, 'We've already spent a great deal of time interviewing any of her friends and family who will speak to us.'

'And for God's sake, leave a good man alone.'

That's what this is about. Bryan Webb. Is this coming from Zamora himself, or has someone had a word with him? How high does Webb's influence reach?

'Even good men can go bad,' Ronson says, 'in the right circumstances.'

'I'm not going to sit here while you publicly trash one of our own.'

'As far as I'm aware, Bryan Webb has left the police force.'

Zamora leans forward, the vein in his neck jumping. 'Focus on finding the wife, and getting an ID for that body. That's your job.'

'All I'm saying—'

'Enough with the excuses. You either—'

A knock on the door cuts him off. Zamora growls for them to come in.

'Sorry to disturb you,' Sergeant Maxwell says. 'We've got a name for the dead woman. Anonymous tip-off.'

Ronson gets to his feet. 'Checks out?'

'We've matched the name to an address. SOCO are heading to swab the place.'

'Great work, Jess.' He points to the door, saying to Zamora. 'You mind if . . .'

The super replies with a stare that could freeze lava. 'I need people in this department I can rely on, not troublemakers with their own agenda. Go that?'

'I'll let you know when we've found something,' Ronson replies.

Outside the office, he tells Maxwell he'll catch her up, and heads the other way. Something's going on here. No one applies this much pressure if there's nothing to hide.

He finds a quiet stairwell, takes out his phone. Thinks about the statements collected by Chen and Goldstone this morning. The age-old question – how much to trust your gut? Enough to put your career on the line?

With this decision he's either going to force the hand of someone he knows isn't telling the whole truth, or destroy the credibility of an innocent man.

The only thing worse than doing something wrong, is doing nothing at all.

36

ASTRID

TUESDAY 31 OCTOBER, 8.45 A.M.,
FOUR DAYS BEFORE THE CRASH

It's easy for Astrid to fool Bryan that she's still sick.

When he backs into the bedroom, tray in his hands, she makes her eyes hazy, her cheeks slack. When he asks for her 'status report', she groans and croaks, 'Stormy night, heavy rain.' When he sits in his usual chair, takes his usual sip of tea, makes his usual speech about the importance of getting out, getting fresh air, getting her circulation going, she says all the things she's supposed to say: 'I'll know, I'll try, you're right', and tries not to scream at the absurdity of these rituals.

What goes on behind those light brown eyes of his? What are the thoughts that power his brain? It seems impossible to believe what she's been told when she sees him like this, clean-shaven, freshly showered, ready to bike out into the world and do good things. Wonderful, life-changing things for those women whose trust has been incinerated by the wrong 'un they had the misfortune to love. This man who has cared for her, who has never once been cruel or violent to her, or anything other than the white knight who saved her from the stalker intent on ruining her life.

Who is she choosing to believe instead of him? Someone she hasn't seen for years, who is open in his disdain for Bryan (and his attraction to her), and another whom she has never met in person. Who says she is one thing but could so easily be lying. How will Astrid ever know?

Until she's staring with regret at the wreckage of her marriage.

Astrid waits for the front door to shut to throw back the covers. To hop out of bed, swoop for her dressing gown, slip it on without fear of a sudden spasm in her spine. *This* is what she knows to be true. Being pain-free, nausea-free, her mind clearer than it's been in years. Clear enough to know that she needs answers.

Downstairs in the Palace of Failure, rooting through the bags of tea leaves for the phone. Her fingers trembling so hard it's tricky to press the right buttons. Zack answers on the first ring.

'Hey,' he says. 'So . . .'

'Well?'

'I saw him.'

'Oh my God.' She sits heavily on the crate behind her. 'And?'

'Wow.'

'What does that mean?'

'He's not the same as you remember.'

'Please, just tell me.'

Zack sighs. 'I mean, I only met him once. Remember that time he showed up at my birthday dinner at El Capo?'

How can she not? That was the night Niall followed her on the bus home. The night she got off and ran into the police station. The night she met Bryan.

She makes a noise for Zack to go on.

'I thought I had the wrong house,' he says.

'What does Niall look like now?'

'Like he's aged fifty years in the last five. He's lost most of his hair, put on a lot of weight. Something's happened to his teeth – I don't know if he was in a fight, but he's got a bad lisp now.'

She thinks back to his preppy V-necks, his Toni & Guy haircuts, his orthodontic smile.

'I told him I was an old friend of yours,' Zack goes on, 'looking to speak to him about what happened. He wasn't keen. Seemed downright terrified, to be honest.'

'Of you?'

'His exact words were, *I've never said anything. You can tell him that. Not one word.*'

'That's it?'

'Then he slammed the door and locked it from the inside.'

It was always going to be a long shot, verifying what she'd been told with Niall. Why would he want to help her? But does his reaction to being asked tell her everything she needs to know?

She thanks Zack and they confirm their plans for tomorrow – a day out in Blackpool, thrilling and terrifying in equal measure. Once they've hung up, she paces the Palace, then makes another call.

Half an hour later, she's driving into a village so similar to Dinckley it makes her shudder. A pub, a green, a bakery and post office, then she's out the other side, slowing to a crawl as she comes to the turning to the address she's been given.

The cottage is off the main road. Along a little lane, just like theirs. She pulls up outside, turns off the engine, and stares at what could be a replica of their own house. The sense of déjà vu is sickening.

How is this going to prove anything? She's watched enough films about con men and hustlers to know there's always an extended cast involved in a scam. If this is all part of an elaborate scheme to destroy her marriage then they're not going to let up now. The person who opens the door will be as convincing as the rest.

When she gets out of the car, a frigid wind picks up, swirling dead leaves around her ankles. The front door has a large oval pane of pebbled glass. Astrid peers through it, hearing the television, suddenly wanting to get in the car and go, keep driving, far away.

No going back, not any more.

She rings the bell and watches as a shape approaches in the glass. The blonde woman who opens the door is about her age, and too similar-looking for it to be a coincidence.

'That was quick,' she says.

'We don't live far away.'

'I guess you'd better come in,' the blonde woman says, and breaks into a smile that makes Astrid wonder if she's made a terrible mistake.

37

BRYAN

Bryan rouses face down on the floorboards of Zack Cookson's decrepit cottage. The side of his skull is throbbing, his vision blurred. His legs are weak as he tries to stand.

He remembers hearing a noise in the hallway, seeing the shadow of someone behind him – Zack? Had to be him. What about the woman he heard screaming? Was that Astrid?

Keeping his back to the wall this time, Bryan staggers up the stairs. He checks the bedrooms, as bare as the rest of the place, then does a once-over of downstairs. No sign of any spilt blood, although if Zack bought a tarp he could have used that to keep things from getting messy. The man himself is long gone.

Bryan heads outside, into the weak sunlight. He scrambles up the ridge to his car. By the time he's reversed along the plateau, spun around and weaved between the trees to get to the track, he's smashed a headlight and scratched all along the passenger side. The crack down the windscreen from the crow makes it feel like reality itself has fractured. Like at any moment his mind might break in two.

At the main road he presses his foot down, hammering the steering wheel. *What the fuck is happening?* He rags round a bend, almost smashing into an oncoming motorbike, in the last second swerving onto the grass. The biker shakes his fist at him as he goes past.

When Bryan takes his hands from the wheel they're trembling. He looks in the mirror and doesn't recognise the pale startled face staring back.

Did he really hear a scream? At the time he was certain, but thinking back, forcing his mind to replay it, he's not so sure. Could it not have been a power tool? A saw blade perhaps? Maybe it was foxes? The sound of them shagging could easily be mistaken for a woman howling in pain. His head is pounding so hard, it's difficult to string a thought together, let alone recall an exact sound from before he was bashed on the bonce.

At the very least, he needs to call Ronson. Tell him about Zack's secret cottage. Even if the scream was nothing, even if he gets picked up for harassment – that fucker would have a case, especially after he sneaked into his room this morning – he's got to try. It doesn't look like anything dodgy had been going on at the cottage, but you'd be amazed what a skilled forensics team can reveal.

Bryan gets out his phone to ring the detective and sees a message from Hoop – a URL link and a single line of text: *Don't contact me again.* He clicks the link – a zip file download. The case file. It must be.

There's a BP garage a few miles down the road. He speeds there, pulls into the car park, transfers the zip file to his laptop. Inside are nearly a hundred documents – reports, statements, interviews, photographs, surveillance footage. Added to that is their internet search history from home, their mobile phone records, and observations about possible suspects.

Niall Turton.

They'd spoken to him already, on Sunday morning. The day after Astrid's disappearance. Spoken to him and discounted him, all on the word of his uncle.

Why hadn't Ronson told him? He didn't have to mention Turton's alibi, but to not even say they'd interviewed him. Disgraceful – cruel. It's his wife who's missing. His life that's being destroyed. Innocent until proven otherwise. But right from the start, the detective's attitude has been, *It's always the husband.*

Well sometimes it's not.

That unreal sensation again. His mind breaking, falling apart.

Funny how they all have their stories. Zack chatting to his landlady, according to his statement. Turton sitting around with his uncle. How very convenient.

Bryan thinks back to Saturday morning, who else was involved.

They're all working together.

Of course they are. Now, finally, it makes total sense. How did he not connect it before? He clicks back to the interview with Turton. At the top of document, handily enough, is his address.

If anyone's going to crack, it's him.

It's less than an hour down the M6 to St Helens where Niall Turton lives, but Bryan knows he shouldn't be driving. The combined effect of the clout to the head on top of bone-deep exhaustion along with this new surge of adrenaline, like a gallon of cold brew coffee injected into his veins, has left him skittish. He stays in the fast line, hunched at the wheel, hitting a steady ninety, not worth it for any black rats to give chase if they spot him speeding past. With twenty miles left he returns to analysing his standoff with Zack this morning, going over how he reacted, scared, weak, pathetic, and imagining what the Bryan Webb of ten years ago – sod that, five years ago – would have done, drifting into the middle lane, only snapping back when the Eddie Stobart artic already there blares its horn. After that, he keeps his window down and the radio blaring, driving the rest of the way being battered by the wind and Beethoven's Ninth Symphony, until, wired and dazed, he turns off the motorway.

He's been to St Helens a couple of times on police business. The centre is pleasant enough, but further out where Turton lives it's all sixties concrete council estates that make you depressed just to look at them. He stops outside what he thinks is the right address.

Bryan rests his forehead on the steering wheel. Got to calm down. The sound of kids banging on the rear window jerks him upright, but when he turns they're already gone. Or maybe they were never there. He throws open the car door. *Fucking pull yourself together.*

You're supposed to hand in your warrant card when you leave the force, but Bryan kept hold of his as a souvenir. He bangs on Turton's door.

When it opens, he shows the card. 'Sergeant Webb. Greater Manchester Police.'

The bloke on the other side doesn't look impressed. He's

older, late fifties perhaps, dressed in a short-sleeved shirt and smart trousers. 'What do you want?'

'I'm looking for Niall Turton.'

Short Sleeves leans against the door frame, arms folded. An old boy who's been there, done that. 'So?'

Bryan realises how he must look – wild, dishevelled, like he hasn't slept for weeks. Maybe he should team up with Ronson after all. 'We're investigating your nephew's involvement with a possible murder.'

'Police have already spoken to him.'

'We'd like to talk to him again.'

'You're him, aren't you?' he says, smirking like he knew all along Bryan was trying to pull a fast one.

'Him who?'

'The bent copper who fucked up our Niall.'

'What did he tell you?'

'Enough.'

'Is he here?'

'Packed up on the weekend.'

Bryan squares up to him. 'You know it's an offence to obstruct the police.'

'Like I'd tell you anything,' Short Sleeves replies, not shifting from his relaxed pose.

'We talk here, or we talk down the station.'

'I'm not going anywhere with you, pal.'

They hold eye contact for a second, until Bryan looks away. For the second time today, he's been forced to back down. When did he become so powerless?

'Look,' he says. 'I just want to find my wife.'

'Yeah, right. Everyone knows you've done her in.' He snorts a laugh at this, then reaches for something inside the door. 'Our Niall left you something.'

He hands over an envelope – on the front is scrawled *Webb*. Bryan tears it open and finds a scrap of paper, the message in messy biro.

I never said Anything

38

BRYAN

Bryan gets home to the press camped at the top of the private road to their cottage. It's dark, the camera flashes blinding. Questions are shouted, but he can't hear them through the window. There are more journalists outside the front door. He doesn't want to talk to them like this – he needs to shower, put on clean clothes, check the lump on his head. Then he can think about giving a statement.

They surge as he gets out of the car, but he's prepared. He rushes to the door, key out, shielding his face with the laptop. Once inside, he sinks to his knees. *Home.*

Clearly, the media have their narrative. He didn't see these crowds around Niall or Zack. As far as everyone's concerned, he's the one with questions to answer. The press can't have him as the prime suspect for no reason – not after his appearance on the news yesterday, which he'd thought went okay.

He takes the laptop to the kitchen. A shape moves across the window when he turns on the light, a photographer perhaps, so he drops the blind. It's way too early in the evening for his usual snifter of St-Rémy, but so what? He pours a large and takes a deep breath over the top of the glass. What could they have on him?

Bryan carries on analysing the case file. When he gets to their internet search history, he pauses, remembering how Astrid had cleared down the computer in the nook. Among the celebrity gossip sites she seems to spend half her time scrolling through, there are a number of searches for things like *tips on going cold turkey* and *side effects of stopping prescription drugs*.

Had Astrid come off her medication without speaking to him, or her doctor? Why would she do that? Had someone convinced her?

He matches that information with details from the police interview with Zack. Apparently, Zack and Astrid met up in Manchester on the day Bryan had to collect her from a police cell – they'd been out drinking. The next morning was when she started researching going clean. Had Zack talked her into that? Doesn't he know how dangerous it can be? Or maybe that was his plan – to destabilise her. Bryan remembers now how sick she was that week. He just assumed it was because . . . Well, whatever. But he sees he was wrong.

She wasn't sick. She was *withdrawing*.

His head is spinning. It feels as though his life is flaking away, leaving a raw, exposed core. Niall has an alibi, Zack has an alibi, and Bryan himself is being served up on a plate. As much as he needs to find Astrid, he needs to protect himself.

Time to call Ronson, tell him they need to work together on this. No more keeping things from him. If he's going to find his wife – and clear his name – it's going to have to be with the detective's help.

A bang on the front door. The letterbox clatters, and someone shouts inside, 'Mr Webb? Care to give your opinion of the new accusations today?'

What new accusations? Bryan loads a news website, reads with shock what's being said. *How is this happening?* He calls Ronson.

'Detective Inspector—'

'It's Bryan Webb.'

A long pause 'Good to hear from you, Mr Webb.'

Bryan tells him to cut the nonsense. He accuses him of leaking lies to the press. Lies which have destroyed everything he's worked so hard to create.

Once he's burned himself out, Ronson says, 'Why don't you come down the station? Give us your side?'

39

RONSON

Sergeant Maxwell stirs her coffee and clatters the spoon into the canteen sink. 'The super's going to have your bollocks.'

Ronson takes a sip from his burgundy Blackburn FC mug. 'I'm too old to have any more kids anyway.'

They sit at a table. Bryan Webb should be arriving here any minute. Ronson flips through his folder, pausing at what he leaked – Chen and Goldstone's interviews with the prostitutes that morning, the reported violence. There's no way Zamora can trace the leak to him. Now the documents have been scanned onto the system anyone with a grudge against Webb could in theory have passed the story on to the press. Despite his protection from the top brass, he's not everyone's favourite ex-sergeant, that's for damn sure. More than a few officers have taken Ronson aside in the last day or so with a tale of his harsh treatment towards them.

Webb's not the nice bloke he makes himself out to be. But does that make him a murderer?

Maxwell's radio blares with static. Detective Constable Goldstone's coming through the gates with Webb.

'Showtime, boss,' Maxwell says, getting to her feet. 'You want me in with you?'

'I need you on lookout, Jess.'

They get to the viewing area in time to watch Webb being shown into the interview room. He's in a neat blue checked shirt, hair combed, respectable. When he sits down, he glances at the camera and forces up a phony smile.

'He's not happy,' Maxwell says, taking a seat in front of the computer.

Ronson perches on the corner of the desk. 'Good.'

They give it another twenty minutes, Webb squeezing his hands, staring at the chair opposite as through imagining what it would be like to throttle the person sitting there. Right before Ronson goes in, Detective Constable Chen comes tearing down the hallway. She breathlessly shows them what they found at the search of the murdered woman's property.

'This is it,' Maxwell says, sifting through them. 'We've got him.'

Ronson chooses the best one. 'Wish me luck.'

40

BRYAN

TUESDAY 7 NOVEMBER, 7.37 P.M.

Right as Bryan resolves to storm out and find the nearest competent officer higher up the chain from Ronson, the detective enters the interview room looking, as always, like he's wandered into the police station by mistake. Shirt half-tucked and sweat-stained inside the collar. Hair standing up as though someone has been rubbing his head with a balloon. Here he is: the man who gets to decide his fate.

Ronson eases into the chair opposite. 'Thanks for coming in at such short notice.'

'Half an hour you've kept me waiting.'

'I'm so sorry, Mr Webb. And no one's been in to get you a drink – again! I can only apologise. Can I—'

'Did you leak those lies? Do have any idea of the damage you've done to the Foundation's work?'

In the wait for the car, and all the way over here, Bryan watched his life being reduced to rubble. Every news website had the same accusations.

'We're going to be taping this, if that's okay,' Ronson says, leaning forward to activate the machine. He speaks into the

271

microphone, giving location, date, who's present, then opens the folder in front of him, and passes over a sheet of paper.

It's a printout from the Montague website, the listing for Bryan's e-bike model. He turns it over in case he's missed something on the back. 'Why are you showing me this?'

'It's a beauty,' Ronson says. 'I bet you've really got to keep on top of the maintenance. Lubricating the chain, checking the tyre pressure. Making sure the bolts are tight.'

'Is this a joke?'

Ronson leans back and ruffles his hair. 'You're going to look after a bike like that, aren't you? Make sure you've got all the kit.'

Bryan tosses the page back on the table. 'Where are you going with this?'

'I couldn't help but notice,' Ronson says, sitting forward. 'When I looked at your bike, it had that nice toolkit built in below the seat. That must be handy when you're on a long ride and something goes wrong.'

Ronson leaves a space for him to respond, but Bryan says nothing.

'You've got a special slot for each tool,' Ronson goes on, handing him another printed sheet. This one has a colour picture of the toolkit, a number by each tool, the names listed on the right-hand side. 'What's number fourteen there?'

'A torque wrench.'

'And what's that used for?'

Bryan gives him the kind of withering glare that used to have constables quaking. 'My wife has been missing for over three days, and you want to discuss bicycle mechanics?'

The detective doesn't look away. 'This is about your wife.'

'A torque wrench is used to tighten bolts, okay? The things that keep the bike together. I thought you were "into it" for a while.'

'And it's common, isn't it with these electric bikes, for the bolts to come loose? More so than with . . . old-fashioned ones?'

'Motor spindle rotation is a problem, if that's what you mean. Too much can damage the drop-out slots.'

'Sounds important.'

'It is.'

'You'd probably need to keep one of these torque wrenches with you, especially if you use your bike a lot.'

'I must have ten of them at home.'

'Tell me,' Ronson says, leaning forward. 'Where's this particular wrench?'

'What's the point of this?'

'Humour me.'

'I honestly haven't a clue what you're talking about.'

'It was missing from the toolbox beneath the seat. Can you tell me where it is?'

'Probably in the house somewhere.'

'We couldn't find it during the search.'

'Not my fault you're incompetent.'

'If we went to your house now, do you think you could locate it for us?'

'How about you put this much effort into finding my wife?'

'Can you answer the question please.'

'How many times do I have to tell you? *I've got other wrenches at home.*'

'But not this one?'

'Who gives a shit!'

Ronson lifts his hand to his chin. Purses his lips, taps his cheek, takes a long breath through his nose.

'You know,' Bryan says, 'I could sue the police for releasing those lies.'

Two prostitutes have come forward since his appearance on the news. One claims he left her with bruises on her chest and legs, the other that he choked her until she was unconscious.

'Are they lies?' Ronson asks, his expression coy.

Bryan takes in the detective. Is this all he's got? Conspiracy theories about a missing wrench and testimonies from women who could easily have been paid to come forward and bad-mouth him?

More to the point, why wasn't this information in the case file? Has Hoop been holding out on him? Bryan called him right before leaving, laying it on the line, making it clear that if he goes down then it won't be on his own. Is there anything else he doesn't know?

'I don't know why they've come forward with this stuff,' Bryan says. 'I have never beaten a woman in my life. I have people, many people – many women – who can vouch for me. Haven't you considered that there might be bad actors out there who may not like the work we do at the Foundation? Who would love nothing more than to bring us down?'

Ronson dips his hand into the folder, pulling out a couple of eight-by-ten stills and passing them over. The first shows a pretty blonde woman leaning against a railing with a takeaway coffee, the second is a different woman, similar-looking but with darker hair, wearing suspenders, pouting for the camera.

Bryan makes a show of looking at the pictures. 'What am I meant to do with these?'

'They are the prostitutes making the claims against you.'

'Never seen them before in my life.'

Ronson removes a photo of Astrid from the folder. The pretty one of her in the back garden taken when they first moved to Dinckley that they've been using in the media appeals. He lines it up with the other two.

Bryan's about to say something, but stops when he sees the detective reaching into the folder once more. Something's going on here. He knows a set-up when he sees one.

The final photo goes down beside them. It's a close-up of a woman's smiling face against an office backdrop, the kind you might see on the Meet the Team page of a company website. She's slim, attractive, her eyes misty grey, her hair a muted blonde. His heart clicks through the gears.

'What do you want from me?' Bryan says. 'You want me to tell you I hurt these women?' He points to the final picture. 'Is that who you found dead? Sorry to disappoint you, but I've never seen her before either.'

Ronson's wry expression doesn't change. 'Take another look at those pictures, Mr Webb. All together. Tell me if anything jumps out at you.'

Bryan makes a show of scanning them. 'What do you want me to say?'

'All remarkably similar-looking, wouldn't you agree?'

'This is your idea of evidence?'

'I'm asking a legitimate question. Your wife is missing. Another woman who looks like your wife has been found dead. Two more women who look the same—'

'Oh, come on.' Bryan jabs a finger at the one in suspenders. 'She looks nothing my wife.'

'Same age, same build—'

'Why aren't you grilling Turton like this?'

'We've spoken to Mr Turton—'

'He made her life *hell*.'

'Have you met this woman before?' Ronson rests a finger on the picture of the one found dead.

'No. No, no, no. That clear enough?'

For a couple of beats, he doesn't reply. Then Ronson reaches again into his folder. The back of the photo he takes out is yellowed with age. He turns it up and slides it across the table.

Bryan feels his lower lip drop, along with that same sickening sense of dislocation that's hounded him for days.

The detective is no longer smiling. 'How about now?'

41

CELINE

Celine looks out of the window at the squared hedge running along the back garden, the wide oak looming behind, the field beyond sweeping into the distance. She used to hate the countryside, all that mud and tedium; there's nothing to do as a teenager except take drugs and look for trouble. Or maybe that's just her.

How long to go? Twenty minutes? She's so nervous her chest quivers as she exhales. It has to be today. Everything is in place; her nerves can't handle any more delays. It's one thing to be doing this, another entirely to be caught in the act. She has no doubt at all of the consequences of being found out.

It's not been easy to get to this point. So often she's asked herself why she's doing this, why she's getting involved. What does she possibly hope to achieve? Revenge? Justice? Her fantasies only stray into those territories on occasion. More frequent are the daydreams that paint her into a picture of normality: a loving partner, some adorable children, perhaps a slobbering dog. Is any of this going to get her closer to achieving that?

Her fear is that it is not.

That's the problem with being in the country. Too much space and silence to fill with introspection. She misses the rush of the city, the buzz of the coffee shops, the general milling of people to make her feel less alone. Being here allows her to dwell on the question she all too often tries to avoid: how has her life come to this?

There are many ways to look at who she has become, and in the last few months of living here she has galloped repeatedly through all of them. The most obvious is to put it all down to her troubled childhood, her messed-up mum and done-a-runner dad, the horror of how she's been treated by people who act like they know better, who strut around in public as though they are bastions of propriety when really they are the opposite, but maybe that perspective is wrong. Maybe it absolves her from every mistake, every wrong decision, every blunder, social, romantic or otherwise, which has signposted the path of her life. Maybe all the bad things that have happened to her could have been avoided with one simple change: not being her.

Ugh. So self-pitying. Celine could kick herself without mercy.

She checks her phone. Ten minutes to go.

What must it be like to live in a place like this for the rest of your days? Wearing wellies and wax jackets. Walking the hounds and perusing country fairs and cooking a fried breakfast every day with fresh bacon. Perhaps it's not as boring as she imagines. Perhaps there's a hush-hush underbelly of sleaze and intrigue. Once you've done your time at the village boozer it'll be down in the dungeon basement where a busty barmaid whips your bare behind.

More than likely you simply get used to the same faces. The same voices, the same gossip, the years rolling by, the ceaseless procession of seasons, unending until the final end. The march of age implacable. Everyone muttering the same words of consolation as the next one disappears.

What if she can't help the darkness inside her?

What if this is simply who she is?

She tried. Honestly, she did. When she finally left Manchester, she was determined to be the machine-stamped version of a person, someone who got a job and took holidays and made friends. Someone who progressed far enough through the game of life to look back on their achievements with pride and happiness, and maybe a few regrets to keep it interesting.

It seemed to be working. She started as a temp in the HR department of an insurance company, a job that sounds boring, and was boring, but gloriously so, at least at first. Hugh was a broker in sales; a few years older, but that's what she likes, why deny it? He had nice hair, was always smiling, and did little kind things, letting her get in the lift first or cut in the queue at the canteen. Unlike many of the middle-aged spreaders in the office, he ran marathons. And money would never be an issue with Hugh; his aging parents owned properties in London, Scotland and Spain. Only someone who's never tried to pay for something and found her purse bare can afford for that not to be a consideration.

They became a couple. Celine made Hugh cups of tea in the morning. She sat with him in the pub, in front of the telly, on the balcony of his parent's villa in Malaga. When he asked her to move in, she brought her stuff in a single car.

For nearly five years everything appeared blissful, but she feared all along it would fail. A vocal part of her had always believed there was as much chance of a double-leg amputee leaping up to lead a conga line as there was of her finding a happy ever after. That she simply couldn't keep up the façade of being normal for ever.

It started with boredom, which sounds innocuous enough, but it's as nagging as a rotten headache. You're always thinking on it, on ways to relieve it; you're always imagining how much better life will be once it's gone. But the boredom wasn't going anywhere, not while she was with Hugh. That was the whole point about settling down, right? You have your routine, more or less. This is how you spend your days.

She began drinking again. Hugh had never seen her drunk before, and it's fair to say he didn't like how it made her. Celine didn't care now the boredom was receding.

Dear, sweet Hugh, he thought he could fix her. When he proposed, she said yes.

They agreed on a long engagement. That told her perhaps Hugh was more complicit in the charade than she assumed. He knew she was wrong for him, perhaps even that their marriage would never happen, but she'd sucked him into the drama by then. When drunk she'd berate him, sober she'd apologise, pleading for another chance; the things she did in bed to make up for her meanness left him loopy-eyed. When she began to squirm at his touch, that only seemed to make him want her more.

The deadline put pressure on an already fragile situation. Celine's behaviour became more extreme the closer it came to the big day. Her bad self was still there, still twisting beneath the surface. One time she pushed him over; a week later she lobbed a litre bottle of lemonade at his head. The third time they'd both been drinking, a nice glass of wine over dinner, which turned into a bottle, then two, then spirits, Hugh perhaps hoping that by getting to her level he could find a way to draw out why she was being this way. She doesn't know how she got to the point where she was hurling punches at his chest; her memory snaps back in right at the point where he struck her, open-handed, three times.

A few hours later, she was standing over her snoring fiancée, the long deboning knife he used to prepare the lamb chops when his parents came over for Sunday lunch poised over his chest.

The dark part of her mind had the story worked out. He came at her, beat her; the bruise on her cheek was evidence. She grabbed a knife, ran into the bedroom, defended herself. But same as with the blonde woman in the cottage, she couldn't do it. Instead, she left and blocked Hugh's number.

The ringing of her phone snaps Celine from the memory. Is it done? She answers, listening intently to the voice on the other end, as she's doing so realising what has to happen.

Twice before she's failed to act, but this time will be different.

This time she knows her bad self will have no qualms about finishing the job.

42

BRYAN

SATURDAY 4 NOVEMBER, 8.13 A.M., THE DAY OF THE CRASH

Bryan glides on light feet to his office, glancing all around, even though Astrid is never out of bed at this time. Once inside, he locks the door. Another unnecessary precaution, no doubt – she's as likely to burst in as she is to sign up for an Ironman triathlon – but he hasn't got this far by taking risks. Risks are for people who haven't wits and organisational skills to formulate a cohesive plan. And for idiots who don't lock the door.

He takes the stool, painted in primary colours by Astrid in one of the creative binges he likes to foster to keep her amused, and places it beside the far end bookcase. Three bookcases line a whole wall, stretching from floor to ceiling. For someone who didn't grow up a reader – aside from his mum's art history tomes and his dad's pharmaceutical tracts there were few books in the house – he's pleased to have quite the library now. He'd never have said this to the lads at the station, but it behoves a man of intelligence to be well versed in the written word.

The bottom shelves are filled with fiction, crime thrillers mostly. Ian Rankin, P. D. James, a bit of Mark Billingham if he's feeling fruity. Further up is dedicated to policing, *Blackstone's* manuals, multiple editions of Miller and Braswell's classic *Effective Police Supervision* – among those are his awards, his Chief Constable's High Commendation, his Long Service and Good Conduct Medal. Even higher up are more esoteric topics, such as philosophy, psychology, medicine. It's for those that he reaches now.

Second shelf from the top, he slides the books across. He runs his fingers along the wood at the back, finding the indent and pressing to release the panel, which he is able to slide open. He's executed enough search warrants in his time to know how to hide something, even if you have twenty officers frisking the place.

Bryan takes the brown leather attaché case from the hollow, the same one his father used to carry to conferences, and brings it to his desk. Inside are neatly labelled bags of powder, along with his instruments, and the ledger. For a few weeks after Astrid started on with that money nonsense, questioning the limit on her debit card, he had her on the hard stuff – flunitrazepam to make her lethargic, an arsenic trioxide compound for the headaches, and a sprinkling of strychnine to cause the spasms in her spine.

Sledgehammer tactics, no doubt. It's not like she demanded to leave Dinckley, which is a constant concern. And he's cut it close a couple of times – the police could easily have drug tested her when they picked her up in Manchester. Most of the things he gives her have such short half-lives, and are in such small doses, that they probably wouldn't show up, not with everything else she takes, but you never know.

Since Wednesday, when she went for her little wander, he's been cutting everything back, letting her OxyContin addiction

284

do the heavy lifting. She could easily have disappeared deeper into the forest, and what a pain in the arse that would have been!

Bryan checks the ledger, makes some mental calculations. He uses a stainless-steel micro scoop with a tip the size of a baby's fingernail to reach into the necessary bags and add the right amounts to the four waiting capsules. Once they're sealed, he updates the ledger, closes up, and heads downstairs to make her breakfast. In her lilac pill box, in each of the time slots for that day, he places one of the capsules along with the rest of her medication.

Upstairs with her tray, backing into her bedroom. 'Hello, love.'

There she is, his beautiful wife. Sometimes he feels so incredibly tender towards her, lying there drowsy as a freshly woken kitten. It's not ideal, this situation, but the steps to stability are tricky to navigate. If only she embraced being here, in this lovely village, with some of the most incredible scenery this fine country has to offer right outside her window, she would be happier. Until then, until she truly gives herself over to being here, to this life with him, then it must be this way. She makes it worse for herself by resisting. But even the sturdiest mares break in the end.

'Status report?' Bryan asks, falling back in his chair.

Astrid's cheeks are loose, her eyelids limp. 'Some light showers. Otherwise, calm.'

They spar for a while in their usual manner, him trying to gee her into getting out of bed, her wanting only to sink again beneath the covers, but he's distracted by the upcoming meeting with the Department of Crime and Policing on Monday.

It could well open the door to a move he's been craving for a while: politics. Surely there has to be a place for someone like him? Someone with drive and conviction. Someone who's both served in the public sector and proved himself in the business world – in two years he's built the Victim Relief Foundation from nothing into a network of charities that have raised between them over a million pounds.

Once he has a foot in the door, who knows how far he could step through the corridors of power?

That's for later. His immediate concern is bringing Astrid back down from her regime – the last few weeks have been punishing on her. For a while he'd never seen her so sick. Even now, when he kisses her forehead, her skin is clammy. Maybe it'll be best to row back on everything for a while, give her a chance to recover – she's certainly been docile this week. Perhaps she's finally allowing herself to settle into their life here.

Back downstairs, he brews a cup of tea and takes it to the back garden to sit and think. It's getting overcast already, the grey clouds massing over the faraway hills, the wind picking up and gusting leaves. He's analysing his call yesterday with Linda, the civil servant at the Department of Crime and Policing who's been doing the legwork for the proposed partnership, thinking of ways he could tweak their conversations to make them more personal, flirtier perhaps – although a touch of that was already there – anything to give him an edge in securing the funding.

His phone vibrates. It's from a private number, but that could mean a government department. This better not be them cancelling the meeting.

He answers with, 'Hello, Bryan Webb. How can I help you?'

At first, he thinks it must be a joke, a sick prank by someone who must know him *very* well. But it doesn't take much to convince him it's real. By the time the call is over his head is throbbing. It feels as though he hasn't blinked or breathed for the entire time.

This needs dealing with. He races upstairs, throws on his cycling gear, pokes his head into Astrid's room to tell her he's going to take that bike ride after all. She's on her side, sleeping. Her meds must have kicked in. He was right to keep her on the flunitrazepam for a bit longer.

Usually on his Saturday ride he likes to meander up to the hills, sip his coffee overlooking the forest spread out below, then take the winding scenic route back through the village. Today he kicks the bike to top speed and takes the Preston Road.

What could she want? Money, most likely. Not a problem. Just promise the earth and keep her dangling. Perhaps call on an old friend like Hoop to help. That would certainly be an ironic way to bring closure to a chapter that should have ended, that Bryan thought had ended, a long time ago.

The address she gave him is not far past Longridge. It's a small, modern house on a quiet country road. Detached, bay window, newly tiled roof. Maybe it's not money after all.

What else? Revenge?

That's always a lot trickier to handle.

There are only a few properties in the vicinity, plenty of green space between them. He swerves off the road, jags in beside a hedgerow, kicks out his cleats and ducks down, panting hard.

The house looks quiet, the windows dark. Is he walking into a trap? What if she's the front, and there's more of them involved? Over the years, he's built a fair collection of enemies, and it might not be as easy to keep them away as when he was a serving officer. He takes the retractable torque wrench from the kit under his bicycle seat, stuffs it in the pocket of his zip-up. The danger of carrying weapons is there's more of a chance of them being used, but if they're coming for him, he's going down swinging.

It's quiet enough for the doorbell to maybe echo to the other houses, so he knocks lightly instead. Then he stands back, hand inside the pocket, gripping the wrench.

The door opens. She looks so different, all that cute puppy fat gone, but it's definitely her. He opens his mouth to speak, but nothing comes out.

'Looks like it's going to rain soon,' Celine says. 'Why don't you come in, Seth.'

43

CELINE

The name Bryan doesn't suit him. It's too cheery, has too much heart in it, and she knows by now that he doesn't have one of those.

Bryan Seth Webb.

She couldn't believe it when she saw him in the news. A few months ago, an article about the charity he runs with his wife. Celine didn't figure it out at first; the article didn't give his middle name, and he'd changed since she last saw him nearly two decades ago. He was leaner, his hair neat and short. It took more than a couple of double-takes at his picture to recognise him. She didn't find out his full name, and piece it all together, until much later.

From the doorstep he asks, 'Why did you call me, Celine?'

'Please,' she says, cringing at the politeness in her voice. 'Come in.'

'You said it was urgent.'

She flashes back to the last night she saw him in Manchester, when she was still only seventeen; he showed up at her door, pissed off and dripping wet, saying much the same thing. His look is identical to then – confused, exasperated, and liberally daubed with anger.

This time she won't be dissolving into tears for him.

'I'll explain,' she says, moving aside. 'But you'll have to come inside first.'

He stomps past her. Celine follows him down the hall to the kitchen, the sudden rush to her chest both exhilarating and sickening. He's here. It's happening. As if it could have been any other way.

'Can I get you a drink?' she asks. 'A tea perhaps? Or a glass of water?'

He whips off his helmet, slams it on the table. 'What the fuck's going on here?'

Celine rests against the counter, feeling the weight of what's in her cardigan pocket bounce against her hip. What indeed?

As she waited for him to come over, hating herself for how much she was wrestling with what to wear – settling for the pretty dress and knitwear combination that she lived in ninety-nine per cent of the time anyway – she tried to plan how to play it. She'd been imagining this moment, seeing Seth again, confronting him, for so many years. Everything went wrong after that night, when he drugged her and trashed her little flat. She ended up on the street, a proper junkie; once she found out 'the good stuff', as he used to call it, was heroin there was no going back. For years she was in and out of institutions. Clinics, psychiatric wards, residential treatments centres. Sometimes it was for addictions, speed, alcohol, heroin, a brief but brutal few months on meth, and sometimes for self-harm, when the scars spread to more visible parts of her skin.

Things only started turning round when she went back home to Chester. Her mum was so relieved to have her back that she made Derek stump up for decent rehab. She got clean, got a job, a boyfriend. For over a decade she lived the dream of being a normal person.

The problem is, she's not normal; she doesn't know what she is, but she's not that. No one normal would do what she did to Hugh.

While they were engaged, she longed to leave him, imagining herself if not happy then at least relieved. Instead she got time alone with her darkness.

Celine tried to distract herself with the old methods, but she didn't have the stamina for drugs like she used to, and slicing her skin with a cold blade straight from the freezer felt more tragic than illicit now that no one, absolutely no one, gave a shit; since Derek passed away during his triple bypass her mum only had eyes for her own grief. The cuts hurt a lot more too, these days.

She went through the motions. More therapy, more anti-depressants, more failed attempts at meditation and sad midnights highlighting chapters in self-help books. A new job, new people, but after what happened with Hugh she didn't trust herself to get close to anyone. Her life began to while away, a long and lonely routine.

Then she saw the picture of Seth in the news; the story about his charitable work; the fact that he wasn't called Seth at all but Bryan.

Bryan Webb, hero to abused women everywhere, by all accounts.

How dare he.

It gave her dead mind a little jolt.

She began researching this supposed foundation, reading about *Bryan's* decorated career as a police officer, a job he definitely didn't tell her about when they were together, and which made everything he did to her so much worse, for someone to hold that power and act that way. With every glowing write-up, every teary testimonial, she'd get another little jolt, each one giving her the incentive to dig deeper.

She'd attempted to track him down before. There'd been many a drunken stumble through the socials searching for someone called Seth; although she must have seen his surname on his credit card, she couldn't remember any more than it started with a W. Her searches always came up blank. Now she knew why.

Could it be possible that she was the only person in the whole world who knew his true nature?

It came to her in a Eureka moment. Someone else who might understand the real Bryan Webb.

Celine didn't remember the address of the blonde woman's cottage, but the route was imprinted in her memory; when she got off the train and walked the same country road as so many years ago, it all came back, how skilfully Seth groomed her into believing his lies about love and their destiny together, to the point where she was willing to kill someone to be with him.

The elderly man who answered the door had been there for years and hadn't even met the person who'd sold it. He kindly let her come in and look through the legal documents for the sale, which is how she found out the blonde woman's name. Wendy Donovan.

Wendy hadn't moved far. This time, Celine drove.

The woman who opened the door was slim and blonde, about the same age as Celine. Wendy's daughter, Sarah.

'Bryan Webb hunted my mum down,' Sarah said, 'every time

she left him. He'd destroy whatever little bit of life she built up, so she'd crawl back to him, because she had nowhere else to go.'

'How do you mean, "destroy"?' Celine asked.

'He'd call up her boss at work, saying she hadn't declared a criminal record, to try to get her fired. Or he'd create these fake email accounts and spread lies about her to her friends.'

'What happened to your mum? Did she manage to get away from him?'

Sarah looked away, a tissue to her eyes. 'She died a few years ago. Mum never even drank before she met him, but that's what finished her off in the end. That and some pills. She was just so scared of him coming for her all the time. Even years after she last saw him, she'd get messages saying that if he couldn't have her then nobody would.'

The search became an obsession for Celine, a new addiction. The only thing of any interest to her.

When she found out Bryan lived in Dinckley on a *Guardian Weekend* write-up about the foundation.

Jolt.

When she visited Dinckley pretending to be an old friend of Astrid's, and managed to get their address.

Jolt.

When Celine moved to the local area, began spying on the Webbs, watching their routine, their life together, seeing the state of his wife and realising he was doing to her what he'd done to the rest.

Jolt. Jolt. Jolt.

When she made contact with Astrid – who listed the Tea Network as a supplier on her half-built website – and told her the truth about her husband.

Jolt.

And now here he is, the man she once believed she'd kill to be with, standing right in front of her. Healthy and happy in his world, having not suffered for a single second while ruining her life and Wendy's life and Astrid's life, and the lives of who knows how many others.

'Do you have any idea what you did to me?' Celine says to him. 'You humiliated me. You destroyed me.'

He steps back, the anger fading from his eyes. 'It was so long ago.'

'You drugged me and left me practically naked on the bed while your mates took pictures and laughed.'

'It was a wild time,' he says, as though she'd consented to the photos.

'How could you do that to someone?' Celine clenches her jaw, looking away. No way was she going to cry in front of him. 'You used me.'

'We were only together for a few months.'

'You got me hooked on drugs—'

'You were on 'em before you met me.'

'You gave me heroin.'

Seth lifts his shoulders, seemingly unable to meet her eye. 'I don't know what to say. You think I'm not ashamed of the person I used to be? That I'm not sorry about how I treated you?' Now he looks at her, so fucking contrite. 'I am sorry. I truly am.'

'That's it? An apology and you're done?'

'I can't change the past, but I'm not the same person now. Have you heard of the charity I run with my wife? It's a foundation for victim relief. We raise money for people – for women

– who are in abusive relationships. To pay the legal fees, or help them with a new start.'

Celine knows she's supposed to calm him down, keep him talking, but now she can feel her bad self writhing in her mind, desperate to take control. 'You expect me to believe this rubbish?'

'It's the truth.'

'You've not changed. You're the same horrible, manipulative—'

'I know I hurt you when we broke up—'

'Narcissistic piece of shit.'

Seth grabs his helmet, starts for the door. 'Well, this has been fun.'

Celine glances at the clock. Not long enough. *Stupid!* Should have left him to ramble on about his supposed good work; he could probably talk about how great he is for hours.

All the times she's planned what to say when she saw him next, and she's run out of words already. She's told him how what he did affected her, he's apologised, what else is there to say?

'I'll expose you,' comes out of her mouth.

That gets his attention. Bryan turns slowly towards her. 'For what?'

'I spoke to Wendy's daughter.'

He cocks his head and feigns confusion. 'Wendy?'

'The woman you started seeing when you were with me. Her daughter told me that you turned her into an alcoholic, separated her from her family, then stalked her every time she tried to leave you.'

This time there's no pretence at an apology. 'Prove it.'

'I'm sure the papers will be interested.'

Bryan snorts. 'I'll sue you for slander and them for libel, if they even go near it, which they won't because you have no evidence for any of this nonsense.'

'I'm sure there are others.'

'Maybe there are,' he says, his smile suddenly tinged with spite. 'And they'll keep their mouths shut if they know what's good for them. That goes for you and all.'

He starts down the hallway. She can't let him leave, not yet.

'Wait,' Celine says. She checks her cardigan pocket, reassured by its presence. Is she really going to do this? 'There's something I need to tell you.'

44

BRYAN

Bryan watches Celine push off the counter. He watches her glance over her shoulder, as though someone might be in the kitchen with them, then approach him, slowly, her face determined – and something else he can't figure out. Something unhinged perhaps. He thrusts his hand in his jacket pocket, feeling the hard metal of the wrench, ready to brain the crazy cow if necessary.

She stops at the table, still a few feet away. 'Two stars dance and spin,' she says. 'Together they burn bright, defying time. For ever they swirl and twirl, lovers enfolded in an eternal sky.'

Definitely unhinged.

'I'm sorry,' he says, 'am I supposed . . .'

'You wrote that for me.'

It's possible. He vaguely recalls scribbling rubbish like that, down the pub after a shift, laughing with the lads about who could produce the naffest lines. It's all a bit of a haze, back then. What does she expect now – for them to be together?

'You told me we had a love that never dies,' she says, her smile a bit too tight, her eyes a bit too wide. He can almost feel the tension in her body.

297

Bryan realises that's exactly what she expects.

'Even years after we broke up,' she says, 'whenever I'd get a message on my phone my heart would jump because I thought it might be from you.'

He lowers his helmet. Now this, while not perfect, is easier to deal with. All he's got to do is get through the next few weeks, or maybe few months depending on how long the paperwork takes – with government it goes at two degrees slower than a crawl – then if Celine turns rogue and starts making public accusations, the contracts will already be signed. It'll take a whole lot more than hearsay from some psycho bitch to get rid of him then.

'Wow,' he says. 'I had no idea you still felt that way.'

She thrusts her hands into her cardigan pockets. 'Oh God, it's so stupid even saying it.'

'No, no, it's not stupid. It's not stupid at all . . .' There's something about the hang of her body that isn't right. What's really going on here? 'Five minutes ago, you were calling me out as absolute scum – now you're quoting me a poem I wrote God knows how long ago.'

'I was seeing how you'd react. To check if you're still the Seth I used to know.'

'Don't call me that.'

'Why not? It's who you are.'

'I'm not the same person who wrote you that poem.'

Celine angles her shoulders back, making her chest more prominent. Her dress is fiery orange, patterned with falling leaves, her oat-coloured cardigan invitingly unbuttoned. Even before he added potassium bromide into Astrid's medication, she wasn't a particularly sexual person, so he must admit that below the irritation, the sheer primitive need to shut this down, there's a definite frisson to this flashback to his younger days. Celine has him there.

'Yes, you are,' she says.

He softens his voice. 'I'm not in a position to do this.'

'I'm a very discreet person.'

'Think about what you're asking me to do. I'm a married man.'

Her expression – like he's a kid she loves who's doing the same sum wrong, over and over – doesn't change. 'You know what I think?'

'Please, Celine—'

'You're scared. You've been so tucked away in your sad little life, with your sad little wife, that you've forgotten the kind of man you really are.'

Despite himself, he stands taller. 'What kind of man am I?'

'A strong man,' she says, stepping towards him. The way she's moving her body transports him – back to Celine as she was then, young and sensual, swaying her hips as she sashayed to where he was waiting on the bed. 'An assured man. Someone who takes control of a situation, who knows what they want and how to get it. And won't let anyone get in their way.'

Bryan bites his top lip, his breaths shallow, aware of the stirring against the Lycra of his cycling shorts. 'Think about what you're asking me to do.'

She stops at the doorway, leaning against the frame, one hand in her cardigan pocket, as though daring him. What would he do if she made a pass?

Would he be able to resist?

'I understand why you'd want to cling to your boring old life,' she says, 'your boring old wife. They're safe, they're manageable – but if you were with me, you could have so much more than that. You don't need these weak, pathetic women who you've got to control with drugs and threats. You don't need to control me at all. *I know who you are.*' She leans forward, so close he can feel the warmth of her breath on his face. 'Just think what you could achieve, if you had me by your side.'

'You do look good,' Bryan says, unable to stop his eyes sliding down her body. 'I can't argue with that.'

'I'm here,' she says. 'I'm yours.'

He closes the gap between them. She tips up her head, and he cups her cheek, the pulse in her neck drumming against the side of his hand. Right before their mouths touch, he senses a motion to his side, a swish. He catches the glint of a blade in the light and shoves her back.

'Christ, Celine. What the fuck are you playing at?'

'Oh, wow,' she says, and looks from him to the knife she's taken from her cardigan pocket and flicked open. It's short, maybe five inches, but very sharp. Definitely enough to do some serious damage. She gives a slow, nervous laugh.

'Please,' Bryan says, 'think about this.'

'Just shut up,' she says, but doesn't go for him.

'Do you want me to apologise again? If that's what you want—'

Celine waves the knife towards him. 'What I want is for you to shut the fuck up for once.'

It's been a while, but this isn't the first knife he's had pulled on him. You normally know in the first few seconds if they've got the balls to do it, and she doesn't, he can see that clearly.

'Why don't you give that to me?' he says, lifting his hand to take it.

The knife is trembling. 'Fuck off.'

'I remember now, your thing about knives. Always cutting yourself. Loved it when I brought over those video nasties – got you hot, didn't they?'

Celine snarls, lunges, but she's slow and inexperienced in a fight. Bryan grabs her wrist and pushes her back into the kitchen, hooking her ankle with his foot. As she's falling back, he drags the torque wrench from his jacket pocket and whips it into her face, holding her down and carrying on – *bang, bang, bang* – long past the time she must be dead.

When he stops, he's quivering. He pulls back, hyper aware of his surroundings – has he touched anything in the house? The end of the wrench is gory with blood, as is his fist and jacket.

He turns on the kitchen tap with his elbow and washes up as best he can. The wall clock says it's nearly eleven. He needs to go home, think about this, come back later with the car and some cleaning supplies. Work out what to do with the damn body.

Halfway back, he slows by a ridge. On the other side is a steep bank leading into heavy undergrowth. He flings the wrench as far as he can. At an Esso garage, careful to avoid any cameras, he shoves his balled-up jacket deep into a bin. Then he races home, pushing his legs harder, trying to blank his mind from seeing Celine's face, the feel of her bones giving way beneath his blows, the sound of each one punctuating his thoughts. What *bang* have *bang* you *bang* done?

He swerves onto the private road leading to their cottage. There's a police car parked outside. He kicks himself free of the bike, and clatters to the uniformed officer about to ring the doorbell.

'Mr Webb?' the officer asks.

Bryan nods breathlessly, wiping sweat with a Lycra sleeve.

'It's your wife. I'm sorry to say we've found her car. There's been an incident.'

45

BRYAN

Bryan stares at the photo Ronson has slid across the desk. He
and Celine are lying in bed, their heads together and shoulders
bare, their smiles wide. He'd still have been a constable, still
young enough to be reckless, living life as though it were about
to come to an abrupt stop.

She really was cute, back then. He'd finish a shift and go over,
any time of day or night, she didn't care, she was up for anything. Now she's dead. He killed her. It's not something he's
proud or happy about. While it may have been thrilling in a
raw, animal way, if he could roll back time and take a different
path then he would have done it already. How was he supposed
to know that when he got home Astrid would be gone?

If he knew his life was falling apart behind his back, he
wouldn't have done something to make the situation fifty tril-
lion times worse.

Ronson clears his throat. 'You said a moment ago that you'd
never met Celine Pennington, but isn't that the two of you
together?'

303

'I didn't recognise her,' Bryan says, keeping his voice calm.

Ronson moves the bed photo next to the later one of Celine, the company headshot. Even though she's much older it's easy enough to see they're the same person.

'It was such a long time ago,' Bryan says. 'And we weren't together long, a couple of weeks tops. It's awful what's happened to her, and I can see how this might look to you, because you're desperate for a lead. But I swear to you, I haven't seen her in years.'

'That is you, though, isn't it?'

'I'm amazed she kept this – I had no idea our relationship was so important to her. Where did you even find it?'

'Ms Pennington was renting a place not too far from where you live.' Ronson leans forward with a touch of a smile, like they're both detectives going over the case, and he's uncovered a particularly juicy clue. 'I'm not one to judge – I used to drive the missus mad with my clothes everywhere – but Ms Pennington was not particularly house-proud. Didn't seem to do much cleaning.' He pauses to sit back, watching Bryan all the way. 'All except one room – the kitchen. Not a speck in there. Bleached to the moon and back, smell it as soon as you walk in.'

Bryan can't deny the man in the photo is him, but so what? All it says is many years ago he knew this woman, that perhaps they'd had a sexual relationship. All circumstantial to the fact she'd been murdered.

Ronson musses his hair, tiredly scratches the back of his neck. 'What I'm thinking is she was killed in the kitchen, then taken to the forest.'

'Seems reasonable,' Bryan says.

'You don't think it's unusual? A woman you used to sleep with turns up dead, while your actual wife has gone missing?'

'I've told you I can see how this might look.'

'Do you really believe in coincidences?'

'I've seen everything in my time.'

'You want to know what I think happened?'

The air stills. Ronson's silent until Bryan says, 'Knock yourself out.'

'I think you cycled to Celine Pennington's house on the morning of Saturday the fourth of November, and murdered her with the torque wrench from your bike. You left there planning to return to dispose of the body in your own time, but came home to find the police on your doorstep. So, you had to bide your time, you asked questions about the search area – remember doing that? I suspected you were planning to hide something, so I told you about the patrols and checkpoints on the routes out of the area, and that we were focusing our search towards the north and west. That left only one place to go – east, further into the forest. Which is where we found Ms Pennington's body.'

'What about my wife?'

'Maybe you killed her as well. Crashed her car to make it look like an accident.'

'This is insane.' Bryan's head is throbbing. He needs to be on his game here, but his mind feels about as sharp as melted butter. Ronson can't prove any of that, Bryan knows he can't. If the detective had hard evidence – witnesses, forensics – he'd be filleting him with it right now instead of trying to manoeuvre him into place with empty theories. 'Why would I do any of that?'

'What do you know about your wife's relationship with Zack Cookson?'

'We've been over this. They were friends, they lost touch. He showed up outside our house last week in a blue car – which you barely seemed to care about.'

Ronson picks up that stupid old notepad and leafs through it, taking way longer than he needs to get to the last page of writing. 'Did you know that between Monday the sixteenth of October and Saturday the twenty-first, Zack Cookson and your wife spoke on the phone every day? They sent each other numerous messages.'

'Are you trying to humiliate me?' Bryan feels his neck flush. As much as he doesn't want Ronson to get to him, the thought of Astrid and that smug git playing lovey-dovey is almost too much.

'Your wife's phone is in your name. So are all the bills, bank accounts. Seems like you run a tight ship, so I'm just surprised that she would have this friendship without you finding out.'

'If she was sneaking around with him then she's hardly going to tell me over dinner.'

Ronson sighs and rests his hand on his notebook, sombre. 'I'm doing my best to find your wife, if you can believe that. I owe it to her, and to Ms Pennington, to explore every avenue.'

'I love Astrid,' Bryan says. 'If I lose her, then I lose it all. Without her, everything we've worked for, my whole life, is gone. You have got to believe me – I would never hurt her. You couldn't pay me enough to lay a single finger on her. And as for this woman' – he gestures to the photo of him and Celine – 'I haven't seen her since this was taken. Who knows why some-one killed her? Have you even bothered to investigate? Or are you one of those detectives who makes his mind up about who's guilty, and *then* goes looking for the evidence?'

A pause. A look across the table. 'Let me show you something else,' Ronson says. He opens his folder and riffles through it, frowning, like he's surprised to see what he's brought. Bryan wants to rip the lot out of his hand and tip it over the table. See what else is hiding in there.

'Here we go,' Ronson says, placing another photo beside the ones of Astrid, Celine, and the two sex workers accusing him of violence.

It's a picture of Bryan's family from when he was young. He's twelve, maybe thirteen. They're in the pose he remembers from growing up – standing in front of his mum, her hands on his shoulders, his dad to the side, upright, proud. They're all dressed smartly, for church, it looks like. He gets a vague recollection of listening to a service while pulling on an uncomfortable collar. A good-looking family, if he can say that. A great childhood.

'Why are you showing me this?' he asks.

'You definitely have a type, don't you?'

'*What?*'

'Don't be embarrassed, Mr Webb. We all do it, apparently. Freud has already absolved us from any possible shame.'

'Are you trying to provoke me?'

'I'm trying to understand you.'

'You didn't tell me you were a qualified psychiatrist.'

'It's always interesting to see where people came from – it gives you a good idea where they're going.'

'Bravo,' Bryan says, giving him a sarcastic clap. 'And there's me thinking you don't know what you're doing.'

Ronson flips the page on his notebook. 'Your mother was

quite sickly, wasn't she? Judging from her medical records.'

'What are you getting at?'

'More coincidences, I suppose.'

'More accusations, you mean.'

'I'm just trying to join the dots, Mr Webb.'

'By winding me up?'

Ronson points to the picture of the second prostitute, the one in a sexual pose. 'She claims you asked her to roleplay a mother-and-son situation, and that you requested to strangle her.'

'Utter bollocks,' Bryan replies.

'You'll be amazed how often we find that kind of behaviour with murderers. Practicing their violence in a "safe" environment.'

'*It never happened.*'

'Did you know Ms Pennington lived near to you?'

'What fantasy planet are you on?'

'Do you know why Ms Pennington moved to a house near to you a couple of months ago?'

'I haven't seen her for years!'

'How old was Celine Pennington when you had your relationship?'

Bryan lifts his shoulders, mouth going like a fish. 'I mean, I don't know. Legal, definitely legal, if you're asking that.'

'Did you know she had a history of severe mental health issues? In her late teens and early twenties, she spent some time in psychiatric institutions.'

'Is that my fault as well?'

'Was she obsessed with you, perhaps?'

Bryan swipes his hairline with his finger. 'Maybe she was

obsessed with Astrid. She could have read about the Foundation in the papers – we were both in the publicity shots. Maybe she was her stalker, the one in the journal. Have you asked yourself that? Maybe Astrid killed her and that's why she's gone.'

'Do you believe your wife is capable of murder?'

'Of course not.'

'So why say that?'

'You're the one insisting we hear every theory, no matter how crackpot.'

'How did your relationship end with Ms Pennington?'

'I don't remember.'

'Who was the one to finish it?'

'I don't remember.'

'Could Ms Pennington have had cause to hold a grudge?'

Bryan goes to give the same answer but pauses – he doesn't want to say anything ambiguous and make it sound like she might have had a reason for revenge.

Something flickers in Ronson's eyes. He sits up slowly. 'She knew about something. Not the prostitutes, but similar.'

'You're wrong,' Bryan says, but his voice has faltered, he can hear it. He needs to jump on this, deny it as ridiculous. It's like his gears are jammed.

'She was going to expose you, so you shut her down.'

Celine spoke to Wendy's daughter. Bryan hadn't really taken that in at the time, there was too much other stuff going on, but he remembers now. What if the daughter comes forward next? He races through the options, but it doesn't take long. He needs one thing: time.

'I want a solicitor,' he says.

Ronson nods, as though that confirms everything. 'Bryan

Webb, you are being arrested for the murder of Celine Pennington. You do not have to say—'

'Where's your *evidence?*'

'—anything, but it may harm your defence if you do not mention when questioned something which you later rely on in court.'

'The CPS will throw it back in your face.'

'Anything you do say—'

The door to the interview room bursts open. The horsey sergeant rushes in, looking stressed, saying, 'Boss, wait.' Before she can carry on a tall bloke in a white shirt – a crown on his epaulets, a superintendent – pushes past her.

'A word, please,' he says to Ronson, in a way that suggests it's not a request.

'Give me two minutes,' he replies.

'Outside,' the super says, jabbing a finger at the door. 'Pronto.'

46

RONSON

Zamora leads Ronson to surveillance. Detective Constable Chen is still at her computer, watching the interview room. She glances up when they bustle in, then quickly focuses on the screen, frowning and moving her mouse to make herself appear busy.

The super laces his fingers and pushes them out, cracking all his knuckles, like they've come here for a scrap. 'I told you to leave Webb alone.'

'He's our man,' Ronson replies, leaning against a desk, folding his arms.

'Are you getting a kick out of this? Dragging a good man's name through the dirt?'

'With respect, that's not what's happening here.'

'You've got an ex-officer with twenty-five years under his belt sweating it out like he's a bleeding shoplifter.'

'He's a flight risk. We've got more evidence coming in every minute.'

'Nothing that'll stick, none that I've seen.'

'He killed Celine Pennington.'

311

'Webb said it himself – this Ms Pennington was obsessed with his wife. She was stalking her. Are you so stuck in your ways that you can't see the truth when it's slapping you in the face? Astrid Webb killed Celine Pennington. That's what we're going with.'

Ronson shakes his head. 'Let me run the case my way—'

'Your way is sloppy – messy, disorganised—'

'Come on,' Ronson says, glancing at Maxwell and Chen, his officers, watching in horror as he gets shredded by the big man. 'There's no need for this.'

'And that bloody leak to the press! It's a disgrace, an embarrassment to the whole station.'

'I can assure you, I am as concerned about that as you are.'

Zamora flattens his face, unimpressed. 'Give over. A detective unit rots from the inspector down.'

Ronson pushes off the desk. Enough of this. He knew Webb was bad news from the moment he met him at the crash site. Not just his attitude to the constables, ordering them around like he was still putting together the weekly schedule, but all his sneaky questions that weren't questions, like where they were planning to expand the search. And look what they found.

Webb was jumpy as well. Of course it's normal for someone to be nervous in that situation, but not like he was acting – almost as though the whole thing was a distraction, his wife's car, the police being there, and he had other, more important, plans to get to once everyone had gone. Webb went through the motions, he said the right things, but Ronson's been dealing with victims day in and day out for well over half his life – he must have met a hundred spouses whose partners have disappeared – and within seconds of their introduction he knew there was something not right.

Now it all makes sense: Webb had come straight from murdering Celine Pennington.

Ronson takes in the super, towering over him. A good man is how he sells himself, an honest man – *Honest Abe* is his moniker – but who knows the truth? Everyone thought Bryan Webb was a 'good man' and look how mistaken they were.

'I don't know what you've been told about Webb,' Ronson says, 'or who is asking you to defend him, but you're wrong about this, and you're going to be proved wrong very soon.'

Zamora's nose wrinkles like there's a bad odour in here and only he can smell it. He points to the screen where Webb is hunched over the table, head in his hands. 'I want him released. Pronto.'

'With respect—'

'Don't *with respect* me.'

'Have you seen the photos? He was in a sexual relationship with a woman who's been found murdered half an hour from where he lives.'

'Release him or pack up your desk. What's it going to be, detective?'

47

BRYAN

Silence in the squad car back home. Darkness outside the windows.

How does someone come back from this?

Bryan tells himself it could be worse – he could be pacing a custody cell, stressing over the possibility of a life sentence – but the consolation doesn't make a dent. He's so weary, the adrenaline from the station long gone. Everywhere he looks there are wolves. It's only a matter of time before he's eaten alive.

A scrum of vehicles is waiting at the top of the lane to their cottage. Reporters swarm around the car as they get close, the camera flashes blinding. Bryan shields his face with his hand. *Bang. Bang, bang.* His heart jolts. He twists in his seat, seeing grey fingers breaking through glass, but it's just some scummy journo trying to get him to look around.

He flees from the car, through the front door. Slams it behind him, kicks over the umbrella stand and pulls the coats off the hook. Bryan sinks to his knees, his fists either side of his head, wanting to do more, to smash the whole place, destroy his crumbling world to dust. He should have strung Celine

315

along. He should have seen through her trick to seduce him. He should have used less bleach to clean, not been so obvious in asking about the search area.

Mistake after mistake, from the bloody start.

Ronson knew all along. A detective with that many years' experience, how could he underestimate him so much? Worrying about his stupid coffee stain and whether his shirt was tucked in. Bryan remembers Ronson giving the bike the once-over, that first day when the police came back, making out that he was into cycling as well, buttering him up while he clocked that the wrench was missing from the built-in kit. The detective got him good and proper there.

Bryan slopes upstairs, gets changed. Goes into his office and pours a brandy. Never has he deserved his end-of-day glass more, but from the first sip it tastes bitter.

What if tonight he committed the biggest mistake of all?

Before going in to the station he'd sent Chief Constable Douglas Hooper, known to his mates with good reason as Dangerous Doug, the leverage he had on him – the picture of Hoop and Celine at her flat, the little party when she was out of it. Hoop's grinning and grabbing her hair, lifting her head. Her face is covered in all sorts, lipstick, marker pen, a smear of brown on her forehead that you had to hope was peanut butter.

The very same girl, now a woman, that has shown up dead.

There were other officers at that party, some of them nearly as high up the ladder as Hoop, and they all still talk. They'll be wondering if there are any photos of them floating around, and whether they too will be called to help an old pal.

What if they make a move first?

His phone is going off the hook, messages from friends,

neighbours, ex-colleagues. He checks online and sees it's all over the news – the pictures of him and Celine. There's an interview with some rough bloke called Flynn and a few others, all claiming to know Bryan from when he was dating her, going on about what a sleaze he was back then, how he took advantage of an innocent young girl, making out like he's some kind of paedo.

When he gets to a website and reads, *the alleged affair between seventeen-year-old Celine Pennington and forty-seven-year-old Bryan Webb*, he throws his phone down in disgust. There. Right there. That's what's wrong with all this digital news. They can say outright lies, and what can you do? He was thirty when they were together. Big fucking difference.

Maybe they'll correct it if he tells them, but what's he going to do? Drop them a quick fucking email? In the meantime, anyone who reads that will think that he's been sniffing out schoolgirls, which is very much not the case. Celine was living away from home, with her own job, a consenting adult.

He scrolls down to the comments, knowing he shouldn't, but he needs to see if he's lost support from the public as well. His answer comes from the top line – someone claiming to be at school with him, telling everyone that he was a bully back then, so it's no surprise he's gone on to be a killer now.

The letterbox clatters open. Someone calls for him to come outside for a quick chat. Give his side of the story. Bryan finishes his drink and reaches for the bottle.

Back when he was with Celine, he was a proper boozer. He'd do his six days on, then go nuts for however long, and be back for duty, showered and shaved, at the start of the next roster. He had the constitution of a whole herd of elephants. Now all it takes is one drink and he can't see straight.

He takes his glass through to the bathroom to pee. Looking in the mirror, he understands what these last few days have cost him. Everything is now sagging – his jaw, his cheeks, even the purple semi-circles below his eyes – as though the muscles in his face have given up. He looks ancient, cadaverous, dug up from the grave.

As a show of defiance to this reflection, who honestly can't be him, it's impossible it's him, he drains the drink. The brandy burns down his throat. For the first time the whole picture comes into focus. He puts the glass down and grips the side of the sink as the realisation takes hold. Fast rebukes flow from all angles, but each one rebounds from the thought, shielded and shining and rising from the mud of his subconscious, until it is all that remains.

He's had this coming for a long time.

Bryan knows what he's like – he's not daft. He doesn't have that cognitive dissonance, which is the fancy term for when your behaviour is at odds with what you believe about yourself. There's no denial, where he's concerned.

He understands who he is, and where he comes from.

'Your mother gets confused,' his dad had told him. 'She needs looking after. Protecting.'

This after Bryan had caught him a couple of times slipping something into her gin. The drink would fizz, his mum would take a sip and grimace, and an hour later her throat would become unbearably sore.

'Mum needs to stay here so we can protect her,' Bryan had replied.

His dad patted him on the shoulder. 'Good boy.'

Bryan always was an intuitive child. Right from start he

realised life was a fist fight, and you either came out swinging or faced many decades getting knocked flat.

If something's working, you don't change it, do you? He'd done well from his methods – a great career, plenty of mates, his house paid off in full. As soon as he saw Astrid, he knew he'd found the final piece, and that he'd do anything to get it.

He was already in his forties, already thinking about the next chapter, that night she rushed into the station, scared and looking for help. There was no way he wanted to see out his days as one of those sad old bachelors everyone thinks is gay, or to leave it too long and end up with an annoying lump like Meera. He wanted to find someone both beautiful and young enough to care for him as the years passed, to hold him when he died, just like his mum did with his dad. Astrid ticked every box in his head and some he'd never considered before.

It wasn't hard to get rid of Niall. Bryan bagged the little shit when he was staggering home from the pub, took him to the abandoned warehouse they often used, beat him with metal bars, and yanked out half his teeth with pliers.

'You ever mention this to anyone,' Bryan had hissed in his ear as Niall lay bleeding. 'And I'm coming back for the rest of your teeth.'

After that, Bryan used one of his standard operations on Astrid. All the phone calls, the texts, banging on her windows at night. Creating fake identities and spreading stuff about her, causing divisions with her friends and family, keeping her destabilised, on edge, desperate for help – and then being the person to offer that help. Classic.

It was almost too easy. She didn't have many people in her life, and those she did have were remarkably quick to turn their backs, which perhaps goes to show that he was right about them all along. From the start her mum didn't care, Bryan could barely get a response from her, and it took little more than a nudge to get rid of losers like Zack. As for her 'best friend' Vivien, she couldn't run fast enough. Bryan had posted that baby comment from Astrid's Instagram account when she was flaked out, thinking that it was only the first step in separating the two of them. Imagine his surprise when that was all it took.

The power of modern technology: years of friendship, vanished in the time it takes to press a button.

Same with someone's reputation.

From now until either the end of time or the internet, long after he's gone anyway, search for his name and all you'll get back is gossip and slander. His awards, his commendations, his twenty-five years serving on the police force will be buried at the bottom. The footnotes that no one can be bothered to read.

Bryan goes back to the office. He pours another drink. The journos are banging on the front door, the windows, even round the back of the house. The wolves closing in.

He just wanted a perfect life. Isn't that the same for everyone? He nearly had it a couple of times – with Wendy, for example – but he made too many mistakes honing his method, and by the end they weren't worth having any more. Astrid was the one, though. And he let her get away.

When Bryan takes a drink, he notices his vision is blurry. So tired. So fucking tired.

Everything can disappear in a moment. The home you've built, the money you've saved, the freedoms you've lived by, they're all illusions. The *only* real thing in this world is power, and his is gone.

Is there anything left for him now?

48

RONSON

Ronson stares from the rec room sofa at the dark shadows on the ceiling. Zamora can give all the ultimatums he wants, but it'll make no difference. It's out there now, and the more that goes out, the more that's coming in – stories from Webb's past, bullying, harassment, abuses of power, all delivered with threats to keep their mouth shut, or else.

That's the difference with how it used to be, when Ronson started as a detective. Back then, even if a victim wanted to say something in public, who's going to listen? Now a tweet becomes a chorus becomes a scream, until the whole world can hear.

There's more to come from this, Ronson's sure of it. Once it does everyone will know the name Bryan Webb.

The rec room door inches open. It's Maxwell.

'You asleep, boss?'

'Yes.'

'You might want to see this.'

*

321

Ten minutes later a convoy of emergency vehicles are streaming out of the black gates and racing up the A road to Dinckley. Ronson and Maxwell are at the front, Jess using the gears to navigate the bends and switchbacks that loom in the windscreen so fast it's like they're in a video game.

Ronson activates the touchscreen built into the dash. He dims the light so as not to distract her – the last thing this case needs is a five-car police pile-up in the middle of the night – and taps into the case file. The email from Bryan Webb is there.

I confess to the murder of Celine Pennington.

No doubt about it, when they arrive Webb will be swinging from his bathrobe belt. First question: has he topped himself, or has someone given him a helping hand? Ronson's been around long enough to understand that just because someone's dangling from the rafters, it doesn't necessarily mean they climbed up there themself. Webb must have pulled in some serious favours to get his reprieve. What if someone made sure he kept his mouth shut?

Second, and perhaps more important: where is Astrid Webb? Is she far from here, maybe in hiding, having learned the truth about who she married? Or is she buried deep in the forest, perhaps now lost for ever, the location of her body gone along with her husband?

It's quiet at the top of the lane leading to the Webb house. News vans are parked up, the reporters getting a kip in the back, hoping to be on the spot for the first scoop. Looks like it's their lucky day. Maxwell leads the convoy to the front door.

They don't bother with the bell – it's straight for the ram.

The door goes down first hit. Ronson and Maxwell pull on gloves and head upstairs while SOCO set up in the hallway. They smell Webb on the top landing before they find him in his office. Vomit, hard spirits, opened bowels. Death.

The office is a long room lined with books, and in the far corner by the window there's a computer desk. Webb's face down by his laptop along with a half-empty bottle of brandy. Expensive stuff, by the looks of it, the label all black and gold. Ronson checks his neck for a pulse. Nothing.

Also on the desk is an open leather briefcase containing what appears to be various bags of powder, each neatly labelled. Drugs? If so there's plenty there. A whole little apothecary, it seems.

'Check this, boss,' Maxwell says, flicking through an A4 notebook. 'Looks like a schedule of some sort.'

Ronson shines a light into the briefcase, examining the labels. Potassium bromide, flunitrazepam, diphenylcyanoarsine. He lifts a bag of white powder from the rest. *Strychnine?*

What was Webb up to here?

Ronson would never have picked him for the suicidal type. Even when Webb was being released, he was bullish, confident of his innocence. People genuinely on the edge don't put up such a fight; they've already given up. He had given up nothing.

And yet he's here, going cold with a puddle of vomit in his lap.

'Did you see that?' Maxwell asks, pointing to the laptop. The lid is open, a USB flash drive sticking out of the side; on the screen is a Word document containing a single line:

She's in the air-raid shelter behind the house.

Ronson turns Maxwell to the door. 'Go, go, go, get out there. I'll call for a dog squad.' He radios it in while she rushes down the stairs.

Not long after, he follows.

49

ASTRID

The air in the shelter is dank and stinks of piss. Astrid wraps the blanket tighter, curling her body on the cold floor, hoping to keep what's left of her warmth. She hears a voice.

It's so dark in here that she can't even see her hand when she sits up and wipes her face. Maybe it was the wind. Or the howl of a night-time creature, a badger or a fox. It comes again, stronger this time. Someone calling a name. Her name?

It must be.

Her back is aching, her legs numb, but she forces herself up. The voices are fading a touch. She yells for them to come back, please come back. She feels around for the hatch and bangs on it, screaming, 'I'm here! Get me out!'

The voices return. Soon there's more of them. Footsteps overhead, the sound of damp leaves being shoved around. She's slapping the hatch, sobbing and pleading, until there's the clunk of something heavy being slid aside. Suddenly the hatch is gone and in its place is torchlight so harsh she has to shield her face with her arms.

A man drops into the shelter beside her. He's asking if she's okay. All Astrid can do is hold onto him, tears streaming, thanking him and thanking him until they lift her out. They lay her on the soft leaves. 'Can you hear me? Are you in pain?' Static from someone's shoulder radio. 'Hurry with the paramedics.'

They police are here, so it must be over. The relief shudders through her like an aftershock. It's over, he's gone. She can't believe it.

Soon the paramedics arrive. They load her onto a stretcher, carry her to an ambulance, check her over, taking bloods, hooking her to an IV. Into the hospital for more examinations, swabs, tentative questions about what he did or did not do to her. She tells them he didn't rape her, if that's what they're thinking. To give Bryan the barest of credits, he never did that.

Aside from being cold and hungry and dehydrated, she seems to be okay. No lasting damage is the verdict from the medical staff. They give her a Cup-a-Soup and let her rest for a few hours, then she's asked if she's able to speak to a detective. She says yes, and a few minutes later the door opens again.

'Good morning, Mrs Webb,' a man says, coming to the side of the bed. 'Detective Inspector Ronson.'

She takes a pained swallow and turns her head to him. He's quite a bit older, in a suit that's seen better lifetimes, but his eyes are kind. 'Thank you for finding me.'

'This is one of those beds you can raise and lower with a button.' He pats along the frame, like they're in a showroom. 'I wonder where they get them from. My knees are murder in the morning.' He glances at her and gives an awkward laugh. 'Sorry, bad choice of words.'

'I've been through a lot worse, the last few days.'

'Do you feel well enough to talk about it?'

Astrid closes her eyes, crunches her mouth, but she has to do this. 'I guess so.'

'Start at the beginning. What happened on Saturday morning?'

'I— I don't know. Bryan told me I'd crashed the car, but I don't even remember getting behind the wheel.'

He asks, gently, 'Can you go back to that morning for me? What happened.'

'I'm not sure. I was in bed, having breakfast, and that's it . . . Next thing I know I'm wandering across a field, feeling like I've just walked into a wall.'

'Do you remember having your medication?'

'Yes – no.' She shrugs. 'Sorry, I don't know.'

The detective takes out a thick notebook, then pats around each pocket twice before locating a pencil. 'What happened next? You're in a field, lost. Why didn't you call someone?'

'I didn't have my phone.'

'What about the phone Mr Cookson bought for you?'

Astrid bites her bottom lip and quickly lets it go. 'You know about that?'

A little smile, more to himself, then he asks, 'Can you tell me about the nature of your relationship with Mr Cookson?'

'We're just friends. Old friends.'

Ronson nods, watchful. 'Let's get back to Saturday. It's quite a way to walk – why didn't you flag down a car? Or find a shop?'

'I was too embarrassed.'

'Then what happened?'

'I carried on walking until I saw a road, and found my way home.'

'You'd have looked a state. No one stop to help?'

'I tried to stay behind the hedges, out of sight.'

The detective ruffles his hair and blows out his cheeks. He closes his notebook, raps his fingers enigmatically on it, and lifts his eyebrows. 'Must have taken you a while to get back.'

'I'm sorry, I don't remember. I was so out of it. It was dark, though.'

'What happened when you got there?'

'Bryan was furious with me for going out. There have been a few . . . incidents lately of this happening. He said I'd defied him for the last time, but then he seemed to calm down. I thought everything was fine again. He made me a cup of tea, and the next thing I knew I woke up in the dark.'

'He had locked you in that . . .'

'It's an air-raid shelter, I think. From the Second World War.'

Ronson nods. 'You must have been terrified.'

She presses her fingers to her eyes, hitches her shoulders. 'Every time he left, I thought he wouldn't come back.'

'You're safe now. He won't be able to hurt you any more.'

Solemn silence. No one has confirmed what happened to her husband, but she saw another stretcher being carried into the back of an ambulance. The blanket was pulled up over the head.

'How did you find me?' she asks.

'Your husband,' Ronson says. 'Left it on his computer screen. Looks like it was the last thing he did. Well, almost.'

'You think he . . .'

'That's how it seems. We'll have to wait for a full autopsy.'

Astrid gives him a frayed nod, and wipes her eyes one more time. 'I hope he's in as much hell as he put me through.'

'I'm so pleased to see you intact,' he says. 'Judging from the crash, we thought you might be more injured.'

'Oh, I—'

'There was a fair amount of blood. We were expecting to find you with a severe head injury.'

'I think I had a nosebleed – I'm prone to them. Most probably I hit my head on the wheel.'

'But you don't remember?'

'Sorry,' Astrid says.

Once the detective has gone, she speaks to a community officer who runs through the next stages in coming to terms with her trauma. There are therapists and group workshops and even some faith healers. She keeps her wan smile to herself as she accepts the leaflets and printouts and promises that she's not alone, help is there. It's easy enough to keep up the hazy expression required to glide through the debriefing. Anything to get out of there. A hot bath is what she needs, and enough soap to scrub off the last five years of her life.

But not at her 'home.' She'll go back there at some point to pick up the few things that are genuinely hers, but it'll be like visiting the prison from which you were recently released. She's not in any rush to return.

Thankfully, she does have somewhere to go. They drive south from the hospital, down the Withington Road, pulling up outside a redbrick terrace house.

She gets out and thanks the constable. Waits for him to go before knocking on the door.

Zack opens the door and pulls Astrid into him arms. He pushes her out again and searches her face for the answer to the question he's too scared to ask. Astrid doesn't keep him waiting. He holds her as she sobs into his chest.

'We did it,' Zack says. 'We did it. That bastard, we did it.'

50

ASTRID

Faking the crash was Celine's idea. At first Astrid found the notion both ridiculous and dangerous, as well as liable to leave her in serious trouble with the police. Once she visited Sarah, Wendy's daughter, she changed her mind.

The parallels between her story and Wendy's were astounding. They were both teachers, both in good health before they met Bryan. Sarah was ten when her mum got together with him and already living with her dad, so she doesn't know exactly what happened at the time, but she does remember a scandal, secrets being revealed – a handwritten note pushed through a letterbox causing deeper rifts in her already broken family. After that argument, she didn't see her mum for nearly three years.

Hearing that made Astrid think back to when Niall was stalking her. The email to her mother demanding money for a supposed debt, the gossips and rumours spread behind her back, even that comment posted on Vivien's Instagram account. Could Bryan have been behind it all?

At the time it'd been a huge shift from how Niall had previously been acting. Mooning after her, showing up unannounced on nights out, not getting it through his head that she wasn't interested in a relationship with him. Why didn't she question more how he'd go from that to ripping her life to shreds?

Bryan, that's how. He seemed so sure of himself when he explained that this kind of 'ramping up' was common when it came to stalkers. The fact that Niall had gone underground only confirmed it.

She'd already gone to the police. They were actively involved in helping her, or so she thought. She was so desperate for it to be over she never really questioned if the person harassing her was still Niall. Why would she?

'Next time I saw my mum,' Sarah said, 'I almost didn't recognise her. She was so frail, she'd aged like twenty years. It was in the morning but she was drinking wine – from a mug, so I couldn't see it. But I could smell it. It was staining her lips. After that I never saw her without a drink. I asked her why she was doing it and she just kept saying she'd had a fall, hurt her back. She wasn't a drinker before then – even my dad says. She only used to get a Coke in the pub.'

Astrid sees Bryan backing into her bedroom every morning, the Lilac Monster on the tray. Watching with a sympathetic smile as she downed her pills.

How could he be to blame for her OxyContin addiction? The doctor prescribed the pills.

And yet when she came off all her medication, all her symptoms disappeared.

One thing Bryan always said to her, as a joke (or so she thought), when she was most sick, most incapacitated, when she'd be thanking him profusely for continuing to care for her. He'd give her a playful smile and say, 'You'd be no good to anyone else in this condition.'

Could he have been giving her something to make her sick? How was that possible without her realising? Who knows what her husband was capable of, now she was beginning to see the truth about him. Even before she handed over the labour of filing her medication into the Lilac Monster to Bryan – once they were married, he insisted on doing it – she didn't look too closely at what she was throwing down her throat.

'Every time Mum left him,' Sarah said, 'he'd hunt her down and bring her back. He'd ruin whatever life she'd built for herself, so she had no choice but to return to him. Even when she finally did get away, he didn't leave her alone. He just did it out of spite. The last time was right as she was happy for probably the first time since she left him. He turned up in his uniform at Graeme's door – he was mum's new boyfriend – with all these lies about how she was a scammer, that she was only with him to steal his savings. Graeme got cold feet, and that was that. Mum never recovered. She started drinking and didn't stop. A couple of months later, we found her . . .'

After hearing that, Celine's plan to fake the crash no longer sounded so ridiculous.

'If we do it this way,' Celine said, the one time the two met at her house near Longridge, 'it will put the spotlight on him. It's always the husband, that's what people think. It's what the police think.'

Celine was different to how she'd seemed on phone, or on chat. That's how Astrid got back in touch with her. The mail Celine had sent her, the address made to look like it came from the Tea Network, was still in the Trash folder.

Astrid had been expecting someone confident, assertive. Instead Celine seemed shy, a bit disconnected, in her vintage burgundy midi dress. Her nails were bitten, and she picked at the torn cuticles as they spoke.

'If it's about getting him in trouble,' Astrid said, 'then why don't we just come forward? There's already three of us, and there might be more.'

'If Sarah doesn't want to speak out,' Celine replied, 'and no one steps up, then it might not be enough. We'd only get one chance. This way he'll be too busy trying to save his own behind to worry too much about you.'

Astrid shuddered. 'Even if it works, even if I get away and start a new life, won't he try to find me eventually?'

'Maybe think of it more as a head start.'

The journal and the smashed door and the threatening Facebook messages were Zack's idea. 'If you want to put Bryan in the spotlight,' he said, over lunch in Blackpool, 'then you need to make it interesting. The police may even think he planted it all, and that you're buried in the back garden.' That evening Zack sent her the first message from Lee Connor.

On the day of the crash, the road was quiet. She jagged the car sideways, bracing as she slammed head first into the hedgerow. She checked her pocket for the vials: still intact. Shaking from the crash, she flung the contents over the steering wheel, the dashboard, the windscreen. Was that enough to be convincing? She'd drawn her blood that week using the equipment Zack bought for her and a YouTube video called *How To Take Blood Like A Pro – Venepuncture Explained*.

Zack was waiting in his car less than a kilometre away through fields. They went back to his cottage and waited to hear from Celine – she'd said she knew people who could help Astrid with fake ID, which was crucial to staying hidden, at least in the short term. Zack explained that Celine had called Bryan that morning to lure him out of the house, keep him busy.

They watched as Astrid's disappearance became a news story. Bryan became the prime suspect, but Astrid didn't know what to do. Go on the run now? She needed Celine, that new ID.

When Celine's body was found, they knew Bryan must have murdered her. Zack rang the police with the anonymous tip-off about her name.

Wendy, dead.

Celine, dead.

Anyone who got involved with Bryan sooner or later ended up dead. For the first time in a long time, Astrid didn't want to die.

Until then, she'd been holed up in Zack's cottage. Once it became clear that that Bryan was closing in (she screamed when she looked out the window and saw him snooping around) she moved to the air-raid shelter. She hated it there, but it was the only way she could be sure no one would find her, and she wanted to be close to the house if she got an opportunity.

The case was being followed by the rolling news. When Zack messaged her to say that Bryan had just been taken in by a police car, she knew this was her chance. She found the spare kitchen door key where it always was, in the hollow handle of the wheelbarrow standing up beside the shed. Once inside she crept upstairs to her tiny bedroom at the front of the cottage.

There, on the nightstand. The Lilac Monster of her nightmares. Now an unlikely ally, a friendly face. All the Saturday compartments were full, Sunday too. Well prepared as always. So predictable, Bryan, in his own way. There was enough to get started.

Astrid took what she needed downstairs and put them in the pestle and mortar Bryan liked her to use to grind the spices for

Thai green curry. It was a good one, sourced all the way from Asia. It did an excellent job of turning the eight OxyContin pills into powder.

She'd worried that they wouldn't dissolve, instead collecting at the bottom of the brandy, but she need not have done. The liquid was a rich brown colour, and the powder vanished quickly once she swilled the bottle. There was already some fine sediment at the bottom, so he wouldn't be likely to notice anything, even if some fragments did remain. Although she was slightly concerned about the taste. What if he spat it out after the first sip?

Again, she shouldn't have bothered worrying. Less than an hour after Bryan crashed through the front door, trashing the hallway and storming upstairs – while she quivered behind the door, lights off, in the spare bedroom – she heard what sounded like a pig being electrocuted on the upstairs landing. She cracked open the door, saw nothing, then realised the sound was coming from Bryan's office.

She couldn't remember him ever really snoring before, but he was then. Slumped back in his swivel chair, his head tipped back, his hand still wrapped around the glass on the desk. Could she simply kill him? Cover his nose and mouth and hope to hold on as his body bucked and clung to life? She wasn't sure.

Astrid noticed the A4 notebook open by the laptop, the page filled with columns of numbers. She noticed the faded brown leather briefcase by Bryan's feet that she'd never seen before, the colourful stool she remembered painting for him by the bookcase, the books slid to the side near the top to reveal what seemed to be a secret panel.

Once she looked inside the briefcase, the secret panel, on the

USB flash drive she found there, all became clear.

She mixed him a batch from all the different bags in the briefcase.

'You're sick,' she whispered in his ear as he groggily swallowed. 'It's your medicine.' She held him as he passed out again.

By the time she raced back to the air-raid shelter, Zack was there to lock the hatch. All she could then was wait.

Astrid's still waiting, even now Bryan has gone. At least that's how it feels.

'One thing I'm not doing', she says to Zack, 'is moving back to Dinckley.'

'I'm putting my place on the market,' he replies. 'I don't know what I was thinking buying that old dump.'

They're having sandwiches by the canals in Castlefield, a week later. She's been staying with Vivien, in her four-bed in Prestwich, taking the eldest's room while the kids bunk together, but that arrangement won't last long. Vivien worries about the media attention, with the little ones.

Zack has offered to rent them a place together in Manchester. Even after what he's done for her, putting himself at risk, probably breaking the law to get her away from Bryan, she senses herself resisting. It's not him. Astrid wants to be with Zack in a way that she never did with Bryan, but right now she's too angry. At Bryan, at herself, at all the people who turned their backs on her. Zack and Vivien included, if she's honest. Pretty much everyone in her life.

'I just need some time,' Astrid says.

'I've only waited, oh' – Zack glances at this watch – 'just

most of the time I've known you for a shot.'

'A *shot*? I'm not a clay pigeon, you know.'

'You'd be the prettiest clay pigeon this side of the Peak District.'

Bryan stole five years of her life. He made her into a slave without her even realising. Doing his cooking and cleaning, providing him with company in the evening, while he lied and manipulated and poisoned her.

How does anyone ever move on from that?

Zack takes her hand, and she leans into him.

'You take as long as you want,' he says. 'I'm not going anywhere.'

Astrid thinks back to Celine, what she told her about her experiences after Bryan. So many years had passed, and still his influence ran deep. She was never able to rinse the stink of him out of her life.

What if she's the same? What if in five or ten or fifteen years' time she's still messed up by what he did to her? What if she destroys her relationship with Zack the way that Celine said she did with Hugh?

What if she spends the rest of her days waiting for a release that never comes?

Astrid presses into Zack, pleased for the arm he wraps around her, for the solid warmth of his body.

'Look on the bright side,' he says.

'What's that?' she replies.

'At least you never have to watch *Countryfile* again.'

Astrid snorts a laugh and slaps him on the shoulder. 'Honestly.'

'What? You can't stand it.'

'I know, but come on.'

Zack squeezes her again. 'Meh, got to take those silver linings where you can find them.'

Astrid kisses him on the cheek. He may just have a point.

EPILOGUE

RONSON

Snow is falling outside the canteen window, settling on the business park down below, making it look fairly pleasant for once, instead of the grey maze of portacabins and concrete misery you usually had to stare at.

'I see they've pulled Sir Robert into the inquiry,' Maxwell says, reading the newspaper. She sips her coffee and glares at the cup like it's just insulted her. 'I swear these are getting worse.'

'I try not to think about it,' Ronson replies.

'The coffee, or the inquiry?'

He drains his cup. 'Both.'

No one can say how the press got hold of that USB flash drive. Perhaps it fell out of an evidence bag? The contents of it turned out to be damning not only to Bryan Webb, but also to a serious chunk of the Greater Manchester Police senior management, including the chief constable himself, Douglas Hooper. Lurid photos, compromising emails, some decidedly shocking screenshots of WhatsApp messages where both victims and the bereaved were being mocked.

341

Ronson has found himself on the train down to London a couple of times already, giving evidence at the House of Commons. Although he wants to minimise his involvement. It's not for him, this kind of witch-hunt. The criminal acts have been identified, charges have been brought – but now they're onto who knew what, who turned a blind eye, all the hairshirt stuff the government thinks the public craves. Ronson reckons 'the public' would rather put the millions this inquiry is costing towards a well-funded, professionally trained police force, but hey ho. That's why he's not in politics.

The contents of that USB weren't the only astonishing revelations to come out of the Webb case. A deep-dive audit into the Victim Relief Foundation exposed what appeared to be a serious case of embezzlement. Bryan Webb had all kinds of tricks for syphoning out the cash – booking expensive venues then cancelling and keeping the money, creating elaborate paper trails for payouts to victims who didn't actually exist. Of the one and a half million pounds he raised in the last two years, it's estimated that he managed to sneak out nearly a quarter of it.

Maxwell flips to page eight of the newspaper. 'You see this?'

Under the headline, 'Cookson of the Caribbean: Zack's Secret Proposal', there's a long-lens shot of a couple dining on a white sand beach, the man off his chair and kneeling in front of the woman.

'Sorry, Jess. You're a bit young for me.'

Maxwell gives him an eye roll version of a pained groan. 'It's Astrid Webb.'

'So it is,' Ronson replies, giving the page a quick scan. The high-profile nature of the case, and the ongoing inquiry into

342

the Foundation, means that everyone involved is now tabloid famous.

'Well?'

'Well, what?'

'Still think they weren't having an affair?'

'That's what she told us.'

Maxwell sits back, folds her arms. 'Not like you to leave loose threads dangling.'

'It can't always be a neat bow.'

'Is that what you really believe?'

Forget what he believes, this is what he knows: Astrid Webb was lying. Her account of the crash, her account of events after the crash, and, as Jess already noted, the exact nature of her relationship with Zack Cookson – Ronson is sure that much of her statement is riddled with untruths.

Rescues, sadly, are less frequent than the reports of people going missing, but even so he's been involved in plenty. Same as with her husband when he arrived at the site on the day of the crash, when Ronson interviewed her at the hospital he sensed something was off about her reaction. She was too calm, too together. She didn't seem surprised, or grateful enough to be free, which is how people usually are. Weeping and thanking God and shaking their head, bewildered, as though even now it's over they can't quite process the ordeal they suffered. It felt as though Astrid Webb couldn't wait to get out of there. Like she had other places she'd rather be.

Some of the logistics didn't ring true either. It's a stretch to imagine a nosebleed matching the blood splatter inside the car, as is the idea that she walked eight hours home, hiding behind the hedgerows, without noticing the huge police presence in the local area, or thinking to flag a police car down for assistance.

If Ronson wanted to, he could have pushed for the details of her burner phone – which she handily revealed to him in her interview. He could have asked her why she thinks the key to open the kitchen door was on the outside of the lock. There are so many questions he could ask her, but there's one thing he understands to be true ahead of everything else: Astrid Webb was the victim here, as much as Celine Pennington.

'What I believe,' Ronson says, 'is that you can dwell on a case long after justice has been served, and never find a satisfying way to close it in your mind. It's something I've learned not to worry about – because of one thing.'

'What's that?'

'There's always another case, coming right—'

Maxwell's radio comes to life on the table. A 10-35 on a housing estate in Preston, suspected homicide.

'You were saying,' Maxwell says, gathering her things.

'Indeed I was, Jess,' Ronson replies. 'I'll tell you the rest in the car.'

ACKNOWLEDGEMENTS

Somehow, I seem to have written another book. Looking back on the past year it's hard to recall individual days, but they must have happened, because here we are. The fog of writing is how I think of it. For this book probably more than any so far, I need to express my sincerest gratitude to the people who supported me in pulling the words from the mist and presenting them to you in the story you've just finished, and hopefully enjoyed.

Huge thanks to Miranda Jewess at Viper, who helped shape the initial idea, and has kept it on course throughout. Thanks also to Therese Keating and Sam Matthews for their crucial input at vital stages. In fact, the whole Viper team are fantastic, and it's been a joy to work with them throughout the publication process.

Thanks also to my agent, Jordan Lees at The Blair Partnership, for his calm words and wise counsel in times of high stress, of which there may have been one or two or ten.

During the writing of this book, I lost a dear friend, Regine Wood, to whom this book is dedicated. She was simply a beautiful person, who did incredible work as a Childcare Advocate for Islington Local Authority, and was always first on my begging list for law-related research. The world is a sadder and lesser place without her.

There are a number of people I regularly call on for research. To that end, I'd like to thank my good buddy Jason for his vast and devious pharmaceutical brain, my cousin Undercover Ben for answering many questions on policing – any errors are one hundred per cent my own – and my crack legal team of Richard W. and Oliver.

Any writer needs people close to them to read those dreadful early drafts, and I am lucky to have a few poor souls I count on to do just that. So thanks to Richard W., Tashy, and my brother Adam for their sterling service to the cause. My same gratitude extends to all the bloggers and book-lovers out there I've had the privilege to get to know, and especially to the members of my ARC group. Your support means everything to me.

As always, I'd like to thank my parents, my brothers and their families for all the good times when I was able to crawl out of my writing hole. And of course, to my own family, Amelie, Boddington, and my lovely wife Delia. It's been a slog, this one, and I really don't think I would have made it without your love and encouragement. And nose hats. Can't forget them.